ORPHAN OF ASIA

. . .

Modern Chinese Literature from Taiwan

ORPHAN OF ASIA

. . .

WU ZHUOLIU

Translated by Ioannis Mentzas

COLUMBIA UNIVERSITY PRESS *New York*

Columbia University Press wishes to express its appreciation for assistance given by the Chiang Ching-kuo Foundation for International Scholarly Exchange and the Council for Cultural Affairs in the publication of this series.

Columbia University Press
Publishers Since 1893
New York   Chichester, West Sussex
Copyright © 2006 Columbia University Press
All rights reserved

Library of Congress Cataloging-in-Publication Data
Wu, Zhuoliu, 1900–1976.
[Ajia no koji. English]
Orphan of Asia / Wu Zhuoliu ; translated by Ioannis Mentzas.
    p.   cm. — (Modern Chinese literature from Taiwan)
ISBN 0-231-13727-3 (cloth)
    1. Taiwan—History—1895–1945—Fiction.   I. Mentzas,   Ioannis.
II. Title. III. Series.
PL2824.C48A3513   2005
895.6'35—dc22   2005045450

Printed in the United States of America

c 10 9 8 7 6 5 4 3 2 1

Foreword

. . .

SINCE THE YEARS IMMEDIATELY AFTER THE
Second World War, the title of Zhuoliu Wu's *Orphan of Asia* has
become a most powerful metaphor for the uncertain social, political, and economic situation of Taiwan in the world community.
The search for an identity other than "orphan" has spurred incessant crises across the Taiwan Straits for nearly sixty years.

When David Wang and I drew up a list of novels to be translated
for the series Modern Chinese Literature from Taiwan, this book
was at the top because it is the most explicit and realistic fictional
portrayal of the fate of an intellectual youth seeking a respectable
and authentic identity while drifting as a solitary sail at the time
of the imposing changes of the Japanese occupation of Taiwan
(1895–1945). Unfortunately, *Orphan of Asia* was not among the
first books published in this series because of the amount of time
needed to translate it from Japanese into English.

The protagonist, Hu Taiming, while leading a life based on local
Taiwanese customs, nonetheless retains a deep-rooted admiration
for his ancestors' motherland: China. He also has a strong desire
to return there. This obsession, however, and the real trials he
experiences after he does return bring only disillusionment and

a realization that he does not belong anywhere. He is the orphan of Asia. No other literary attempts that I am aware of portray such a vivid and detailed account of the bewilderment, anxiety, and humiliation of such a vehement pursuit of ethnic identity. The painful, emotional journey in this novel represents the experience of many of us in Taiwan. Accordingly, it is very close to our hearts, especially today during the stand-off between China and Taiwan.

During the second half of the twentieth century, Taiwan developed into a democratic reality, looking forward to international understanding of our efforts. With the beginning of the new century, this English version of *Orphan of Asia* will be an important contribution for an international audience interested in Taiwan's history and aspirations. I only pray that our future will be brighter.

Pang-yuan Chi

Chapter One

· · ·

1. When the Flowers of Toil Bloom

The spring sun was warm on Hu Taiming's back as he kept count of the stepping-stones that studded the backyard path to the little hill, up which his grandfather led him by the hand. The path ran through a small woods, and nameless little birds chirped and flitted from branch to branch around them. Forever, it seemed: before he knew it, Taiming was short of breath and had lost count of the stones, and his grandfather was nowhere to be seen. Puffing, he caught up with the old man, who was waiting quietly for him at a level spot on the slope.

Grandfather had untied his long black bandanna to expose his head to the breeze. Taiming did the same and took off his bowl cap and wiped the sweat off his forehead. Although his head at the base of his pigtail itched, thanks to the breeze he soon stopped sweating.

The old man seemed ready for a smoke. He tied his bandanna back on, sat down on a rock, packed purple tobacco into his beloved long bamboo pipe and, after having Taiming light it for him, began, with relish, to make it hiss. The protracted hissing was familiar to Taiming. It carried him into a realm of curiously nostalgic feeling like the enticing prelude to the unraveling of a long tale.

For a while the old man seemed far away in memories, but then he slapped the pipe bowl against the rock and remarked: "It's changed. When Grandfather was young, this place used to be a deep forest of huge pine and camphor and oak trees. . . . What's more, it was overgrown with wisteria and rauwolfias, and badgers and squirrels came by in broad daylight. Even brave men hesitated to come this way alone. But listen to this, Taiming, when your grandfather was around twenty, he used to come on this path alone."

Back then, the slope was the secret passageway of bandits and thieves. If a cow was stolen here, you knew you would never see it again. The scariest place of all was Dragon's Neck, at the top of the hill, where even if a person was killed by bandits, the authorities usually didn't investigate: the crime was assumed to have been committed by barbarians, whose lands were not far away. But one day the old man, still young and reckless, walked up the hill alone. Halfway up, a big gust of wind—unbelievably cold—hit him. He yelled and instinctively shielded himself, but something resembling a cloud of dust covered his already partly obstructed vision. Cowering, he could not move. When he finally steadied himself and looked at where he was standing, there a huge umbrella snake lay. Horrified, he stepped back and picked up a stone to defend himself, but suddenly! the snake was nowhere to be seen. He threw away the stone and stood for a while dumbfounded, so strange was what had taken place, which had lasted no more than a few seconds. Nothing else happened. A courageous young man, he continued on to his destination and did what he had to do there. On his way back, though, when he reached the same spot, the stone, which he knew he had thrown into the undergrowth, was sitting right in the middle of the path.

An unexplainable chill went up his spine, and he flew home, terrified and gripped with fever. His head was spinning, and his waist hurt as if his legs had dropped out from under him.

He did not doubt that he had met a "demon," but he purposely refrained from "exorcising" it. Day after day, delirious with a high fever, he cursed, "Demon! You decided that we would meet. Try another unlucky fellow if you want money, because I'm not giving you any!"

Although he tried to fight, the demon persisted. Grandfather's mother was worried and decided to ask a fortune-teller to appease the demon who, they were told, was Barefoot Bighead. A thousand sheets of gold paper, three hundred of silver, five sticks of incense, a pair of large white tigers, a bowl of rice, one of soup, and an egg were prepared and sent to a point exactly 120 paces from where Grandfather lay ill. The gold and silver sheets were burned. His fever was gone the next day. By holding out for a week, he had exhausted the demon's patience—so said the old man and laughed like a hero.

"Well, Taiming, shall we?" he said, finished with his reminiscences. He stood up with a yo-ho and started leading the way again. When they went over the Dragon's Neck, it was as though their field of vision had suddenly been brightened: in front of them were endless, eye-opening, fresh green tea fields, at whose far end lay the Central Mountains as clean as though they had been washed and completely erasing, as if it had been a daydream, the eerie legend of Dragon's Neck recounted just a moment ago.

From behind the trees came the songs of young women, the coarse mountain songs of tea pickers. They stopped singing when they heard footsteps; a certain expectation had made them keep still. When they found out who was there, they did not hide their disappointment: "Humph! An old man and a kid." Laughing lewdly, they exchanged obscene remarks.

"What an awful place," the old man muttered bitterly and hastened his steps, eager to get away as soon as possible. It is not the practice of gentlemen and scholars, even the cruder ones, to sing mountain songs. The old man, who loathed mountain songs as though they were reptiles, felt as though his ears had been polluted.

They walked down a broad incline covered with pine trees and eventually reached the Ladder to the Clouds, a school that faced a courtyard containing a banyan tree. Across from the study, with the tree in between, was a temple, one of whose wings served as a classroom. In the small room were as many as thirty or forty pupils. Their reading voices and the whole disorderly atmosphere of the classroom spilled over into the courtyard.

With Taiming in tow, the old man went into the dark building. The abrupt transition from the bright outdoors temporarily blinded them, but as their eyes got used to the dark, the details of the room gradually became visible. In the corner was a bed and, above it, a square ashtray on which a shaded light, an alcohol lamp, flickered tiny, pale flames. The same dim flames were reflected gloomily on leaves, a pipe, a tray, and other carelessly strewn implements for smoking opium, as well as on a skinny old man who lay next to them. Books piled high on a desk by the bed, a holder for a number of crimson brushes (although summer was still some time off, it also contained a dirty bird-feather fan, which stood out), a picture of Confucius on the wall straight in front of it, incense smoke that trailed like a piece of string—these thickened even more the room's cloistered, swirling air. The old man walked up to the bed and saluted reverently: "Master Peng."

The old man on the bed opened half an eye and seemed merely to stare at the other's face, then suddenly sat up and said, "Aha, Master Hu!" in an unexpectedly strong, beautiful voice. "It's been a long time."

Rising from the bed, Master Peng recovered his dignity, went to take a peek in the classroom next door, and uttered a word of reprimand. At once the din of the boisterous students subsided and there was only a hushed silence.

Licentiate Peng used to be Old Hu's impoverished but brilliant classmate. Old Hu helped him in those days. If your work bore fruit and you finished as a top student, it was customary to visit the houses of the rich to receive congratulatory monetary rewards. Thus Licentiate Peng became rich, too, in a small way. But he quickly squandered the money to become poor again, as though to say, "This suits me better."

The only occupations for literati in the countryside were surveying, medicine, fortune-telling, and pedagogy. Like many others, Licentiate Peng chose to teach and became a master at the Ladder to the Clouds. He also remained a scholar, hoping to win a recommendation to the interior. But when Taiwan was placed under the administration of imperial Japan, the educational system changed, too. The ancient gateway to success was shut and bolted. With his dream of three decades crushed, Licentiate Peng devoted his life, without enthusiasm, to teaching at the local school at the Ladder to the Clouds. Rather than grooming talent, he was simply eking out a living. But when he spoke to Old Hu, he lovingly used literary words to bemoan the decline in the study of Chinese classics ("The way of the lords is no more," he asserted, "oh, my way has grown thin") and spoke formally even to Hu Taiming ("Thou art how old?"). When Taiming responded as his grandfather had taught him to, the master was overjoyed. Such was their fondness, and pride, for what had been lost.

Today the old man had brought along Taiming to entrust the boy's education to the scholar. Citing the distance the boy would have to commute, Licentiate Peng recommended waiting another year, but Old Hu wanted his grandson to begin studying the Chinese classics right away. Now that the village bookstore had closed, there was no place else except the Ladder to the Clouds. Moreover, the current state of affairs was such that the Ladder to the Clouds itself could be forced to close any day, so one could not afford to wait until next year. Bowing to Old Hu's convictions, they decided that Taiming should enter school immediately as a boarding student, since commuting was not a possibility. Although it was not easy for the old man to give up his cherished grandson, sacrifices had to be made for the sake of scholarship.

Before they left that day, Licentiate Peng put 120 copper coins on a red string and placed the necklace around Taiming's neck. Thus it was that Taiming, in the cloth shoes his mother had made for him and with a brand-new bowl cap on his pigtailed head, entered the Ladder to the Clouds in April when the flowers of labor still smelled sweet.

2. The Ladder to the Clouds

Hu Taiming's education began with the three-character book: Repeat after the master. After a couple of times, study on one's own, and recite before the master three or four times a week.

The text, which proceeded in strings of three characters each and consisted of maxims regarding history, the humanities, and complex moral philosophy, was too difficult for Taiming. Its main purpose, however, was to teach characters, and because Taiming had learned some at home, he did not have much trouble with them. Although the class went smoothly, the kids at the Ladder got into mischief in their spare moments. Chinese chess and hide-and-seek, of course, but they also stole fruits and vegetables from the neighbors, mainly for the fun of it. There was no lack of theft-worthy fruits, peaches and plums in spring and longans in the summer, but the most numerous were the fruits of autumn: pomegranates, pomelos, and persimmons. Winter, too, offered tangerines. The kids' usual strategy was for their antics to coincide with Licentiate Peng's daily nap, which he loved above all else and always began at noon and lasted for two hours. The expeditions sometimes became a problem for the neighbors, but the kids, whose mischief did obey rules of a sort, avoided the field right next to school. Although they could have stolen as much as they wanted from the absentminded old man who owned it, they chose instead for their exploits the field that belonged, say, to the old cat lady, a notorious miser. The more elaborate the measures taken to keep them out, the greater their pleasure in circumventing them, for it was not the end but the means—the process by which their cunning, carefully drafted plans bore fruit—that amused them.

Nonetheless, the kids were scared of Licentiate Peng, who used strict pedagogic methods, mercilessly spanking those who did not do well. Moreover, unlike most opium addicts, Licentiate Peng woke up unusually early. His water pipe, which filtered the smoke, began bubbling before sunrise, and the end of the bubbling meant that the rear gate was about to open with a creak: this was a signal for the boarding students to rise quickly, shine, and water the flowers. Lifting up, by flicking his waist, the hems of a robe that was as long as a mosquito net, Licentiate Peng would soon be coming down the stairs. Because he spent his life smoking opium in a dimly lighted room except when he was teaching, the master's almost fleshless face was a pale blue that betrayed no trace of blood even in the morning sunshine; his lips were dark blue, and his teeth, black. The nails on his left hand, in which he held his water pipe, grew uncut to well over an inch. Indifferent to all worldly matters except opium, mixing with no one, hardly ever exchanging any but pedantic remarks with his students, he still looked every morning at the flowers in the garden, his favorites being the orchids and the chrysanthemums. It was part of his daily routine. He had lived in this way for almost thirty years.

One day, Taiming had an accident. He was playing with several classmates in a meadow close to the school when a grass-eating water buffalo lazily accosted him. To Taiming, the buffalo was just another familiar detail of his pastoral surroundings. Standing up, he reached for its horns with his hands in an innocent show of affection. But the moment his two hands touched the horns, a blast of black wind whished before his eyes, and his off-balance body collided with the earth so hard that he lost consciousness. The astonished buffalo had shaken its head and thrust its horn into Taiming's side. Taiming vaguely felt someone pick him up but then fell unconscious. When he came to, he was on a bed, and his parents were anxiously looking into his face. There was a dull, numbing pain in his side.

Seeing his mother crying made Taiming remember the accident he had had. He relived the terrifying instant, but only as a memory of a faint and receding past.

His father, seeing that Taiming had revived, said, "Everything is OK now. Don't worry." And looking over his shoulder, he added for the others to hear, too, "We've rubbed bile of bear on your wound and made you drink carrot juice. . . . " He was a doctor of Chinese medicine. Licentiate Peng, who also was at Taiming's bedside, uttered heartfelt words of relief.

When he saw Licentiate Peng, Taiming reflected dully, "So I must be in the Ladder to the Clouds." His father and mother had come rushing over the Dragon's Neck.

The next day, Taiming was carried away from the Ladder in a palanquin to convalesce at home. Because there were not many doctors of Western medicine, bluish green herbs were applied to his wound. Meanwhile, his mother prayed for his recovery almost every day, making promises to various gods and grinding incense sticks for him to swallow. Fortunately, the wound did not become infected, and Taiming recovered in due course, but the year was nearly over by the time he was on his feet again.

As Taiming's wound healed and the new year approached, everyone at home grew busier and busier. His mother was preoccupied with making, under a feeble lantern light, shoes for Taiming and a hat for his sister. He hardly ever saw his father, who left home early every day and didn't seem to come back until late at night as far as Taiming could tell. His older brother was out until very late harvesting the sweet potatoes with the man-servant; then the brother's wife processed the potatoes, steaming them and placing them in large barrels, hoping they would ferment well. Amid this bustle, only Old Hu had nothing to do. The children discussed sweet cakes, bragged about their new shoes, and counted the days until their pig would be slaughtered.

The Ladder was closed until after New Year's Day, and so Taiming, though fully recuperated, was still at home. His job was to change the water in the old man's pipe. Old Hu, who was happy to be talking to Taiming after so long, repeated as often as before that "manifest virtue is the way of great learning" and told him about his own experiences. Sometimes he also complained: "Taiming, Japan's time has come, and it's not all bad. We have fewer thieves and robbers, and the roads are wider. But your way to scholarship and government has been blocked. And how are we supposed to pay such high taxes!"

The new year came at last. Speaking ill of others was prohibited during "New Year's Greetings," December 25 to January 5 on the old calendar. Misfortune lay in store (or so it was believed) for anyone who was criticized during that period. Every New Year's Eve, Taiming's family slaughtered a pig to make a votive offering to the Son of Heaven. Around an altar set up in the middle of the yard, they placed candies, fruits, the five fragrances, alcohol, votive coins, and gold and silver sheets at the head; chicken and meat at the lower seat; a sacrificed sheep on one flank; and the pig on the other. Then, at around four in the morning, the whole family left the house to worship the Son of Heaven. Old Hu and his son, dressed in ritual robes for the Triple Address, prayed for the family's prosperity, making vows to the Son of Heaven and to gods ranging from the merciful Guan Yin to the warrior Guan Di, and expressed gratitude for the past year's peace. On New Year's Day, starting in the early hours of the morning, firecrackers were set off everywhere, honoring the ancestors and gods. People forgot their work and abandoned themselves to the new spring until January 15 or so, with the men making their New Year's rounds and gambling and the women visiting their parents' homes and burning incense. The red planks with verses and the lively bursts of firecrackers, though nothing new, fanned their congratulatory spirit.

On the third day of the first month, Poverty Demon's Day, people usually stayed home and burned coins at the gate to drive away the demon of poverty. Shortly after noon, however, Licentiate Peng strolled in on a surprise visit. He stood for a while in the courtyard, admiring the poem on the red plank. When he was invited into the main building, he exchanged greetings with Old Hu, praised the tea cakes that were offered to him, and said, "Excellent. 'A yard of chicken and dogs? / Tour the enchanted garden. / The smoke that fills your path? / The mist keeps out the worldly.' Such ethereal lines come only to the most detached."

In response to the licentiate's praise, Old Hu requested meekly, "And your own, how does it read this year?"

"Terribly," the Licentiate warned: "'Fresh dew does not blight the large tree, / But coats the ancient ladder to the clouds.'" He also wrote it down for the old man to see.

"Excellent. I am reminded of those brothers in ancient times who refused to be fed by a traitor who had turned against their lord—I'm talking about the young princes Boyi and Shuqi, who preferred to eat their own sandals and starve." But in a voice suddenly clouded with gloom, he asked, "Even so, will the Ladder to the Clouds truly guard its ways as the poem says?" Without really meaning to, he revealed his most recent concern.

"In that case—in the event that the Ladder to the Clouds is ordered to shut down," Licentiate Peng replied dolefully, "classical learning will perish."

Right then, Taiming, his brother, and their father came out to exchange greetings, and from the gathering rose a merry din befitting the new spring. After a while, Licentiate Peng started to yawn repeatedly: his last dose of opium was wearing off. Old Hu, who was as considerate as he was shrewd, caught on immediately and invited Licentiate Peng to come to the old man's room and, there, gave him the needed fix.

At that moment, the yard suddenly grew animated. A new guest had arrived, Old Hu's elder brother's son, who had not called on them for some time. A heavy smoker, Opium Tong had turned to ash every ounce of a holding that was worth six thousand bushels of rice when his family had established itself as a separate branch—thus his name, whose unmodified form was Hu Chuantong. Opium Tong was also a gifted conversationalist and instantly livened up the atmosphere.

Taiming absentmindedly compared the two unexpected guests, Licentiate Peng and Opium Tong. As he could deduce from the exceptional treatment shown to the first, Old Hu revered the scholar. But Taiming did not want a scholarly or bureaucratic career, regardless of what his grandfather thought; rather, he sensed only hell in such a life. Conversely, he was fascinated by Opium Tong's son Zhida, who spoke Japanese and was a police deputy. People called Zhida "Sir," and he certainly cut a fine figure, carrying expensive Japanese cigarettes, flashing a brilliant white handkerchief, and leaving whiffs of perfume everywhere he went. To soak such a handkerchief with one's sweat seemed terribly wasteful to country folk. The refreshing, peculiarly cultural smell of soap that Zhida left in his wake the villagers called the "scent of Japan." At a time when clothes were washed with soapberries and faces, with teaberries, the new soap smelled expensive and special. Taiming sensed in Zhida's frivolous airs the harbinger of a new era.

But Zhida was not especially popular with the villagers. His own family treated him like a stranger, and the rest of the village paid him only the falsest respect. They bowed incessantly to his face, but while the scent of soap was still fresh—in fact, the moment he turned around—they denigrated him, and not just because he was part of the establishment.

Meanwhile, Zhida found it easy to talk to Old Hu, who had been to Hong Kong and Canton as a young man and knew something about Western culture. He called frequently on the old man. Soon, losing all sense of restraint, he began to advise him, "Sir, you ought to send Taiming to a real school. That's how things stand today."

Old Hu's reply was always this: "However they stand, you can't study the classics there." Although Western culture impressed him in some ways, he did not have much use for it—and wasn't Japanese culture merely copying it? His mind was full of admiration for the *Chronicles of Lu*, the teachings of Confucius and Mencius, Han and Tang literature, Song and Ming science, and the magnificent culture of ancient China, and he wanted this heritage transmitted to his descendants at all costs.

Not averse to his host's insistent offer, Licentiate Peng, who had arrived on the third of the month, stayed on for four days or so. He might have stayed longer if Opium Tong's friends, who had gotten wind of the Hu family's largesse, had not begun to gather and horn in on the elders' refined conversation. With the mood spoiled, Licentiate Peng said he was going home. Now, the villagers had nicknamed Opium Tong's friends Tail Winders, for they were a bunch of sycophants. Well aware how awkward their position would be if Licentiate Peng left, they tried their utmost to persuade him to stay, but to no avail. Old Hu's entreaties could not change the scholar's mind either.

Although Meng Chang-jun of the Three Thousand Guests was the old man's ideal, he had no desire to entertain the likes of Ah-San and Ah-Si. Once his former classmate took off, Old Hu withdrew, leaving his son, Taiming's father, in charge. His son had a reputation for being tough-minded and practical, so the uninvited lodgers, ill at ease, shuffled off on their own accord.

The lingering New Year came to an end. The moon had quietly been waxing, and it was now the fifteenth of the month. Various attractions were being prepared in town for the night of the full moon, the Flower Welcoming. The young girls, all dressed up, appeared, escorted by their parents, and there were plenty of young men. Besides being a great time to choose a bride, it also was one of the girls' rare opportunities to step out of the proverbial "boxes" or homes in which they were guarded.

Taiming and his grandfather set out before sundown to attend the festivities. As they neared the town, the noise of drums and gongs and pipes and flutes whetted their appetite for an evening under the full moon.

The promise of special attractions had drawn such a large crowd that it was almost impossible for them to make their way through the streets, in which people from as far away as Taipei were packed. When the human wave rolled, the child and his grandfather could hardly stay on their feet; Taiming and Old Hu were carried to the center of the festival when it was reaching high tide, with interminable lines of torches and floral lamps swirling breathtakingly. Trumpeters, choruses, masquerade parades of giants and dwarves, and wizards and fairies in their best clothes were gently swaying on floats. It was theater adorned with flowers and antiques, and as the floats passed, Old Hu explained that the man who was murdering his wife had lived in Wu and that the barbarian's lady bride, whose willow was dying, was Zhaojun. Taiming stood on his tiptoes and gazed, captivated, as a spectacular Lord Guan cut down six enemy generals. Last in the procession was a high platform decked with real singing geishas. Hoisting white paper lanterns, each with a large red dot—the Japanese flag—the policemen and young volunteers below were directing the traffic. It seemed as though the feverish crowd, pushing and shoving to get a better look at the geishas, was gathering force like a tsunami, when suddenly more than a dozen bodies, squeezed out by the human wall, stumbled toward the procession.

"You stupid chinks!" yelled the officers and swung their clubs to chase away the intruders. Chaos ensued. Old Hu had been pushed out of the human wall—his legs had not been strong enough—and found himself in the middle of the melee. He was hit hard and crumpled to the ground.

Although he finally managed to stand up and get to a safe spot, he was unable to calm down and kept moaning, "What a disaster . . . what a disaster!"

Clinging to the old man, Taiming begged, crying, "Grandpa, let's go home, let's go home right now."

The incident thoroughly damped their high spirits. Forgoing what should have been a pleasant celebration, they left the town and trudged home in the moonlight, feeling as miserable as beaten dogs.

The incident had a tremendous impact on Taiming. The old man, too, looked downcast, his pride wounded. But as the days sped past while they visited ancestors' tombs and the like, their painful wounds healed. By the time the bright white narcissus on Taiming's desk was tinged with yellow and the once arresting red of the plank at the gate had faded, Taiming's long New Year vacation was over, and at long last, he returned to the Ladder to the Clouds. The school, which had lost many students, seemed completely different, desolate.

The public school's incessant recruiting had drawn away students who lived closer to town. Licentiate Peng showed no signs of being upset, apparently having resigned himself to the way in which things were going, and refused the public school's invitation to teach Chinese literature there. Oblivious to his own fate, he recited Tao Yuanming's poem of leave-taking. His water pipe still bubbled in the morning, and he continued to tend his flower garden.

It was not exactly clear why, but when the watermelons were beginning to ripen, Licentiate Peng accepted an invitation from a private school close to the barbarian lands. He departed as if he had no attachments. Although Old Hu was disappointed, he had no choice but to take Taiming back. The task of guiding him through the classics now was up to the old man himself.

3. The Old and the New

In the meantime, the tremors of the new civilization that was rocking their sluggish existence were beginning to reach Taiming's everyday life too. He realized this for the first time when his young cousins, who had come to celebrate Taiming's mother's birthday, played and sang Japanese games and tunes in the "enchanted" yard. Painfully aware that there was a world he did not know, he recalled Cousin Zhida's words and felt left behind. Taiming's father, Hu Wenqing, was beginning to repeat, like a chant, "Those who can't speak Japanese are as good as fools in the civil service today." Times were changing, and the grandson could not understand why Old Hu was pushing him to study the Chinese classics. Although Hu Wenqing had vague hopes for the new education, he let the matter slide because he had other things to do.

These things—like buying back the land that Old Hu had lost—seemed worthwhile to the son, in his capacity as a son, and did not hurt his own interests, either. He made mistakes, however, such as when he bought a plot without asking about third-party obligations. He also found out that some mismeasured tracts actually belonged to him but had been included in the adjacent property.

One day, because he was a doctor, he rushed to the site of an avalanche merely to sit and idly watch the efficient government physicians handle the situation. In another case, a single injection saved a patient that he had given up on; sexually transmitted diseases, in particular, were beyond the capability of a doctor of Chinese medicine.

Hu Wenqing finally understood that real estate matters had to be settled according to a new, living, and practical science and that the sick were saved by Western medicine more often than by Chinese medicine. To begin with, doctors of Western medicine made so much more money! Thus, despite his interest in the new disciplines, he continued to entrust Taiming's education to Old Hu and those classics lessons; Hu Wenqing knew only too well his father's stubborn nature. Taiming thus became a small, rudderless boat drifting between the currents of two epochs.

An unforeseen development set him on course. Not far from the Hus' house was a lake; one day, the principal of the public school, who was fishing there, dropped by the house on his way home. He was warmly invited to tea, along with his interpreter Lin, who taught at the public school and whose conversation with Old Hu that day was only the first of many. Master Lin had a background in the Chinese classics as well as a knack for getting along with older people, and he finally managed to convince Old Hu to surrender his grandson to public education. Since it was common in those days to skip grades or to begin school without the proper qualifications in the middle of the school year, Taiming started at the beginning of the second semester. His view of the world abruptly widened, vast and vivid.

The school's bustling atmosphere was nothing like the Ladder with its restrictive atmosphere. The playing field and the classrooms were large and bright. Taiming lived in a commoners' dormitory which housed, in addition to Masters Lin and Horiuchi who occupied a corner of the building, five or six students, all of whom were about twenty years old, some already married. They all adored the quiet, sincere, and diligent Taiming. He advanced through school with flying colors.

Everything he saw and heard was new and wonderful. The place efficiently shattered the sorts of superstitions that Taiming had been taught; for instance, a camera did not rob you of your soul. Everyone was photographed without fear.

Taiming was not the only one who changed. When he returned home on vacation after a long absence, his family's pine woods had been reduced to a miserable state. Having heard the rumor that all forests were to become state property, the Hus had cut down their carefully preserved pine trees, citing a family emergency—but too hastily, it turned out, for the state had decided merely to monitor them, not to appropriate them.

Hu Wenqing was busy every day visiting the sick at their homes, and he gradually bought back the lands his father had lost. Although at one point, the Hu family seemed to be in decline, it now was showing signs of recovering its fortunes, its wealth and luck—or so said the villagers. As the Hus' financial condition improved, Taiming's father's short black tunics turned into flowing robes, at first made of cotton and, later, of the softest silk. Hu Wenqing looked very proud in his flowing patterned silk robes.

Under them, he nurtured hopes in his bosom for a certain young woman whom he had first seen on his way home from work. Her name was Ah-Yu.

Having somehow detected Hu Wenqing's secret, the parasite Ah-San whispered sweet, seductive words in his ears: "Doctor Hu, I don't blame the roosters for making so much noise. Ah-Yu has a pretty face, her skin's second to none, and what's more, she's obedient. She's certainly good enough to be your mistress. Ah, and no entanglements—she's got no family other than her mother. A man like you ought to have *two* extra beds—and you don't even have *one*! No sir, we won't have that."

"Really?" Hu Wenqing replied, grunting indifferently. But his heart was beating wildly with lust.

The palpitations of the doctor's heart were no secret to Ah-San, who gestured that he understood everything. With a knowing smirk, he added, "Don't worry, doctor, it'll turn out just fine. Just leave it to Ah-San. . . ."

Everything turned out just fine—for Ah-San, that is. The frugal Hu Wenqing began to support Ah-Yu, and brand-new furniture accumulated under her roof. Knowing, for the first time, the skin of a woman other than his wife's, Hu Wenqing was as happy as an idiot, oblivious to the fact that when he was not on the fancy bed he had bought for Ah-Yu, Ah-San smoked opium on it.

A greedy man, Ah-San was not satisfied with his cut for having played the go-between. He whispered into Ah-Yu's ear, "When it comes to money, you ought to get as much as you can, while you can. You think pigs know how to love? I bet you don't know how to squeeze so much money out of a pig that you won't have to work for the rest of your life."

Ah-Yu, who was the daughter of one of his relatives, called Ah-San "uncle." When she heard him say that, she thought, "Uncle has a point." Uncle also convinced Ah-Yu's mother that they should add another act to the unfolding drama.

Having completed the day's rounds, the unsuspecting Hu Wenqing visited his mistress's house. Dinner was served with chicken saké, which he loved, and Ah-Yu was more passionately deferential than ever. When he finished his meal, Hu Wenqing lay his pleasantly inebriated body on the bed he had bought for her, ready to wade into a bliss so wonderful that he could almost forget that it was, like the bed, expensive. Ah-Yu knew the routine well and would slip like a soft wisp of air into the reach of his voluptuous tentacles.

Moments of languorous bliss, not unlike the opium smoker's, flowed slowly. Then Hu Wenqing drifted into the sleep that beckoned him.

It was midnight when a knocking so violent that it seemed about to tear down the door woke him up. In between the thundering knocks, someone yelled, "You thief! Here's the cuckold! You tomcat, open the door so I can beat you to death!"

Shocked out of his wits, Hu Wenqing jumped out of bed. Ah-Yu tidied her disheveled nightgown and screamed in a voice pitched high with fear: "Oh, it's him!"

So completely unnerved was Hu Wenqing that his body shook like a dying man's. Between the knocking and bellowing at the door, he could also hear Ah-Yu's mother's pleading wails. For some reason, at this late hour, Ah-San also was around. "Wait, leave it to Ah-San! Let me handle it, I say!" he excitedly insisted.

Thanks to Ah-San's opportune mediation, Hu Wenqing survived the perilous encounter. Before he scurried home, he promised to pay five hundred yen as a settlement, wrote an IOU, and handed over as a guarantee his gold watch, gold ring, gold chain, gold-rimmed glasses, and all the other valuables he had on him. The next day, Ah-San brought Hu Wenqing the piece of paper, exchanged it for five hundred yen, and badgered him for a hundred more, this for himself—the doctor owed the schemer that much for the rescue, did he not? In just a couple of days, the whole village knew about it.

Having paid six hundred yen for a lesson he apparently took to heart, Hu Wenqing did not mention Ah-Yu's name for a while. But two months later, when Ah-San told him that Ah-Yu had been divorced by her husband, Hu Wenqing's desire revived. The lesson had been hammered in so deeply that he hadn't been able to stop thinking about her.

Through Ah-San, he asked Ah-Yu whether she would live with him as his concubine. She had no objections; instead, the problem was how to convince his own wife, Ah-Cha, to accept such an arrangement. He consulted Ah-San, who proved wise again.

One day, escorted by Ah-San, a fortune-teller who seemed to think highly of himself came to the Hu house. "Geography is absolutely crucial," he said, praising the house's location, "for the auspicious fortune of a place and its inhabitants." Said to hail from China, he spoke the dialect of the continent's southern marshlands, wore heavy black-rimmed glasses, and held a large fan. "And yet every person's life has its own laws, rhythms, and duration—what people call 'fate.'" Citing the story of the wise Kongming, the brave Guan Yu and Zhang Fei, and their lord Liu Xuande, who did not, despite the lord's virtues, prevail in the War of the Three Kingdoms, the fortune-teller warned against the folly of resisting fate. He added that death lurked on Master Hu's countenance, that he had probably suffered a severe bout of ill luck recently, and that he might have lost his life were it not for his ancestor's virtues, not to mention Master Hu's own good deeds. But the bad luck was far from over, and the only way to escape it was—the fortune-teller paused here and concluded in grave style—to have a concubine.

"I would like to examine madam's physiognomy as well," he went on. "It will round out our results." Elated, Hu Wenqing advised his wife to submit, which, obedient to her husband, she did. "Madam has the look of a woman affluent in old age, but she should not monopolize her husband unless she wants to jeopardize his well-being. His luck is expected to improve for just one year and flounder for five, during which time he will be extremely vulnerable." Finally, in a matter-of-fact tone, he declared, "It's fascinating how consistently Master Hu's signs cry out for having two women in his life."

If this was true, Ah-Cha had to consent. After all, it was not uncommon for a husband to keep a concubine, and she should not take it personally. Although Old Hu had a pensive look, he did not seem to mind all that much. It was Hu Wenqing's elder son, Zhigang, who opposed the plan. As usual, Ah-San knew how to cope with such annoyances. Hu Wenqing followed Ah-San's advice and promised to add to the land that Zhigang, as the elder son, would inherit when he moved out. The promise immediately dispelled the son's fastidious objections.

That was how Ah-Yu joined the Hu household. Sustained in the face of changing times, such practices—so remote from the transformation that Taiming was undergoing—puzzled and alienated him during his infrequent homecomings. Sensitive to trends among the progressive elements of those times, Taiming had cut off his pigtail and wore his hair cut short. There was a hollow ring where the pigtail used to be, and the village's gossips nicknamed it "the limestone." The village elders, who believed it was unethical to damage any part of one's body, were scandalized, as though he had lopped off his own head. In fact, a traditional, private means of bringing justice against adulterers was to shave their heads.

Taiming, of course, had had his pigtail cut off voluntarily. The first time he went home with his new haircut, his mother Ah-Cha told him in a trembling voice that she tried hard to control: "Taiming, you won't meet your ancestors when you die." She wept. When Zhigang introduced him to others, he always snatched off his younger brother's cap, more for the fun of it than for reasons of etiquette, and his younger sister kept saying, "Gross!" In the streets, comments like "Hey little monk!" were hurled in his direction.

Ah-Yu usually stayed in the innermost rooms of the house and never emerged except for meals, but when Taiming came home, she offered to look after him as though she were his mother. On his part, Taiming resisted the familiarity of the stranger who had become a family member without his knowledge. A kind of rift separated him from the rest of the family. A vague uneasiness propelled him back to school as soon as he was through with whatever he had come home for. This unfulfillment fueled his desire to study and to know more.

4. Into Roiled Waters

Because Taiming was exceptionally honest, all the teachers loved him. His Japanese improved quickly as he helped Mr. Horiuchi (a bachelor) cook. When Taiming graduated, he sat for medical school exams, and when he failed them, he entered the teachers' program at the Department of Japanese. During his four profoundly influential years there, he became a man of the new kind of culture, however shallow his actual learning may have been. Some of his classmates left for Japan with high hopes of pursuing their studies further, but like most of the others, Taiming accepted his duties and was assigned to a school in the countryside. He dropped by his native village for a brief visit with his family.

His cap and suit were edged with gold, and a short sword hung from his belt; the civil officer's full uniform was quite a sensation in the village. As the firecrackers were set off at the gate, more and more friends and relatives gathered at his house for a welcoming celebration as elaborate as the feasts Taiming had known as a child. Seventy or eighty people were chatting in the hall by the time the drinks were poured.

Opium Tong stood up to make a toast: "Here is the first civil officer our village has produced. The learned men of old were not more honorable. To the glory of our clan!"

Everyone heartily welcomed this excuse to drink and feast. Taiming, a product of the new education, felt not only alienated but repulsed by the mindless spree. He cut short his stay and departed to fill his post.

From the desolate station where he got off the train, it was more than an hour's ride on the local sugar refinery's flatcar to get to his first workplace, K Public School. The student body consisted mostly of children from nearby farming villages, and the teaching staff numbered thirteen, including the principal. Two of the instructors were new, Taiming and a Japanese woman named Naito Hisako who had just graduated from a women's college.

The two went to the principal's office to introduce themselves. Even though his bald head made him look much older, the principal, who was Japanese, was not many years past thirty. The Taiwanese headmaster who stood obediently at his side was going on forty-five and looked as lackluster as his dirty uniform, whose gold lace had lost its color. The principal offered formulaic instructions, and when he was finished, the students were marshaled into the main hall to greet the new teachers. On the platform, Taiming was flustered by the innumerable gazes fixed on him. He did not remember a word he said.

As he left the hall, the headmaster said to him, "What energy, what eloquence!" Taiming sensed that he was being ironic and felt even more embarrassed.

It rained the next day. From the classroom quiet after dismissal, he gazed thoughtfully at the white petals, fallen from the oil trees, that littered the muddy brown dirt from one end of the playground to the other. He heard footsteps and turned around to find Headmaster Chen, Instructor Li, and Trainee Huang coming through the doorway.

Grinning, Headmaster Chen approached Taiming and said, "Hu! So what do you think?"

"Well, I'm not used to it yet. I don't know what I'm doing."

"Ah yes, that's how it was for all of us. You'll get used to it soon enough. By the way," he added, turning to Instructor Li, "the Cat is getting pretty nasty: he hosted a Japanese-only welcoming party for Miss Naito Hisako last evening. Did you know that?"

"He was calling for staff harmony just yesterday, after the entrance ceremony! 'Japanese-Taiwanese unity!' It's depressing."

Their conversation seemed to be directed to Taiming. Apparently, "Cat" was the principal's nickname, and the trio continued their mean-spirited talk in a manner that did not become educators. Somewhat disgusted, Taiming turned his face to the window and pretended not to hear.

"Hu, what do you think?" the headmaster asked.

"Well, I'm pretty new here . . ."

Taiming did not have to clarify his position, for the trio immediately resumed enumerating their grievances against the principal and the other Japanese members of the faculty. Finally they said, "We're leaving, go home and get some rest," and filed out of the classroom.

This pungent whiff of the school's smoldering racial tension gave Taiming a sinking feeling. His mood darkened further upon reflection: he could not care less whether the principal had invited him, but it was *his* having been snubbed that had prompted the headmaster and company to air their latest grievances in his presence.

Three days later, after Saturday classes, Headmaster Chen came to Taiming's classroom to tell him, "There'll be a welcoming party for you this evening—just among us—so get ready." The headmaster seemed to think he was hatching some plot, and his clandestine, unabashedly retaliatory intent annoyed Taiming. The insinuating "just among us" had the peculiar overtones of an ideological cadre, and Taiming dreaded the prospect of clearer self-definition through successive meetings. Strife between the Japanese and Taiwanese faculty was bound to cast a dark shadow on the children. Considering this, he replied that he had to decline the honor, though he was grateful to the headmaster, who was being too kind. Headmaster Chen took this as a sign of Taiming's modesty and urged him to accept the invitation; preparations had already been made, and the welcoming party was to be held in Taiming's room.

The room had neither closets nor paper screens. The blanched surface of the six tatami spoke eloquently of his dull living conditions. There was nothing on the dirt-floored patch adjacent to the room except a cooking stove and a water jug. Before Taiming moved in, the room had belonged to Trainee Huang's family of five.

At the designated time, Headmaster Chen and five or six instructors, one of them a woman, trooped into his room. Taiming fretted, too late, that he had no cushions for his guests. And yet—wasn't he supposed to be the guest?

They brought their own drinks and told him they had ordered food from a restaurant in town. The drinking commenced and continued with the help of the lady instructor, who poured. The alcohol had the effect of centering their conversation on the principal's antics. The Cat used the school's janitor as his personal servant, making him chop wood, prepare his bath, and run errands. The Cat also monopolized the occasions for formal, funded trips and preferentially assigned the rare paid leaves to his Japanese colleagues. The voluntary instigator of these verbal attacks was Instructor Li. The others nodded and assented, but only halfheartedly, and they did not seem particularly interested. As a matter of fact, the arrival of every new dish occupied their attention and repeatedly interrupted the attack. Taiming grew sadder and sadder that evening. It was not a welcoming ceremony but an excuse for an uncouth gathering for food and drink.

When all the dishes had been eaten and empty bottles littered the room, Headmaster Chen and the lady instructor went home. The four or five who remained were not yet satisfied and took Taiming out on the town.

The night breeze felt good against his hot cheeks, which still glowed from all the drinking forced on him. His inhibitions disappeared with the wind. He suddenly wanted to shove his thoughts, which had been gathering heat, in his colleagues' faces. In the strongest words, they lived by the trifles that dangled before their eyes, and their way of thinking was utterly petty. What came out from Taiming's mouth, however, were fragmentary, unconvincing sentences that failed to express even a hundredth of what he felt.

"You're such a great citizen," retorted Instructor Li. The expression, borrowed from an occupation-era song that went "Be a great citizen," meant that Taiming was a lackey of the Japanese. "I'm afraid you're still too green," Instructor Li jeered some more. "The notes you took at school are useless in the real world. I wish it were that simple!"

They suddenly found themselves in a weird place, although it was sudden only for Taiming; the others had been steering him to this destination. With Trainee Huang at their head, the party went through a scarlet curtain that swayed seductively across one of the doorways. In the middle of the tidy room was a bed and over it hung a silk mosquito net, decorated at the top with what looked like a horizontal painting but was, in fact, Fuchou embroidery of a beautiful phoenix that seemed to be dancing. Relaxed, playfully muffled, but provocative laughter came from a lady in a high-collared dress who stood in front of the net.

Taiming made out a couplet on the hanging picture of a Xihu beauty that adorned one of the walls: "A brave recalls his once sweet one, a ginger stamen in the sun." He grasped the couplet's hidden message and felt rather satisfied with himself.

When Trainee Huang, who seemed to be well acquainted with the lady, tried to introduce Taiming to her, the new face Taiming surprised everyone by preempting him: "Nice to meet you, Miss Yingkui."

"Hu, how do you know her name? How?" Trainee Huang demanded, suspicious.

Taiming only laughed and answered that a good prime minister knows his people even if he never steps out of his palace. The woman, too, looked more than a bit puzzled that Taiming had guessed her name, so he proceeded to divulge his trick as well as his erudition: the first line of the couplet on the hanging scroll began with the character "ying," the second with "kui."

Later, Trainee Huang started singing a mountain song, and their conversation gradually lost all vestiges of sophistication.

That night, in his dingy room, Taiming had trouble falling asleep for a long time after he went to bed. He thought about the suffocating atmosphere that had surrounded him ever since he arrived, about the sense of injury the Taiwanese faculty nursed against their Japanese counterparts, and about the sad melodies and lyrics that Yingkui had sung from *Lament of the Courtesan*. After a while, Yingkui's face became Naito Hisako's, and when he thought about Hisako, his youthful blood coursed quickly through his veins.

5. Hisako

The semesters that segmented teaching life came and went like whirlwinds, and the seasons hectically tumbled past. The watermelons, which had lined the grocer's storefront until just now, disappeared when you stole a furtive glance back at the summer vacation; the quick-handed grocer had replaced them with rich vermilion persimmons. Meanwhile, local government was reformed in the direction of greater autonomy, and the gaudy gold laces of the civil officer's uniform gave way to black frills. The short sword was recalled, although some people had grown attached to theirs. Taiming found the sudden lightness of his belt to be physically and emotionally liberating.

Autumn failed to dissipate the heat, but at school, Sports Day was coming up. In the playground, from which one could see the peak of Mount Cigao thrust into the azure sky, the students practiced their games and dances after school. The teachers in charge of dancing were Ruie, the only woman at Taiming's welcoming party, and Naito Hisako. As the head of the music department,

Taiming was busy every day, playing the organ accompaniment for the dances. Sometimes his mind drifted off the keyboard into a dream, and the children danced awkwardly to the slowly fraying rhythm until it became too difficult.

"Mister, you're completely off!" said Ruie, wiping her sweat unceremoniously and coming over to Taiming's side. She scowled at him, but the look in her eyes was more flirting than scolding.

"Ah! I don't know what's wrong with me," Taiming replied. He put his elbow on the organ, rested his chin on his palm, and looked far away. Ruie's breasts, which rose and fell with her heavy breathing, occupied a corner of his vision, so close he could have touched them. When Naito Hisako saw that Taiming was not about to start up again very soon, she blew her whistle, called for a break, and walked slowly toward her colleagues.

Ruie said to her pointedly, seeking agreement, "I say there's something wrong with our Mr. Hu." But her chiding remark was imbued with a protectiveness rooted in their assumed kinship. It was not that Taiming did not notice her persistent attempts, sometimes coquettish, to befriend him; rather, he was deliberately avoiding them. He felt sorry not to respond to her advances, but he could not help it. His heart was filled so completely by Naito Hisako that he could hardly think about anyone or anything else. Ruie's kindness and affection only annoyed Taiming.

Almost pushing him off, Ruie demanded to sit down at the organ. Taiming surrendered his seat grudgingly and thought, "If only that were Hisako just now . . ."

Naito Hisako began to dance to Ruie's organ accompaniment. Whenever Hisako bent her body to the swaying tunes of the "The Celestial Nymph's Gown," her gymnastically trained limbs flashed elegant arcs. It was incredible. As she turned, the hem of her skirt spiraled upward, revealing a couple of pistils, the whitest of legs.

"Ah! Ah, those white legs!" Taiming observed to himself. He felt dizzy and shut his eyes. The skirt did not spiral downward under his eyelids, where the white legs went on voluptuously flexing more enchanting curves. The plump and fragrant legs of a Japanese woman—and how like a butterfly, how charmingly her hands hopped from breeze to breeze! He recalled the talent show at which Hisako had worn a white robe to dance the celestial nymph, when her glamorous limbs and their immaculate movements overpowered the packed hall, which grew quiet with pleasure. And on those rare occasions when she was walking around in her beautiful kimono, her obi puffing out at her back, Hisako's inexpressible allure also was not to be underestimated.

He opened his eyes. Hisako was still dancing unawares, but Taiming could not watch anymore. For the more she aroused him, the more depressed he felt and the deeper he slid down into the unbridgeable abyss that separated them, he Taiwanese and she Japanese.

He actually was sick, and thus chance intervened to augment his longing. That day he excused himself on account of a headache, and lying down on his back as soon as he tumbled into his room, he glared at the ceiling. He couldn't stop thinking about Hisako: "That she is Japanese and I am Taiwanese is a fact. Can anyone change that? No one can change it!"

The fact tormented him. If, if they did manage to get married, then what? He would be virtually helpless when it came to providing Hisako with the high standard of living that a Japanese woman naturally expected, and as a public school teacher he had no chance of becoming rich. The best he could hope for was to become a principal somewhere in the countryside, and that only after thirty years of hard work. A thorough examination of his options drove him to despair.

Taiming washed Naito Hisako in his pool of ideals. She was the spotless gown of the celestial nymph, the perfect woman, almost an idol. Curiously, the real Naito Hisako said things like, "I bet you've never taken a bath in your whole life, Mr. Hu, people on this island just don't," and complained that he stank of garlic. But Taiming never ate garlic. She never tired of saying, "What can you expect of these people?" though not maliciously; it seemed more that she could not help but acknowledge her sense of superiority. Baozheng's party, to which both of them were invited for the old New Year, was the site of one of many telling scenes. When a whole roasted chicken (which still was in its original form) appeared on the table, Hisako leaned toward Taiming and whispered, "Are we barbarians or what?" Once she had a bite, she declared it delicious and started chewing like a pig, succumbing to the exquisite, artless taste born of that people's wisdom that she had just now ridiculed as barbaric. She never noticed the contradiction, namely, that her arrogance fed on ignorance. The heedless stupidity with which she gorged herself showed that she was just another woman.

Taiming was not unaware of this. It was just that her faults tended to fuel his passion rather than dampen it. "Then my blood is," he thought, "polluted after all. It's my karma I must overcome; the filthy blood of a man who made a concubine of a loose ignoramus courses through my body. . . ." For a long time that night, his inner conflicts kept him awake.

6. The Longing Lasts

Once Sports Day was over, the pupils began preparing for exams with the hope of entering normal school. Every pupil did everything he could, but each year the number of students admitted from a district was approximately one. The competition for the single seat was naturally stiff in a district that counted sixteen schools and more than twenty sixth-grade classes, but Taiming badly wanted the chosen one to come from K Public School.

The first step he took against these formidable odds was to make up a schedule that extended from daybreak to sundown and beyond. He offered Japanese and math reviews before school, analyses of recent exam questions after school, and, at night, tutorial sessions in his room. It was not too long after he had begun living according to this punishing regimen that he learned, to his dismay, that some of the future examinees had failed to digest the fourth-grade, and even the third-grade, material. In this way, Taiming found out about the lower-grade teachers' negligence.

Hardly ever speaking to his colleagues, Taiming tackled his task feverishly, hoping to escape his unending longing for Naito Hisako. His colleagues did not think well of him for trying; some suggested that his real motive was self-promotion, and others derided what they called his misguided efforts. Instructor Li scornfully pointed out to him that nothing would change in the larger view, since there was a "natives quota" and Taiming was simply trying to rob another school of success in what was no more than a petty turf war. This suffocating atmosphere emboldened Taiming, who thought his colleagues were merely rationalizing their own neglect. "Wait and see," he challenged himself, "the exam results will be impressive." His eyes were bloodshot from teaching day and night.

One evening, a clearly prosperous, middle-aged gentleman visited Taiming in his room. "Though you are young, teacher," he began courteously, "you look after our children as though they were your own. What you have been doing for the test takers has reached my ears, and I am here tonight to ask a favor of a man I have long held in great esteem." A member of the town assembly, Mr. Lin was also considered a man of integrity.

He had three sons. The eldest had failed every examination for Taiwan's secondary schools and, as a last resort, had been sent to Japan. In his ten or so years in Tokyo, all he had learned was how to play pool and seduce waitresses. He, his eldest son, had come back bored and broken. The second son, who also had to be sent to Japan for schooling, joined a political movement and was never heard from again. Thereafter, Lin's hopes had centered on his youngest son; he at least should study at a secondary school in Taiwan, within reach of his parents' watchful eyes. This son was attending K Public School and in fact was in the sixth grade, but not in Taiming's class. Ito-sensei did not offer extracurricular sessions. When Mr. Lin, bowing deeply, requested special tutorial guidance for his son, Ito simply refused. The assemblyman was well aware that the boy's abilities were wanting and that the requested transfer of responsibilities was irregular, but the boy was his son—and the father was desperate.

With the passion of a young teacher, Taiming responded to the man, his story, and his faith in Taiming. Granted, things might get complicated if he accepted another teacher's pupil, and Ito happened to be one of those who regarded Taiming as selfish. Nonetheless, Mr. Lin's fatherly love moved Taiming to do him a favor that appealed to his own, neophyte's, uncompromising sense of justice. His blood rose.

The deal concluded, Mr. Lin, with visible relief, turned to small talk. He looked around the room and said, "These lodgings are, if I may be frank, terrible. Don't they ever replace the tatami?"

"They haven't in three years, I've been told."

"Three years? If I remember correctly, the budget permits them to be replaced each year."

"I asked the principal last December. He said we're running low on money."

"Running low?" Mr. Lin repeated with rising irritation. "That's impossible—the principal, Ito-sensei, and the new lady all had brand-new tatami when I made my New Year's rounds. Outrageous! This is embezzlement." Mr. Lin fulminated at length against the principal and the Japanese faculty's arrogations before he finally left.

The pupils, though, were advancing quickly, repaying Taiming's efforts twice over with clear signs of mastery that he found almost overwhelmingly heartwarming.

Although Taiming felt like a satisfied warrior who has fought well and can tell himself as his lifeblood is draining out that he has served honorably and should have no regrets, his heart beat wildly on the morning of the exams. He was beset by doubts, an empty feeling that every step he had taken was misguided and pointless. Yet what could he do now but await the stern verdict?

The exam results surpassed all his expectations: one student qualified for normal school, and two, for secondary school. The total of three successful applicants was unprecedented for any public school, and the letters on the posting grew misty as Taiming's heart filled with a desire to thank someone or something. Someone tapped him on his back, and it was Mr. Lin, who squeezed Taiming's hands warmly in his and said with genuine feeling, "Mission complete! Congratulations!"

"Mr. Lin's son?" Taiming thought momentarily; then a chill shot through him. Too preoccupied with the overall results, he had not even looked to see how his pupils had performed individually. He looked down—his hands were still in Mr. Lin's—and said, "I'm sorry I failed you." These last words were barely audible.

"What are you saying!" chided Mr. Lin, now the consoling party. "Teacher, you don't know how much you've done. My son wasn't up to it, that's all." But his voice sank toward the end.

No one could deny that the exceptional exam results were due to Taiming's efforts, and he certainly was proud. He also turned shy when, both at school and in town, people talked about nothing else. One day, after school, as he was packing his things, someone sneaked up on him:

"Congratulations, Mr. Hu."

Taiming stiffened, electrified. The voice was Hisako's. It was filled with affection, however, and continued in the same uncharacteristic vein: "You must have worked hard. Really!"

Taiming examined his heart and found that it was open to her praise. He sincerely accepted her kind words, and the two of them stood there for a while, saying little and feeling much.

A jovial, high-pitched cry shattered the conciliatory moment. It was Ruie. "Hu the Great! Congratulations! Wow, what a feat!"

"How predictable this woman is," Taiming groaned to himself. He could hardly speak now, for Ruie's enthusiastic manner always wore him down, but this weakness also made him long even more for Naito Hisako's company. Hadn't his immersion in work helped him overcome his longing? It had been only a temporary respite. How quickly his reserve crumpled before her, her face and voice. This was proof for him! He staggered home overcome by his futile sentiments.

By chance, Taiming's and Hisako's paths kept crossing. On his train ride home—the commencement exercises had been full of joy and tears—he ran into her. She suggested that he drop by her parents' house. The invitation, which Hisako probably offered to a colleague as an innocuous gesture of goodwill, meant so much to Taiming that he could hardly bear the weight of it.

Her parents welcomed the stranger heartily. It was lunchtime, and they offered him a Japanese-style lunch. Although the kidney beans and tempura did not strike Taiming as particularly unusual, the yam soup and sashimi did. "Please," Hisako urged girlishly as she drank the sticky soup, "it's so delicious, Mr. Hu, please try it." Taiming dipped his chopsticks in it but did not take more than a sip.

"Try a slice," Mrs. Naito prompted, indicating the raw fish he had been avoiding: "it's tuna." The slab of tuna that Taiming politely put in his mouth did not inspire him to linger over it, so he gulped it down, but it shot back up with a rush of nausea. He recovered in the nick of time; pretending to wipe his mouth, he spat the slice out into his handkerchief. Tears came to his eyes; this was the bittersweet taste of love. The good-natured Naito family did not notice Taiming's little maneuver, and they seemed not to doubt for a moment that what was delicious to them also must be delicious to him.

He took his leave, and Hisako walked with him to the station. The new semester was not far off. She waved her handkerchief as the train sped toward his village. He was smarting from the tender wound of parting, and his gaze was turned for a long time toward Hisako, who was still waving her handkerchief.

7. At Home

Back home, not much had changed since the last time he was there. Ah-San and Ah-Si had not changed, and Opium Tong still smoked his namesake.

Grandfather was doing just fine, and his water pipe was still bubbling. Taiming wanted to have the leisurely conversations that they had not had for a long time, so he was puzzled that his grand-father treated him like an important guest. He felt better when Old Hu began talking, first about tea and then about the twenty-four obedient children of history. Evidently glad to have someone to talk to, the old man demonstrated how much he still loved to chat, and there was no end to topics of conversation. Licentiate Peng was still teaching in the wilds. Taiming's father, Hu Wenqing, was preoccupied with the family business: medicine, on the one hand, and adding to the Hus' fortunes, on the other.

Not much had changed, but there were subtle indications of time passing. Just as Ah-San's and Ah-Si's foreheads were slightly more wrinkled, the furniture and utensils in the Hu household seemed—was Taiming imagining?—darker with age. The ceremonial hall, where twenty years ago a few hundred Hus had assembled to celebrate, was now completely dilapidated and covered with the children's scribbling; the loosened gold leaf no longer read "summum bonum," and the candlesticks, heavy with the wax that had collected on them, sat on a dust-caked altar. Over the years the Hu clan had scattered, with some members going to the southern and eastern parts of the island and resettling there. Others, like Ah-San and Ah-Si, stayed, but as hangers-on.

"Ah-San's and Ah-Si's world is disappearing," Taiming mused, captivated by the objective vision he suddenly had of the lives around him. Licentiate Peng was trying to escape reality, whereas Grandfather was trying to transcend reality. Hu Wenqing was overwhelmed by wrestling with reality. And Taiming—he was tired of chasing reality. What spurred him on was youthful ambition, hopes, and dreams, but, come to think of it, didn't it sometimes seem meaningless? He almost envied his grandfather's detachment.

When Old Hu mentioned the twenty-four obedient children, he also stated that having children was a person's filial duty and gently urged Taiming to marry. The old man, who had been pressing this idea for quite some time, saw his grandson's homecoming as a good chance to make sure the idea was realized. The custom was to arrange the marriage, which was sealed upon the first meeting—not a custom of which Taiming approved. To begin with, he could not take his mind off Naito Hisako, although the fact that he did not know what she thought about him was certainly a problem. No matter how much he loved her, he had no solid reason for rejecting the matches Old Hu might suggest to him. Taiming really did not know what to do, but Old Hu, who was just sounding him out, just left it there. He returned the conversation to the classics in a way that surprised the public school teacher. The new thinking had apparently found its way to Old Hu, who declared, "A thousand paragraphs written in the best civil examination style are no match for a single bomb. We've entered the age of science, Taiming. Literary dilettantism is not enough. The works that Confucianism long branded as heretical are being put to good use in Japan, even Shang Yang's idea of rule by law. Science is what the coming generations should take up."

This rekindled Taiming's respect for his grandfather, but the young man did not have time for philosophical pontification: he was too busy thinking about Hisako. He was remembering her voice, her words, and her figure even while his grandfather was speaking.

The next day, Taiming was confronted by his brother. Zhigang was not an optimistic person; it was only after much delay and nagging by his wife that he finally brought up the issue of inheritance, which occupied his heart and soul. This was how things stood: although their father's mistress, Ah-Yu, was now a mother, she had not been properly entered in the family register. Although her son was not yet a Hu, Hu Wenqing was trying to remedy the situation. Thus it would be advantageous, in property terms, for Zhigang and Taiming to form separate branches immediately. They could do this successfully if they formed a common front.

Taiming recognized his sister-in-law's hand in Zhigang's plan and found it distasteful. Because Ah-Yu's son was also Hu Wenqing's, the child had to be treated like a brother. It was unbearable to watch a treacherous scheme being hatched behind Hu Wenqing's back while he, their father, carried on without suspecting. To participate in such a plan was unthinkable. Taiming lost his temper and burst out, "I'm single, so I don't need to inherit anything. If you want the property so much, brother, split it with father and leave me out of it." He stormed back to his room and felt miserable for having experienced at first hand the ugliness of family feuds. His indignation flared up when he recalled that Zhigang had also mentioned the tuition money reserved for Qiuyun, their younger sister, who was to enter a girls' school in a year. If Zhigang was going to be like that, Taiming would side with his father, to the bitter end, he swore. Of course, keeping a mistress was not good. It was their father's weak point, and Hu Wenqing would probably give in to Zhigang's demands if Taiming cooperated. Taiming could almost see the smirk on his sister-in-law's and the other faces that would profit from the scheme. Even though keeping a mistress was not good, the child born of the arrangement was innocent. This thought made Taiming want to speak to his father, his poor father, whom Ah-Yu, Ah-San, Ah-Si, Zhigang, Zhigang's wife, and the rest surrounded only to attack him! Striding into Hu Wenqing's living room, where the father sat holding the baby, his mother close by, Taiming poured out his views in a torrent, not bothering to wipe away the tears filling his eyes as he spoke. Both parents were deeply moved.

The father's eyes also teared up. Hu Wenqing had recently been showing signs of old age and now looked at his son with infinite gratitude and trust. He held up the infant: "Your little brother. . . . I'm counting on you." Taiming reached for the small, warm lump of life that laughed innocently at him, and it felt like a blood relation.

Besides having a difficult workplace, Taiming also did not feel at home with his family. He left for K Public School as soon as his father declared once and for all that the Hu property was not to be divided up until his death, effectively ending Zhigang's plan to branch out immediately. The beginning of the new semester was still some days away, and the school seemed lonely without Hisako. Taiming felt as though he had been exiled from life. He decided that he at least could visit Ruie, scurried down the dirt path to the apartment he believed to be hers, and waited nearby. He did not have the courage to knock. Back in his dingy room, dejected, he tried to forget everything by dropping into a lonely, shallow sleep, trying his best not to call out a Japanese woman's name.

8. Storm Season

A new semester usually brings fresh expectations and the kind of tension one feels when looking at a blank sheet of paper, but the semester that began that April was filled with a murderous tension more like the quiet before a storm. Some of the teachers had been transferred. Faculty meetings and morning assemblies, held routinely every day, were torments for Taiming.

At the faculty meetings, the principal regularly denounced the native instructors. He would begin with a cliché like "Those who have not learned the national language (Japanese) lack national spirit" and end by exhorting the native faculty members to make Japanese their language at home. What kind of educators were they if they couldn't educate their own families? These charges of low pedagogic morale hurt Taiming, who felt as though he were indeed their target. The faculty meetings also reviewed the reports on student conduct written by the instructor on duty for the week. It was reported, for example, that the bathrooms in the native pupils' homes were filthy, and it consequently was concluded that the native pupils were responsible for the filthiness of the bathrooms at K Public School. Investigations of family life were common, and Instructor Ito went so far as to conduct one on the basis of an irrelevant response by a student who knew little Japanese—understandably so, since he had just enrolled. Such excesses greatly hurt Taiming.

At one of the morning assemblies, the head of Taiming's class was summoned to the platform. Held responsible for a trivial incident, the boy started giving the facts in the best Japanese he could manage. The instructor on duty that week was offended by the boy's efforts.

"Stop talking back! Don't get uppity on me," he said. And suddenly he slapped the boy in the face, and the boy ended his explanation. His eyes were full of tears.

Perhaps out of remorse, the instructor added in a soothing voice: "You should say whatever you want to say." Much more than that is required to win over a boy who has just resolved not to "talk back" at all. He did not answer, and this offended the instructor, this time beyond all self-control.

"Stop sulking, you twisted brat!" he yelled hysterically. Violent slaps rained down on the class president, who started sobbing audibly. This was simply too much for the Japanese instructor. "A weakling won't make a good citizen!" he exploded.

Taiming felt as though he himself were receiving the blows. It was too much, he thought, as he watched the scene. He did nothing to stop it.

An aura of violence hung over the school for some time. Guardians and concerned townsfolk protested, but nothing changed until, finally, a pupil who had been boxed heavily on the ear was diagnosed with timpanitis. This stopped the beatings. The faculty adopted Trainee Huang's suggestion for a new type of punishment: instead of slapping recalcitrant students, why not make them kneel on the concrete floor? In some ways, this punishment seemed worse than beating. From then on, in the corners of K Public School's classrooms, one could always find the imploring gaze of pupils "under punishment," learning about the properties of concrete through their bodies.

At long last, Taiming began to harbor doubts about education, or at least about the methods that it seemed to require. Now that he thought about it, he had never been able to justify some things to himself. Why did they have to resort to beatings at K Public School when the local grammar school, which did not, also yielded results? And while the grammar school simply followed the prescribed guidelines, Taiming's school placed undue emphasis on agronomy. He had some suspicions about this but had no presentable reform plan in mind.

At one of the bimonthly meetings of the Critical Forum for Pedagogic Practice, it was argued that the native instructors were responsible for the terrible accent with which the public school students spoke Japanese. This set off a debate whose focus shifted gradually to the strained relationship between the Japanese and Taiwanese members of the faculty.

At one point, a tense silence fell over the forum. A single spark could have made it all end in disaster. It was then that Instructor Zeng, who rarely spoke on these or any other occasions, stood up to address the principal. There was a nervous look on everyone's face; the usually so gentle man looked frighteningly pale.

"You say the native instructors speak bad Japanese." His words reverberated, so still was the room. "But did we grow up speaking your language? Who taught us to speak it as we do? At the end of morning assemblies, Mr. Principal, I hear you say to the pupils, 'Dismiss.' I am not sure if our national language permits that usage. Do you mean to say 'Dismissed?' And for someone as insistent on correct pronunciation as Ito-sensei to brag that 'sahweens awe his powince's speshalees' . . . is his locution acceptable from an educational standpoint?"

The principal was as stiffly silent as a statue. Instructor Zeng continued, "Japanese-Taiwanese harmony. You repeat that phrase every time you open your mouth but don't seem to understand the principle behind it. Permit me to teach you by example."

He strode to the board where the small, rectangular planks that bore the instructors' names hung. The eyes of the persons whose names appeared there were pinned on Instructor Zeng as he stared at the thirteen planks. The principal's face turned blue.

"The Japanese names come first, but that must be a mistake. The order of name plates should reflect seniority and rank. This," he said, rearranging them then and there with no view to ethnicity, "is what Japanese-Taiwanese harmony means." He looked the principal straight in the eye and added, "If there is to be true harmony, Mr. Principal, there must not be any prejudice—no preferences."

There was no refuting Instructor Zeng's reasoned opinion. Neither the principal nor anyone else said a word. Instructor Zeng bowed and made his way through them, gently. The calm steps taking him out of the faculty room also were firm; perhaps he didn't mean ever to come back.

After the meeting, Taiming stood up and stood still. The petty logic of self-rationalization, which he had been perfecting until that very day, teetered and toppled around him like a sad toy house of blocks. He sank amid the noise into a groaning pit, his own lost self. He walked home dazed, seeing no one and nothing on the way.

A storm raged within him. He had not paid much attention to Instructor Zeng, the most inconspicuous of persons. Where in his quiet self had he hidden all that intensity? How strange! But Taiming always did know, through others, that the inscrutable man read deep into night.

Instructor Zeng did not turn up the next day. He submitted a letter of resignation, Taiming was told. A few days later, Taiming received a letter.

Dear Hu,

Are you aware that a wave called the world will soon be washing over the shores of our isolated island? It will no longer do to hide here.

In the narrow confines of Taiwan, education is just a synonym for worldly success. For its young men, education means choosing between medicine, which is lucrative, and law, which hands you a weapon. But let's consider education as a way to higher culture. In the twentieth century, that means science.

It's especially the physical sciences, which we Taiwanese have avoided, that we urgently need to master. In the future, men will probably carry out their struggles under the banner of science. Even if we set up a large company here, where would it find Taiwanese technicians? So few of us understand higher mathematics. I've decided to live and die as a student of the physical sciences.

You are you, and I don't doubt you'll make the most of your gifts. Live and love as a great educator. But if and when anxiety about our homeland crosses your mind, I hope you will find at least some comfort in recalling the path of

Your friend,

Zeng

Taiming mulled over every one of these words, addressed to him by a former colleague who was only a couple of years older than he was.

9. Burying Licentiate Peng

Taiming visited the homes of his pupils every day during the first week of summer vacation. Mahuang trees murmured in the wind along the dirt paths he trod. The noise sounded like a lagoon, strangely intensifying his loneliness.

One day, on the way to see one of his pupils, he passed a banyan tree whose bright green leaves overlaid a deeper green. Under it were a shrine to an ancestor who had become a local god of fortune and about ten farmers taking a break. Back at the Ladder to the Clouds, Taiming had been taught to spend a moment at these shrines to gods of fortune, so he stopped to reverently pay his respects.

His behavior amounted to a major event in the eyes of the farmers. Impressed, they whispered excitedly to one another, "The officer is worshiping our ancestor!"

"I'm a schoolteacher," Taiming explained and asked them the way.

When he finally found the pupil's house, it turned out to be a large compound, three roofs on one wing and four on the other, home to a clan of more than ten families. Taiming's appearance in the inner courtyard was greeted immediately and profusely by yelping dogs. A stooped old woman came scuttling out to shoo them away from him. "Sir!" she greeted, turning toward Taiming and bringing her palms together, "Sir!" Her eyes glittered with a mixture of anxiety and reverence. Preferring, as with the farmers, not to elicit such a reaction, Taiming quickly explained who he was. "Ah, Mr. Schoolmaster, I thought you were an officer," she finally remarked with relief.

By this time, the news of Taiming's visit had spread to every corner of the residence. He was subjected to curious gazes that came from somewhere around the side entrance of the main building and belonged to housewives carrying infants and to children whose noses were dripping into their mouths. Taiming heard someone say, "That teacher doesn't have a sword." Still, they maintained their distance in awe and fear. After making sure the old woman understood how a pupil on summer vacation should keep busy, Taiming left.

Although this was the last home he had to visit, it was his turn to watch over the deserted school building. For a couple of hours before noon, he offered preparatory courses for students going on to secondary school, but he had nothing to do in the sweltering hours that followed.

Now and then, however, a student came by to visit his alma mater. Generally, those who were attending schools in Taiwan had a narrow worldview and a stagnant air about them, whereas those who were studying abroad, in Japan, seemed well informed and spirited. Whenever the latter discussed social issues and global events, Taiming belatedly regretted that his own knowledge was obsolete.

One day, a friend from his own alma mater, the normal school, came looking for Taiming in the classroom where he sat. The friend, Taiming's senior by several years, had completed his studies at Meiji University in Tokyo, moved to China, lived there for four years, and just returned. He said he was never going back.

The story shocked Taiming. This reliable source told him that wherever they went, Taiwanese were only Taiwanese—were made fun of, that is—and, in China, were even discriminated against, thanks to mounting anti-imperialist sentiments. As for his flirtation with scholarship, what did he gain but worrisome knowledge that he couldn't help thinking about, and these days there were no jobs because there was a recession. He seriously considered becoming a farmer. These confessions did not completely kill Taiming's desire to study abroad. As he listened, he told himself that he had to see it with his own eyes. He had to give it a try, he just had to!

Halfway into the summer vacation, Taiming learned from a messenger that Licentiate Peng had died. Old Hu, who had sent the messenger, was too old to travel to the frontier territory where his former classmate had chosen to spend his last days. Taiming was asked to represent his grandfather. Although the young man did not feel attached to Licentiate Peng, he was someone whom at one time he had called "Master." In any case, how could he not go when it was his grandfather's wish? "A master for a day, a father for life," he mumbled to himself as he packed and left right away.

It was a long journey to Licentiate Peng's study, which lay deep in the wild recesses of a mountain. Taiming first had to take a train, then a bus, and finally a tram. The last, of course, was not part of a commercial line; its real function could be found in the soot that covered the floors and walls of the empty carriage.

Just when the tram began the last leg of Taiming's journey, a haggard woman appeared from nowhere, with a baby in her arms. Although her eyes pleaded with the civil officer, her lips seemed to have been intimidated into silence by his uniform. "Get back from the officer! Get back, I say," the conductor yelled at her. She flinched, stepped back, but directed her now teary gaze right on Taiming.

"Fine by me. Let her get on," said the civil officer. Taiming was disturbed by the way he dispensed charity from above. The longer he looked at the woman who had gotten on and the longer he reflected on the manner by which the officer had let her, the sicker he felt about himself. The woman began, hesitantly, to excuse herself by explaining that the child had a high fever because of pneumonia and that the doctor's orders were "complete rest." It was as though the woman were silently objecting to Taiming's existence, and he squirmed under the weight of her accusation. He felt freed when she finally got off.

The tram rolled on, weaving through the valleys and rattling loudly between the echoing hills. Heavy cliffs curled up over the car like tidal waves, and crevices reached down to pools of blue water. A kite screeched overhead. The only human being besides the conductor felt the emptiness eat at his soul.

The conductor, however, was not the rough fellow that Taiming had thought he was; in fact, now and then, in a surprisingly warm tone, he offered stories about this or that bend. When the tram approached what he called Bullfight Gate, he told Taiming that barbarians loved to set ambushes there. A few dozen innocent men once perished in a single encounter. Not to be forgotten was the uplifting story of the police rangers, thanks to whom the region was now safe. They used to hold the line courageously in small detachments of one or two.

As they approached the coal mines, they began to meet several other trams, some containing miners. When the tracks began running parallel to a street, the conductor and his passenger were breathing the uniquely coarse air of a mining town.

It was almost dusk by the time Taiming stood in front of the dilapidated hut that claimed to be, in penmanship he recognized, "The Ladder to the Clouds." The desolate hinterland that surrounded Taiming and the hut was too depressing a resting place for one who had devoted his life to studying the ways of men.

It was too cruelly fitting a picture of a dying age. A thousand feelings came to Taiming as he stood before the sign and the familiar hand.

Nonetheless, Licentiate Peng's funeral was almost lively, having attracted quite a few relatives and former students. Most of the latter, who were not much older than Taiming, had grown up in or around the mining town. Only one of Taiming's former classmates was there, Li Qishi.

The burial took place at ten the next morning. The procession was led by a large banner announcing "The Late Retired Master Licentiate Peng," with many more flags carrying phrases like "A Dream Goes South" and "A Freed Crane Flies." It was neither unfitting nor insufficient for a master who had ended his life in a town like this that a number of miners stopped out of respect.

Taiming was the first to leave when the funeral ended. He ran away from the ghost of a prior age, its shell. There had been a time for Licentiate Peng, with its own efforts and sacrifices and achievements of cultivation; perhaps Licentiate Peng did not mind living continuously behind closed doors in a thought system in which he felt at home. That is that, thought Taiming, and now my time has come. The new age, blindingly bright, beckoned to him. When he snapped out of his daydream, the tram had already thundered past Bullfight Gate. On both sides, at breakneck speed, mountains and forests were racing toward the mining town.

10. Love and Confession

The laziness of the long summer vacation still hovered over the faculty room in the first days of the autumn semester; the most popular topics were swimming and fishing. Naito Hisako's sprightly face was as sunburned as a careless girl's, and Ruie's was as unchangingly pale as a melon.

One day, Taiming went with the principal on a visit to a household deep in a longan forest. The family was busy making articles out of bamboo. When the unexpected guests appeared, however, the entire family scrambled to welcome them.

Taiming, who had come to translate for the principal, squirmed when the head of the household and his family rushed out to buy beer and snacks in order to demonstrate their hospitality. The people in this hamlet made a living by selling longans, which they could do only every other year. They supplemented this meager income only slightly with bamboo crafts and stints as coolies. More often than not, pupils who did not have even the basic school implements came from this area. Knowing this, Taiming could not enjoy their hospitality, but the principal seemed quite indifferent to their circumstances. It was with reluctance that Taiming translated his superior's words.

On their way back, the slightly tipsy principal said half-jokingly: "I've been told you get along pretty well with one of our female colleagues. Is it Naito Hisako? Or is it Ruie? If you like, I can help you."

Astounded, Taiming gasped and blushed. He resented the principal's suggestive, furtive offer and was troubled by the hint of malice. The whole school must know if the principal was saying such things to him, and that was a problem. The Ruie matter did not bother him—they could talk as much as they liked—but Hisako had such a delicate place in his heart that he was vulnerable to the principal's jest. In regard to marriage, Taiming certainly dreamed of it but he also knew that at best, it was still far off. His tender feelings for Hisako, which the principal's teasing words worked into a painful frenzy even then, existed on a different plane.

One day later in September, Ruie hurried to Taiming's side. She said that Hisako was going to be reassigned.

"Did you know Hisako-san is going away?"

The earth sagged under Taiming's feet with those words, and in the next instant, the principal's insinuating look came back in a flash. Anger, sorrow, and love gushed up together from deep inside him and formed a single, confused conviction: "I must confess my love!" If he missed this opportunity, he would forever lose the chance to win Hisako. Having decided, he could hardly stand still.

Ruie's presence irritated him.

She walked home alone, Taiming having made up an excuse to stay behind in his empty classroom, which he filled with his furious thoughts. The petty principal was sending her away to tear them apart! Did she know that was the reason? And if she did, what did she think about his shameless action? He wanted to know how she felt.

Taiming was pacing the corridor when he caught a glimpse of Hisako and abruptly halted. She was sitting, pensive, at a desk by the window in her classroom. It appeared that she had packed up her things to leave for the day but could not, detained by her own thoughts. Taiming plucked up the courage to walk in.

She noticed his presence now. "Mr. Hu, I—" Choking on her own words, she was silent. Her manner seemed to show that she was aware of the principal's motives.

"Hisako-san. I know. I—" His words met resistance, too, somewhere in his overfull bosom. He managed, however, to blurt out, "Hisako-san, I have to talk to you. Are you free this evening?"

She started. Still facing away from him, she made a faint sound. It was only from the nodding of her shoulders that Taiming realized that she had responded in the affirmative.

"She too, she too!" He wanted to cry out with gratitude. She, too, seemed to feel as he did.

That evening, Taiming ate only half his dinner and left his apartment to disappear into the dark. He was headed to their meeting place.

It was almost completely dark when he arrived, but he discerned a dark shadow hiding under a tree to avoid being seen. Taiming suppressed his elation and went up to the shadow, to which he could say only, "Hisako-san. I'm glad you've come. Thank you."

The two figures walked wordlessly toward a lonely, dark place. Taiming was absolutely silent, and so was Hisako, who walked behind and away from him, her head bowed. But a hot weight seemed to pass from one bosom to the other and back.

Suddenly, an impulse seized Taiming. He stopped and turned around sharply. Within an arm's reach in the dark floated the faint white glow of Hisako's face. Her lips were parted slightly, and he could smell her heavy breath.

"Her lips . . ." Taiming felt weak. In enticing proximity breathed those lips if he wanted them. Were the fruits eternally forbidden to him, or—

"Hisako-san, how do you feel about me?" he could not help asking.

The silence that followed, seemingly endless to him, was in fact quite brief. Taiming struggled to quiet his trembling as Hisako spoke the following words, hesitantly but clearly: "I'm overjoyed, I really am, but. . . . It can't be. Because you and I are different."

Taiming did not have to ask what she meant by "different." She had not forgotten that they belonged to different ethnicities.

Taiming's shriek of despair could not be heard outside his heart. The verdict had been handed down. The ground under him sank, and Hisako was already far, far away.

11. The Wail of Youth

Winter came to both Taiming and the ground on which he was walking.

With that mild but irreversible rejection, she departed from his life. "How hollow are heaven and earth since our parting."

Taiming lived through days of unspoken sorrow. When he looked up, winter had withered all of heaven and earth. The cold winds that blew day after day were ash colored.

Each day, on his young man's legs, Taiming walked around the neighborhood as though he might stop breathing if he stood still.

White eularias waved their branches along the low embankment as far as he could see. A white heron rested on top of a hedge. It was a picture without substance. Unaware of Taiming's feelings, the farmers busied themselves with the season's work. They pushed their plows and urged on their water buffaloes. The workers piled up the plowed earth to form a kind of charcoal furnace. The fire was so red that Taiming felt sad.

He wondered, "Should I immerse myself in my duties, to forget? Or should I return to my country home?" From the depth of its sorrow, youth was already beginning to show signs of crawling out. Yet it was out of the blue that a particular ray of hope lighted up his heart: "I can study abroad. Yes. I'll forget the past, everything, and start over in Japan, from page one." His outlook seemed to widen.

12. Over the Waves

In the ceremonial hall, large red candles burned brilliantly in lined-up holders while next to them Taiming's grandfather, his long hair and ritual attire flowing, carefully lighted the five incenses. Opium Tong, Ah-San, Ah-Si, and all sorts of other relatives had gathered under one roof to send off Taiming with a feast. In the garden, gold and silver sheets went up in flames, and firecrackers popped as loudly as they were supposed to. No one in the village had ever decided to study in Japan. The commotion was unprecedented.

The gossips had not changed. "He'll be district governor when he comes back. In the old days, we'd have put another flagpole right here," Opium Tong noted, pointing to a stone block and alluding to the era of classical examinations.

"District governor?" Ah-San questioned. "Uh-uh. Assistant chief of police."

But Ah-Si disagreed: "What, assistant chief? He ought to become an inspector. Then he'll get to head his own detachment."

Among these vicarious passions—the merriments of a party— Taiming felt lonely. After the banquet, his brother Zhigang, Ah-San, and Ah-Si, representing his family, escorted Taiming to the lonely railway station; the train pulled out a short while later. As Taiming watched the scenery of his home retreat, first slowly and then quickly, tender feelings for the past and anxious expectations for the future mingled in an intricate pattern of inexperience. The past seemed to be catapulting him into the future. His only solace was the dizzying allure of what might happen in the future.

It was sunny—usually it was not—in the port town of Chilung. A kind of send-off, it seemed. Taiming got off the carriage onto the crowded platform and waded through the crowds of people. When he finally reached the exit, he uttered a muffled cry, for whom did he see there but the unexpected figure of Ruie?

"Hey!" he exclaimed, "What brings you here?"

She smiled broadly. "You. I knew you were leaving. Aren't I clever?" Her tone was as sassy as ever.

Ruie's little surprise heartened Taiming. In fact, she had never seemed so dear to him. They decided to take a stroll in the harbor, since the ship was not supposed to leave for a few more hours. Unusually talkative, Taiming talked about his plans, and Ruie seemed to relish each detail as though entranced. She seemed now so unlike a country schoolteacher, and to Taiming's delight, her suddenly urbane air blended perfectly with the bright, modern scenery of the harbor. She was taking a day off from work.

"Here," she said when the time came, "nothing more than mementos, really." The homemade purse she handed him had been woven of silk lace, and the bag for his pocket watch contained a charm of Guan Di. The woman's practical generosity was deposited in these humble but thoughtful gifts.

Ruie's eyes gleamed as she looked at him. Taiming had never seen such an impassioned look. So, here was a woman who, quietly and from afar, always favored me. The thought, so belated, was a heavy blow. Why hadn't he tried to get to know her? He didn't know what to say, not even to himself.

Their time was up. They walked to the pier and boarded the ship together. The deck was almost overflowing with clusters of people saying bon voyage. The parting moment would be any time now; Taiming and Ruie had much to say to each other, but neither spoke more than a few words.

When the departure bell sounded, Ruie walked down the gangway with the other well-wishers, who flowed out onto the wharf, and she stood there among them. From the deck, where Taiming could see her, she looked almost tiny. The ship pulled up anchor, slowly peeled away from the wharf, and was slowly tugged out to a distance from which Ruie's handkerchief, which she waved frantically, was no more than a speck.

"Good-bye, Ruie. Good-bye, my homeland." The raw sorrow welling up kept him on deck for a while. At some point the ship began slicing quickly through the water. Taiming watched the white wake extend farther and farther behind the ship. Far away behind him was Japan.

Chapter Two

. . .

1. Study Overseas

The traffic was frightening—the masses of people and the busy machines, streetcars and automobiles—moving aggressively in an endless stream. Unwary pedestrians were bumped into, even on the sidewalk, by other people. To the swimming eyes of the young man from Taiwan, they seemed not so much to be walking but trotting. He wondered why so many people in Tokyo were busy.

On the way to the capital, he had stopped in Kyoto, where a friend of his lived. The people, streets, and sights of Kyoto, though pleasing and delicate, made sure that you went away knowing just how long the city's fragrant culture had been nurtured. Taiming loved Kyoto, the ancient capital. The people were too kind, down to the bus attendants, boarding-house girls, waiters at cafeterias, and department store salesclerks, all of whom behaved as though they were well educated. To Taiming, the poise of the city's young women was the greatest surprise.

"A wonderful country and a wonderful people!" This impression quickened his pulse.

Tokyo lacked peace. Even so, exhausting though the crowd

was, the people were generous. Every stranger whom Taiming asked for directions—and he did this more than once—responded knowledgeably and politely, never using the contemptuous tone that he would have heard in Taiwan, and the country bumpkin arrived safely at the lodgings of a certain Lan. This former classmate of Taiming's had been expelled from normal school just a few months before his graduation, regarding a trifle about which he had ended up clashing with one of the professors. Lan eventually came to see this as an opportunity to study in Japan. His dream being the usual one of becoming a lawyer or a high-ranking bureaucrat, he entered the law department at Meiji University.

In normal school, Taiming had always argued with Lan. A passionate person, Lan was fond of taking extreme positions on just about everything, whereas Taiming was something of a centrist on everything, so they never tired of debating each other. Although their worldviews differed, their rivalry united them. By chance, they sometimes agreed, but they had taken different paths and arrived there by different means.

As soon as Taiming arrived in Tokyo, his feet automatically took him toward Lan's lodgings.

Conveniently, Lan happened to be home, even though they had hardly maintained a correspondence—indeed, it could not be termed as such. But when they were reunited, it was as though they had parted only the day before. Lan, who had arrived just recently himself, nonetheless decided to act as Taiming's big brother.

"You think your ideas will go over here? I'm telling you, Hu, Taiwan is hicksville. Be prepared to start all over again. As a freshman."

Taiming did not mind this at all, but when his friend added, "By the way, I advise you not to tell anyone you're from Taiwan. They say our Japanese sounds like Kyushu dialect, so tell them you're from Fukuoka or Kumamoto," he felt as though obscene words had been whispered to him.

This suggested deception was a low blow to Taiming. His discomfort only increased at dinnertime when Lan introduced him to the young servant girl at the establishment who brought in the dishes and asked, not unexpectedly, "So where are you from?"

"Same as me—Fukuoka," came Lan's response like lightning.

Taiming thus became an accomplice to Lan's lie, which now, painfully, extended to the accomplice himself. His cheeks reddened with shame. He would have liked to correct his friend but, considering his feelings, could not. The young servant girl stayed and served; Taiming ate silently, annoyed. He felt a chasm opening between him and Lan, not at all like the familiar one that had existed between them ever since they had become friends.

Lan, a good friend in most regards, readily allowed Taiming to stay with him while the newcomer sought lodgings. There were no rooms left at Lan's place, an inconvenience that Taiming did not regret, as he did not want to live with Lan's lie and, from the outset, had intended to identify himself as Taiwanese.

That evening, Taiming made himself comfortable and wrote a letter to his grandfather telling him of his safe arrival. When he was finished, he felt an urge to write to Naito Hisako, about whom he had not heard since she was transferred, but hesitated because of his less happy memories of her. To begin with, Hisako was nobody to him now. Why write to a stranger? Maintaining silence would be more natural. After this self-examination, he put down his writing brush. Then Ruie came to mind. He now sincerely appreciated her affection for him, but he didn't write to her either. The only way open to him now was to acquire knowledge; he had to break away from his past and work hard.

That night, in Lan's room, two pillows lay side by side. Despite the new gap between them, in Taiming's view, their reminiscences brightened the night. It was only at dawn that the reunited classmates slept a bit.

The next day, with Lan's help, Taiming began his search. He was fortunate enough to find a room only two days later, at the house of an army officer's widow, whose daughter and young son did nothing to disrupt the military atmosphere of order and calm. Taiming immediately signed the lease and moved in the next day. He had not concealed his ethnicity. But the widow showed no trace of prejudice or reservation.

As soon as he unpacked his suitcases, Taiming started studying furiously. Soon he also enrolled at a preparatory school, his goal being to enter a physics department, an uncommon aspiration for a student from Taiwan. Other than occasional visits from Lan, no callers disturbed Taiming. His environment was ideal. The family left him almost entirely to himself—almost, because the daughter, Tsuruko, looked after him in a most inconspicuous manner, watering the otherwise dry expanse of his everyday life.

On Sundays, when he was tired of physics, he lay idle, the notes being played on a koto wafting up from downstairs. The gracious, peaceful melodies resembled Tsuruko's beauty and modesty. Taiming listened absently and thought about Naito Hisako until he stumbled on the more bitter memories, which made him recoil, twist, and roll as though an old wound had been poked open. He scolded himself for seeking solace from a young woman who was even prettier than Naito Hisako and apparently far more sophisticated.

"No women! Study, study."

When Lan came by, it was to argue this or that as vigorously as ever. Once, however, he brought over a particular group's magazine, called *Taiwan Youth*, and recommended that Taiming join the staff. Flipping through it later, Taiming found all the articles to have an overly political tone. Their youthful vigor, particularly, was meant to drag the reader into a whirlwind of enthusiasm that he didn't think he could join.

Although he understood why young Taiwanese might be attracted to politics, Taiming thought he had a cause, too: the pursuit of knowledge.

If all youths plunged into politics and neglected knowledge, how thin the soil of Taiwanese learning would be! As Instructor Zeng had said, not only politics but also art and philosophy and science and business, all important fields, awaited the young. He, Taiming, would march unhesitatingly as a student of science, paying no attention to the political noise. That was the theory, but he was not comfortable with it. If, as Lan had once vigorously argued with him, the primary task was to eliminate the political restrictions placed on young Taiwanese, then politics, indeed, seemed to be the path that they had to take. Which was more important? It was usually at this point that Taiming's thoughts grew confused and entered a large maze.

Meanwhile, he refused Lan's insistent invitations to join the magazine's staff. He was sorry, but he had to study for exams.

Several months later, when Taiming entered a school of physics as its first Taiwanese student, Lan came to congratulate him, without forgetting to bring along a friend named Zhan. That it was the night of a happy day did not discourage the recruiting efforts of the activists, who tried out a variety of arguments on Taiming. Zhan, a sharp critic blessed with formidable powers of intuition, started by recounting the contradictions of Japanese-Taiwanese coeducation, going as far as to cite the co-opting mechanism with which the Han dynasty had neutralized the aristocracy's opposition. He went on to contend, with considerable clarity, that the adoption of regional limits, which regulated Taiwan's sugar-refining industry, was merely an excuse to prevent the natives from making money. In those days, "regional limits," which supposedly protected the sugar refiners by banning the sale to Company A of sugarcane produced in Company B's region, gave an unfair advantage to one of them and led to uncompetitive pricing. Combined with the three-year crop rotation system ordered by the Edict for the South, the policy had cornered the Taiwanese, most of whose capital had been invested in the land. Taiming knew little about economics and did not fully understand what Zhan was saying, but he sensed the immensity of the contradictions. It certainly was irrational, but what could he do?

"It's knowledge that matters to me." This was Taiming's usual refuge. Irritated by his indecisiveness, Lan and his friend left angrily. The celebration was suddenly and unhappily over. Feeling empty, Taiming lay down on the tatami and thought about the hopeless abyss that separated him from Lan and others. Compared with their single-minded passion, his was perhaps a greed for peace. Underneath his feeling of emptiness stirred another, a dull self-hatred.

2. Flowers of a Strange Land

A new season began for Taiming, the comfortable one of formal study, of deliberate study. The room that he left so messy in the morning was always clean by the time he came home. From the alcove came the fresh fragrance of that day's arranged flowers. Tsuruko's gentleness spoke in this way, and he heard her.

His studies benefited from her unassuming presence which, like her flowers, colored and stimulated his life. Satisfied, he did not take any further action. His daily life was complete and full of hope.

Tsuruko's mother, the mistress of the house, was an understanding and considerate woman. Worried that Taiming did nothing but study, she suggested one day, "Hu-san, shouldn't you take better care of your body? Why not put aside your books for a moment, and take a walk—with Tsuruko?"

Such candor stunned Taiming, who had been raised according to Confucian customs. He thanked the widow in his heart but could not bring himself to do such a thing.

But one fall day, when the widow suggested that the three of them go to admire the autumn leaves in Tama, he did not offer an excuse. That day's impressions were to become indelible. Covering entire mountains, the leaves were burning scarlet, endlessly enflaming one another. Taiming, who had grown up on Taiwan where it was always summer, at first thought they were flowers.

He nurtured an illusion of his companion: "She is the true Japanese autumn!" He was intoxicated. It was not as though he had exchanged meaningful words with Tsuruko. Still, the moment when her beautiful profile mimicked the scarlet of the flames that dripped on her was forever imprinted on the film of his soul.

Although the trip seemed like only a few days ago, it already was gray winter. Momentarily weary of projectile motion, Taiming was walking alone through a park when he ran into Lan. They had not seen each other since their awkward parting.

Not one to dwell on the past, Lan spoke first: "So how are you? Still a bookworm?" Seizing Taiming by the shoulder, he added, "Haven't seen you in a while. How about tea?"

In a nearby café, without being asked, Lan recounted the ups and downs of *Taiwan Youth*. It was currently facing a budgetary challenge.

"Oh yes," he seemed to have just remembered, "I'm going to an interesting place today. You ought to come." A lecture sponsored by the Academic Association of China did not particularly appeal to Taiming, but he was rather curious and so accepted. In the first place, disappointing a friend he had not seen for so long would have been most inconsiderate.

The lecture had not begun yet. The hall was full of clusters of youths who talked quickly in Mandarin, the Chinese spoken in Beijing. All the young men must have arranged beforehand to pomade their long hair down to the last strand and to polish their shoes to the point of wearing them out. They all looked alike—lanky, pallid, and somehow unhealthy.

Lan approached one of the groups and greeted the youths familiarly in Mandarin. They greeted him in return. Taiming felt that he should introduce himself, too, but because he was not confident about his Mandarin, the words that he uttered were in the Chinese spoken in Taiwan.

"Ah, you're from Guangdong," one of the students said, mistaking him for a southern Chinese. "Allow me to introduce you to your compatriots." He came back with several: Liu was from Mei Xian, Di from Yangcheng, while Huang was a Jiaoling man, and so on. Taiming managed, albeit awkwardly, to introduce himself in turn. He did not say he was from Taiwan.

The lecture began. A very important person from China who happened to be in Japan hurled accusations from behind the podium. They concerned nation building and Sun Yat-sen's Three Principles of the People—ethnic unity, democracy, and welfare—but Taiming, whose grasp of Mandarin was weak, did not find himself moved in the least. The rest of the audience was captivated and willingly repeated the slogans that the sponsor stood up to call out when the lecture was over. "For a new China!" "Down with militarism!" "Down with imperialism!" These, which Taiming understood, rang in his ears during the reception, a race in which students, Lan and Zhan among them, rushed to give their name cards and show their faces to all the important persons.

Lan approached Taiming and advised, "Don't miss your chance; go introduce yourself."

"No," he answered, not moving, "I'll pass." His attitude seemed to annoy Lan.

After the reception reached its climax, the important persons began to leave one by one, but the students, whose excitement had nowhere to go, remained standing around. They confessed their dreams to one another and complained about this and that.

Out of the blue, one of the young men strode briskly to the corner where Taiming sat alone.

"Hi, I'm Chen, nice to meet you. I'm a graduate of Waseda University and I'm also from Guangdong—Fanyu to be precise."

So sincere and unreserved was his manner that it rubbed off on Taiming. "Actually, I'm from Taiwan. My name is Hu Taiming and" (Chen's face changed color) "I guess I'm here to study physics."

With a different kind of frankness, Chen spat out, "Huh? Taiwan?" He sneered in disgust and, with obvious contempt, quickly strode away.

The news rippled forth—murmurs of "He's Taiwanese" and "He might be a spy." A heavy silence fell on the lecture hall, which was more than Taiming could bear. He stood up and silently sneaked out. Filled with hurt and anger, he stomped homeward. The streets were almost empty.

Suddenly, he heard footsteps behind him. A rough hand seized him by the shoulder and spun him around. It was Lan.

"Are you a fool?" Lan cried. "Don't you know what Taiwanese have been doing in Amoy? With Japan's backing?"

Taiming glared silently at Lan's face.

"Tyro!" Lan cursed and turned around. "Tyro" was what the minister Fanzeng had called Xiangyu to his face two thousand years ago, to say that the lord was too stupid to work with. Curiously, this pejorative did not anger Taiming. Rather, it made him feel lonely, empty; again he felt the insurmountable distance between Lan's and his passions.

And that was it. Lan never came to see Taiming anymore, and Taiming did not seek out Lan. They did not see each other again until after the physicist had returned, diploma in hand, to Taiwan.

3. Homeland

Leaning on the balustrade, Taiming saw the port town of Chilung emerge from its perennial light mist. The shower, which looked like smoke wrapping the harbor, sometimes suddenly stopped, revealing the pier of the Hermit's Cave, which the ship eventually rounded to glide into the inner bay. The faint bump on the horizon must have been Mount Chilung. The view of his homeland, especially the harbor, brought back to him the figure of Ruie—of Hisako, now an old memory—no less cherished. He saw Tsuruko under the scarlet leaves still on the trees in Tama, and her mother, a widow. Once, he had gone cherry-blossom viewing with the daughter alone, but the pink that enveloped the path was now as distant as that burning red. Tsuruko's profile lived on vividly with the leaves and the blossoms, but it was no more than the afterimage of a moment of youth, Taiming's youth, which seemed to be as ephemeral as the dream of flowers.

"My homeland . . ." He was surprised that everyone moved so slowly. Strangely disillusioned, he weaved his way through the throng of coolies.

Little by little as the train made its way south, the joy of coming home overtook him. How shyly the trees along the tracks welcomed him! By the time the carriage jolted to a stop at a lonely country station bathed in the morning sun, he was bursting with he knew not what.

Preceded by Ah-San and Ah-Si, who had come to pick him up, Taiming ducked through the gate to the enchanted yard and stepped into a barrage of firecrackers that continued for a maddeningly long time. As usual, the welcome overstepped the proper bounds.

"Fools! But am I even worth it?" Checked by this anxious thought, Taiming almost dreaded the festival that inevitably would follow.

His grandfather and all the rest were in good health. Although Taiming had assumed so, he could not be sure. So that was good to know.

Another, longer, volley of firecrackers awaited Hu Taiming at the public hall. Grandpa burned incense sticks and reported reverently to the ancestors.

"Study in Japan," Opium Tong said as though to himself. He continued, gradually raising his voice in what turned out to be a speech:

"Not one man has studied there in the entire history of our village. The exception, of course, is among us this evening. It is not an easy business, this studying overseas. The difficulty is fourfold.

"First, a wise son must be born.

"Second, and this is no less important, the son must also be decisive.

"Third, his father must be a man of property.

"Fourth, the father must be well educated as well. Money is not enough.

"And that is why Taiming's feat brings the highest honor to the Hu clan. What we inherited from our ancestors—the love of study, no, the determination to learn—that, ladies and gentlemen, is what has borne the fruit we enjoy today."

Taiming blushed and bent his head as the flatterers took their turn.

"District headman isn't what I'd call bad, but I say chief of police," Ah-San mused.

"Nonsense," countered Ah-Si. "What matters most to me is experience. First he should get a taste of field duty. Head detective."

In the brilliant light of the large red candles, which weighed two pounds each and lighted the hall's interior almost as brightly as the sun did the exterior, Taiming did not get a moment of respite from relatives, friends, and village dignitaries. The elderly women, forming a kind of chorus, regarded him with religious fervor, their throats emitting bizarre noises: "E-e-ooh, e-e-ooh." These absurd old wives, this chorus too, Taiming politely entertained. He was getting tired, but, just as an inchoate cry was rising in him, suddenly a band of musicians sauntered in, playing Taiwanese melodies, courtesy of the village dignitaries.

More firecrackers were set off. The spectators who crowded the courtyard pressed close to hear the free music. In the hall, the band was cheered loudly for playing favorites like "Maiden Liu" and "Puzzle Ring." But when a *kokyu* fiddle sounded the first sensual note of a mountain song, everybody fell blissfully silent. Uncle Xu Xin, an elder, insisted that the band play "Tea Picking," a very old number. To his great satisfaction, it was received ecstatically by the men, women, and children. But for the young girls at the windows, it was not the music but Taiming's face that they were interested in.

The feast, which had been scheduled for three o'clock, did not begin until six. Saké was passed around. The musicians ceased to interest the revelers, who now preferred their own voices. Ah-San sang a mountain song to the accompaniment of Ah-Si's whistling. In one corner, the young ones were busily engaged in kung fu matches. This persuaded Taiming's former classmates, who were not so young, to do the same in another corner. Relatives from the countryside were shocked by this, but the chorus of old women looked on with obvious delight.

Taiming's father and mother and brother were in high spirits, too. Hu Wenqing insisted on repeating that two of his three wishes—that his father reach the age of seventy, his son complete his studies, and this last person also marry—had been granted.

That night, exhausted by the feast and glad to be back, Taiming forgot everything and slept soundly.

4. Hopeless People

From the next day on, Taiming hunted for a job, with the help of various acquaintances. A little walking taught him that it was not going to be easy, and his aspirations shrank with every step he took. At last, he decided that he was prepared to settle on a high school teaching post. There was none. But surely he could not go back to teaching at an elementary school! He would have been lucky if he could: in order to accommodate the numerous normal school graduates like Taiming, the public schools were having to retire old-timers. Many normal school alums had been glad to be hired as associate instructors. Banks and firms, meanwhile, were too busy tightening their operations to interview anybody. Sick and tired, Taiming sank into a gloomy despair.

Seeing him like this, the same people who had had such nebulous but high hopes for him decided that he was a disappointment. In the streets, some of them went out of their way to ask him innocently, "Taiming, share your plans with us—when are you going to become an official?" The venom of their sarcasm hurt him, but the subtle changes he sensed in others were equally painful. He lamented his fate. He had fallen into a hole.

One afternoon, he received a surprise visit from Lan and Zhan. Although neither Lan nor Taiming had forgotten their last encounter, they chatted as though they had missed each other, which was not so far from the truth. Lan and Zhan did not say so, but they seemed to be tired of political activism. A certain impatience was visible on their faces which nevertheless still bore a trace of belligerent youth ready to suffer any and all vicissitudes.

In fact, after the greetings, the first thing Zhan said, casually, was: "Hu, have you stopped dreaming?" When Taiming did not answer, Zhan went on derisively, "What's gotten hold of your mind is the moral principle of the mean. You don't seem to understand that this 'mean' makes you exactly that, in the sense of 'vulgar.' Well, you'll see some day."

It was Lan's turn next, and he raised his hand—along with the bag that it held—to emphasize his sarcasm. "So you're tired of looking for a job, eh? Poor you. Those sweet dreams—of rainbow colors!—all gone. Sure, they might have put up signs, *billboards*, 'seeking employees.' The lucky fools who get to hang them—and the unlucky fools who envy them! How many do you think there are—I mean the lucky fools on our island paradise? Not many, and you think it's because they're talented? Oh, if you don't believe me, meet the fellows who've become district chiefs and section heads!"

Their objective was clear: to make Taiming give up and join their camp. Try as he might, though, Taiming could not see it Lan's way. The activists were obviously dissatisfied by his continuing hesitation, but they did not berate him as they had earlier.

"Well, think about it" was what they said before they left.

The next day, Taiming received an even less expected visit from an officer of the local police. Apparently, Lan and Zhan were wanted men, and the officer, who had been ordered to track their movements, asked for Taiming's cooperation. Taiming sent him away with not incorrect but ambiguous information. Here was another cause for a headache, and he felt an urge to sit down with his grandfather for a long chat. When he was upset, listening to Grandpa usually helped. When was the last time? Ah, so that was it.

Grandfather cited numerous sayings and classical examples to explain how difficult it was to become a bureaucrat. One had to wait at least three years to work for the state, it had always been said. As usual, Grandfather was a sensitive sympathizer, and his stories had a curious way of loosening the knots in Taiming's heart, but in the modern world, was waiting such a good idea?

As though Taiming's idleness were not enough, another misfortune befell the Hu clan: Opium Tong's son Zhida quit the police force. His sudden return to the village provided an excellent gossip item for the talkative. The news that spread from mouth to mouth was "Another Hu fired."

One day, as the first "fired" Hu was strolling along the dike, he overheard an exchange between two women who were doing their laundry in the shade of a tree.

"Now that he's fired," the first said, "no one will pour saké for him. We won't even give him water."

The other examined the shirt she was washing. "Did I tell you," she asked rhetorically, "he didn't return my mother's hello—his aunt's, you know."

"That Zhida, now that he's lost his sword . . ."

Zhida—who also had not been fired—was particularly disliked, but the resentment seemed to extend to authority in general. Taiming left. Former civil servants tended to be discussed in a special way.

For a few weeks, Zhida did not step out of his house, not even to see Taiming's grandfather. Then, unbeknown to his relatives, he disappeared as suddenly as he had returned.

When he reappeared, it was in crisp new clothes and as the most joyful man at the Hus' New Year congregation. He now was a prosperous lawyer's interpreter. In those days, lawyers were feared like gods, and so were their interpreters. At the public hall, Zhida lectured about the law, citing an array of verdicts, just as though the clan had assembled to listen to him, and in fact, the ignorant villagers were thoroughly impressed. Zhida was elated that the time was already ripe for a great idea he had in mind.

The next day, he gathered around him the heads of some of the branch families. The gist of his idea was that the ancestral rituals that the clan had so far entrusted to one family, Taiming's, be divided up and conducted separately by all the families. Putting a single person in charge placed a heavy financial burden on his family and invited corruption. The responsibility therefore should be shared, with each family conducting in its own name a designated portion of the rituals. Since this would mean that the land providing the funds also would be distributed, the representatives of the less fortunate families enthusiastically endorsed Zhida's plan. The others did not oppose it. Each family head volunteered to give ten yen to Zhida so that he could look into the legal aspects of this matter. They also agreed that Zhida was mature enough to shoulder some of the responsibilities.

A week later, Grandfather Hu received in the mail a document from Zhida requesting that the ritual responsibilities be shared by the heads of all the families: their signatures appeared at the bottom of the document. Grandfather Hu, who was only nominally in charge of the business, handed over the document to the real manager, his son Hu Wenqing, who went pale with cold fury.

"It's the end of the world!" he cried.

Hu Wenqing had no idea how to respond to this unexpected tactic and sought the advice of his son, who was so well educated. But Taiming knew nothing about the law. He commented instead from what he considered common sense, that there was no reason to oppose what the majority requested, since the activities were meant to be communal. This answer did not satisfy Hu Wenqing. To break up the rituals would be sacrilege; what was at stake was not just the honor of the Hus but also their well-being. Taiming disagreed: the rituals were threatening to degenerate into mere form, and to cling to formalities, that is, to follow the letter and not the spirit, was a worse offense to their illustrious ancestors. The spirit or the letter? Father and son brought the question they could not settle to Grandfather Hu.

He was surprisingly calm about the whole matter. His simple answer was that the incident meant only that the manager's agent could not resolve such disagreements, which in turn meant that he, the nominal manager, lacked virtue. The request that he step down was opportune. He asked Taiming to summon the representatives, all fourteen of them.

They came. The patriarch began the meeting by rising gravely. He spoke with great candor to his fourteen nephews:

"When my father came to Taiwan, he had to lay the foundations.

"Many of his nights and days were indescribably difficult. Helped by my father-in-law, he left the Hus a fortune, an immense fortune. My brothers and I didn't keep up their good work but sat on the fortune and slowly spent it down. I have many regrets but don't know how to make amends—to my forefathers, that is.

"To you, I apologize that I lack the virtue to manage even the remaining trifle. I am to blame for the trouble you have had lately."

The representatives, who had been preparing for a nasty fight, were chastened by the old man's words. Not even an awkward cough was heard. Some of the coconspirators already were ashamed that they had had anything to do with Zhida. The silence was broken by Opium Tong, who did not know that his son had originated the plan. Springing from his chair, he ridiculed the idea of dividing up land yielding a mere 150 bushels, as though he had not cosigned the letter. He could not understand why his fellow cousins were scrambling for just a little more than ten bushels each. Fine, you could consider the matter on the level of the four major branches: still, it would be no more than seven and a half each. What were they trying to do, heap more dishonor on their ancestors?

The others began to fidget. At this point Taiming's brother, Zhigang, burst out with the truth: "Come on, none of you wants this! No one thinks Grandfather is lacking in virtue! So far I've kept out of this, but I can't stand it any more. It's all Zhida's doing, isn't it?"

Opium Tong was dumbfounded. As he scanned the others' faces, his puzzlement turned into shame and anger. "That Zhida! I'll teach him this time!" With those words, he hurried home.

Opium Tong's scolding had no effect, and Zhida's cunning won out in the end. Far from repenting for his abuse of legal knowledge, he threatened to sue his cosignatories for breach of contract. Terrified by Zhida's confident claim that "they'll pay for it, five hundred yen each," they relented, one by one, until all of them had once again agreed to share the responsibilities. Opium Tong, who had stormed out so angrily that day, was the first to go over to his son's side. When the supportive father thought about selling his portion of the spoils, which he assessed at a full year's worth of opium, he could not help offering to his son his skills of persuasion.

That was how the partition came about.

A ritual was held to notify the ancestors. Although the practices had been dwindling in scale for some time and were now little more than formalities, their virtual abolition, the cessation of that which had been handed down from generation to generation, cast a grave air over the patriarch and his nephews as they advanced to the altar to burn the five fragrant incenses. Grandfather Hu apologized to the ancestors that he lacked virtue; his tone was so pathetic that the others shuddered, too late. As he stepped back from the altar, he began to stagger. The representatives helped him out of the public hall. "It's all because of Zhida!" lamented Opium Tong, castigating his son at this late hour in a futile attempt to cheer up the sorrowing elder.

This tragedy of naive folk who had fallen prey to the plot of an upstart was gleefully discussed by the entire village. "The Hus have no partners left for the martial arts they've inherited, so they're sparring with the ancestors themselves." The misfortune that the gossipers found grandly entertaining, however, afflicted them as well. Emboldened by his victory against his own clan, Zhida took it upon himself to look into the sort of disputes that used to be settled by the village arbitrator. Every case that Zhida succeeded in bringing to court diminished the arbitrator's influence, and every dispute added to the coffers of the prominent lawyer and his wily interpreter.

Meanwhile, Taiming's grandfather was failing rapidly and stopped accepting invitations from other families. The Hu family had had absolute faith in the old man's goodwill and his principle that one must not let any circumstances cloud the spirit of compromise, so his decline cast a long shadow across the faces of the

Hus, both young and old. Although the elder tried to give the impression that he had calmly carried out the will of the majority, the partition had dealt him a heavy blow. When one day, out of carelessness, he caught a cold and took to his bed, the illness consumed him at an alarming rate. This time, there was no demon to defy.

Watched over by his close relatives, Taiming's grandfather breathed his last only a week after he took to his bed. His death left a hole in Taiming. To the very end, his grandfather was a warm, capacious man.

5. Ah-Yu's Sorrows

Taiming's days of unemployment lasted longer than the period of mourning. Worse, there now was talk of dividing up the Hu house itself. Taiming did not like the tradition of branching and argued that whatever there was to be inherited should be donated, say, to public works. But his mother, Ah-Cha, was not of the same mind and tried to teach her son the importance of money. She also insisted on the importance of branching out before her husband's mistress had any more sons. The mistress, Ah-Yu, wanted the matter to be settled while Hu Wenqing was still alive and functioning. He had aged suddenly after his father's death, and everyone was nervous. Taiming's brother Zhigang also was pushing for the partition, and Ah-San and Ah-Si had installed themselves as his advisers.

In this swirl of interests, it was Ah-Yu's position that touched Taiming the most. If his father died, Ah-Yu would be helpless. She feared that Zhigang's greed might be given full rein and that he would not be beneath keeping everything for himself. Since she was a concubine and her sons illegitimate, she would not stand a chance. Given that she might have to live on the street with her two children, it was understandable that she wanted Hu Wenqing to settle the matter. Taiming pitied her and realized that he alone opposed the branching and was attracting animosity from all quarters. He finally gave in when Ah-Yu, in tears, pleaded with him. Although there was something ridiculous about her crying, the tears came from a simple heart that wanted life at all costs. The bloodless, formulaic idealism that he had been bandying about was utterly powerless before her frantic efforts to make her life secure. Taiming longed to be liberated from the whole troublesome business. He stayed out of the negotiations.

While they were being carried out, Zhigang argued that since Taiming had used the family's money for his education, the eldest son's portion, which customarily was large, should be even larger to compensate. His mother, Ah-Cha, to whom Taiming had entrusted his interests, would not listen to such nonsense. Opium Tong, Ah-San, and Ah-Si reasoned with her every evening for two weeks until she finally relented. The settlement was decided as follows: land worth 500 bushels as the traditional portion of the eldest son; land worth 250 bushels each as a pension for the father and the mother; with the remainder to be divided equally among Zhigang, Taiming, and Ah-Yu's two sons. Taiming opposed treating Ah-Yu's illegitimate children as half persons, but he was not so compassionate as to insist. After all, his own lot was at stake.

Relatives—Ah-Cha, Ah-Yu, and Zhigang's wife—sent them gifts for the happy occasion. Friends came to congratulate the birth of the three new households. Hu Wenqing now moved officially into the back wing, formerly Ah-Yu's quarters and now the property of her sons. Zhigang took the left wing. He had schemed to gain access to his mother's pension, but she, not listening to him, took her daughter to move in with Taiming, who occupied the right wing. He was happy with the arrangement because it reminded him of his Tokyo days. Above all, it was a relief that they were done. He spent most of his time hiding in his study.

One afternoon, out on a long walk, he strolled toward the village café, a lone hut by a path that went straight through spacious rice paddies. By the entrance swayed a few red lotus blossoms: one of the places in hell is so cold, they say, that one's skin cracks and bleeds like these "flowers of toil." On a long bamboo bench by the flowers, peasants and young people were chatting. Seeing Taiming, they stood up to greet "Master Hu," the new landowner. They used to call him "Sir teacher," which he preferred.

The proprietress of the establishment, which served something that looked like grass, for two *sen* a bowl, begged the master to have a taste of this specialty. Oh, for him, she would not even charge the giveaway price of a mere fiftieth of a yen! Though neither hungry nor tempted, Taiming could not refuse. Observing her face fearfully to see whether she sensed his distaste, he took a mouthful. It was delicious. "When in the country, do what the country folk do," the peasants murmured in amusement. In those days, no man of standing would touch such foods. Taiming's unassuming ways endeared him to them.

"Master Hu, do you know why the ridge between your paddies is crumbling?" asked one of the peasants suddenly. Taiming knew that he could not mean this literally, since it had not rained for a while. Detecting an instance of that allegorical style of speaking of which these folk were so fond, he replied:

"I honestly don't know."

The peasant grinned. "It's because you let yourself be pushed around! We're furious you do. Your brother's no good, but Opium Tong and the rest are worse. And that Zhida's been pulling strings again. Five hundred bushels for the eldest son? Never heard of such a thing! Look at Ah-San, now he's wearing Western clothes—that's what I call imitation. And I'm not making it up if I said he pocketed eight hundred yen from Zhigang and five hundred from your mother!"

The peasant continued to offer unsolicited information, but

Taiming was not angry that his brother had taken so much. What made him sad was that he himself was living on inherited money.

Choking on this unexpressed self-loathing, he left the café and continued down the path. The paddies were green. The seedlings were now several feet tall. Alarmed by Taiming's footsteps, the frogs playing on the path hopped for their lives into the paddies. Taiming remembered that when he was young, his brother used to bring him along on frog hunts. First, they bundled together some bamboo twigs. Then they went after the baby frogs, beat them to death, and tossed the pulp to the ducks. Such happy days. . . . Zhigang used to be such a wonderful big brother, so full of life, so ready to protect Taiming from whatever might happen. Was he the same man who was plotting to enrich himself?

These thoughts were crossing Taiming's mind when the braver frogs that were warily crawling back onto the path hopped back terrified. Taiming looked up and saw a man in baggy Western clothes that hung loosely on him like a traditional robe. It was Ah-San. The man seemed unable to wipe his smile off his face as he walked toward Taiming.

Unexpectedly overcome by a sudden fit of rage, blasted by waves of hatred, Taiming hardly heard the other's greeting. Violent anger shook him long after Ah-San's ridiculous attire was out of sight. It was not the meddling with the inheritance that Taiming resented. It was the idea that Ah-San had lived off the Hu family all his life and was going to do so for the rest of it, too.

6. Put Out

When the long spring rains ceased, the fragrance of the new tea leaves blended with the singing of the young women who were picking them. At night, the leaves poured their fresh scent into the country's thick, lively darkness, which moved with the Chinese violin's languorous tunes. Although the season was sensuous and young, Taiming ignored it. Ensconced in his study, tormented by suspicions about life, he sought the help of Buddha, Confucius, and Jesus, even Kant and Hegel. None of them answered his questions, but he could not stop wandering aimlessly from book to book, from *idée* to *idée*, day after day.

One morning, for the first time in many months, he set out for the nearby town. The villagers he saw on the way seemed to have forgotten who he was. Their apparent lack of interest put him at ease.

He was annoyed that his shirt fit too loosely around his shoulders. He had lost weight. He examined the wares in the market and joined the flow on the street. The crowd was large enough to carry him along.

"Hu!" a voice called out from behind him. "Wait!"

It was Trainee Huang, Taiming's colleague at the public school. Huang caught up, shook Taiming's hand, looked into his face anxiously, and asked, "Six years? Seven?" He was not as much of a clown now; in fact, he almost looked like a gentleman.

The friends could hardly stand still in the relentless waves of people, so they took refuge in a soba shop that opened out onto the market square.

"For old times' sake!" Huang ordered "Duck with Black Mushrooms" and "Assorted Sautéed Vegetables" for the table. He was in a good mood. Every cup of saké added to the eloquence with which he recounted the past several years. Shortly after Taiming, he too had resigned from teaching to try managing a sugarcane farm. Always good with people, Huang had flourished, admittedly under the thumb of the sugar refiners who exercised a local monopoly. But it was yielding profits, his little farm!

They caught up on people and past events.

Then Huang realized with a start that he had forgotten something. Changing his tone of voice, he asked belatedly, "And what have you been up to lately, Hu?"

Taiming told him the unpleasant truth. After a pause, he asked jokingly, "Mr. Huang, would you like to hire me?"

"You? Under me?" Huang laughed nervously.

Two cups later, Taiming brought the matter up again.

"Hey, wait, wait—you can't be serious. You're kidding me, aren't you? You're going to say, 'Ha, look at you, you're so drunk on success that you think I'd work under you.'" But apparently Taiming was not kidding. "Actually—" Huang said, sobering up, "well, I just lost my accountant. You'd be doing me a big favor if you worked for me."

Taiming immediately made up his mind: "I owe you one."

"I'm glad you weren't kidding," Huang said. The way he grasped Taiming's hands, he seemed to mean it. Huang's friendly squeeze brought tears to Taiming's eyes. To cast away petty pride, to labor among farmhands—it seemed a wonderful thing. The darkness in him was already brightening. Both of them had drunk too much that afternoon, and it was on unsure feet that they promised to see each other very soon.

7. Livelihood

Hundreds of parallel lines of plowed red soil formed a regular, striped pattern as far as Taiming could see. On the horizon was the trailing end of the Central Mountain range; in the opposite direction, a shining white thread attached to a faint patch of blue. The distant ends of some of the furrows looked like clusters of moving dots, which as he drew closer, turned out to be female laborers with bamboo hats. An oxcart loaded with fertilizer clattered past Taiming. As big as the farm seemed, it measured little more than four kilometers on each side. Taiming's accounting tasks kept him busy for only an hour a day, so he spent most of his time walking around the farm and chatting with the female farmhands. Sometimes he helped the women sort and pick the cane. He worked both his mind and body until they were thoroughly tired, for he had the nights to recuperate in his quarters at the edge of the farm. His depression was giving way to more positive thoughts and feelings, and he recovered rapidly.

Huang, who was busy dealing with the outside world, entrusted Taiming with the farm's day-to-day operation. There was much to do: planting, weeding, fertilizing, replowing. In just a few months, Taiming's complexion made him almost unrecognizable; it was as though his blood had finally turned red. Meanwhile, the women worked for starvation wages of only thirty or forty *sen* a day and ate sweet potatoes for lunch. Taiming, who was paid four or five times as much—forty-seven yen a month—ate his midday rice with pangs of guilt. He was the best-paid person on the farm. Once when, out of his own pocket, he bought pomegranates and persimmons to share with the women, their joy was such that he decided to go to the fruit store more often. It was humiliating that his salary was exactly the same as his teacher's salary, despite the intervening years of study, but the recession had also reduced the average pay of high school graduates to a mere twenty-seven yen a month.

The women liked him. They sought his advice on various, including personal matters, and he helped them as best he could.

One of the workers was in an advanced state of pregnancy. Somewhat older than the others, who called her "Aunt Xin," she was like a big sister to them. Taiming advised her to take some time off, but the next day she was still working in the fields. She couldn't afford to stop, as she earned her son's rice by the day. Taiming gave up and assigned her to light duty.

One night, Taiming's deep, healthy sleep was interrupted by female voices. He jumped out of bed. At the window were three faces screaming at him.

Aunt Xin was having a difficult delivery. Her three favorite protégées had come to him for carrots "to stop her bleeding."

Taiming rushed to Aunt Xin's room, which was close to his. Many neighbors were already crowding the entrance.

"Don't fall asleep!" somebody was yelling inside.

Men were not allowed to enter. Aunt Xin's husband and little boy were fretting outside. Taiming walked up to the wall, made of woven bamboo, and looked inside. The baby had been born safely, but its cries were muffled by shouts from the "midwife," whom Taiming recognized as one of the older workers, not a midwife at all. She was commanding, begging, the pale mother not to fall asleep. Unable to stand the sight, Taiming asked what was wrong. The would-be midwife answered that the afterbirth had not come out and that there was no carrot juice to stop the bleeding. According to a superstition, Aunt Xin would die if she fell asleep now. Taiming's common sense warned him that a bleeding woman should not be shaken this way, but he knew nothing about deliveries, either. What they needed was a doctor.

He ran to the nearby police box to phone the local doctor, who lived far away. Taiming stood for a long time with the receiver at his ear, but the ringing never stopped. He returned dejectedly to the farm.

The husband was now pacing back and forth like a madman, and the little boy was screaming for his mother. How they all carried on! Taiming caught himself feeling a sort of anger, almost a hatred, toward these people. When he had offered to fetch the doctor, the failing mother had turned to him to gasp out between breaths, "No! No men! I'd rather die." Alarmed by her strange admission, he had said to himself, "It might be too late, anyway." These stupid customs had taken the lives of countless mothers and babies. At least, if a real midwife were present, Aunt Xin might still be saved! But these people thought that midwives were for ladies; they believed that mere peasants had no right to ask for such fancy services. So instead, they played it by ear, and when there were complications, as there were now, they just agonized, clung all the more ignorantly to superstition, and stubbornly rejected modern medicine. The people who died were simply unlucky; they had been dealt a bad hand. "What a silly game! What a silly game!" he kept repeating under his breath. Aunt Xin died.

That her bed of pleasure had become her deathbed Taiming blamed partly on himself, for he had never offered his learning to these people. These crazy ideas, the tragedy of ignorance, taught Taiming that education was not just for children but also for these unschooled adults whom he had advised but not taught. He had still been too much the schoolteacher to see that there was no reason that systematic learning should not take place outside the classroom.

Every day, during the lunch break, in the shade of a large tree, Taiming offered crash courses in arithmetic, Japanese, and basic medicine and hygiene. The women listened attentively to the enthusiastic young man who, to his own great surprise, had a knack for teaching grown-ups. He became immensely popular. He was overjoyed at being an educator, and they soaked up knowledge as sand does water. For Taiming, every day was fulfilling.

Life on the farm was not all good, however. Autumn was off-season, and the workers went away. Bored, Taiming decided to look into the overall management of the farm. Gradually he realized the extent to which Huang had been lying to him: far from making a profit, the farm was bleeding money. The minor drought that year, which his friend had said would not hurt the farm all that much, was making matters even worse. The question was, how could Huang have lied so easily?

The suspicious overseer put the question to his friend at the earliest opportunity. Huang responded with hearty laughter.

"You're certainly no businessman!" he said, his eyes twinkling. "Think like a schoolmaster and you won't have a chance in this world. Well, I'll tell you: the sugar refiners have helped me out with a little money that doesn't appear in the account books you saw. Twenty thousand yen. I'll tell you something else: it's not just this farm. If you made all our loans public, we'd have to declare bankruptcy on the spot. As it is, we claim that we're making money. Of course, some farms do go under and never repay that little loan to the company, but the company doesn't even notice. In other words, suck on the company like a leech to win your daily bread and feed and school your kids—that's my philosophy."

"I see," Taiming said, half to himself; so that is how the world works. He regretted having nagged Huang to raise his wages.

When Taiming expressed his regret, Huang shrugged and said—this time his tone was "philosophical" as well—"I'll pay them while I can, that's all."

"When we ship the sugar," he went on, "we *will* make a few thousand—so it's not hopeless. I do feel sorry for the peasants, though: they work and work for their commission as though it'll make any difference! Unlike me, they don't have any real security, so sooner or later they'll fall behind. One accident or long illness and they're finished. How they swallow the sweet words—and die of sugar. . . . Anyway, I wish it had rained more! If all this doesn't work out, we'll have to start teaching again!"

He roared.

8. More Wandering

Hard reality was encroaching on the pastoral setting. Halfway through the autumn, a political group hosted a day of lectures downtown. Afterward, a couple of speakers had a minor dispute with the detective in attendance. Taiming did not go to the event, but in the days following the skirmish, he too sensed the tension in the air. An arbitrator by the name of Liu, who was no stranger to the farm, came to see him. A little over fifty, this finely dressed country gentleman confidently waved his white fan as he walked into Taiming's office.

"How are you, Mr. Hu? Ah, busy? So you missed the lectures, ah ha." That was his preface to a detailed account of the lectures and the ensuing tension downtown. "The night before the lectures, which the group was so insistent on holding, a detective dropped by my place to ask me a favor. Mr. Hu, he was grinning the whole time he asked me to make sure the townsfolk didn't express their welcome too enthusiastically. When the same group landed in Xin-zhu, the people there apparently celebrated with a huge demonstration—firecrackers and so on. The authorities didn't want such embarrassing exuberance to be on display again. False modesty aside, I have influence in this district, so the detective, knowing that I do, contacted me beforehand to see if I could give him a helping hand."

As Liu smugly continued, Taiming grew more and more annoyed by the middle-aged man's self-image: a mere observer who was also a man of the world and not above collaborating with the authorities. What struck Taiming about Liu's story was that one of the speakers had been Zhan and that he was still in town. But Zhan was just a friend of a friend, and Taiming did not feel a strong desire to see him. If it had been Lan, Taiming would have gone downtown, but he had heard that Lan was in jail.

"Some people are so reckless," Liu was saying, "like one person in the audience. The poor fool couldn't sit still; he stood up and cheered, against police regulations. Who do you think stood up? That hunchback who makes shoes in the street. Ha ha! Well, nothing happened to him then. But they were waiting for him the next day in his favorite soba shop, you know, the one he goes to so happily for lunch, leaving his tools outside. He'll have to be satisfied with less food for twenty-nine more days."

Taiming frowned. The cynicism he was objecting to was not that of the police. Although Liu looked like a gentleman, he was not, according to what the women on the farm had told Taiming. It was rumored that Liu had gotten his job by hanging around the police headquarters and running errands for the detective's wife. Taiming was now beginning to believe that it was not only in sexual matters that the arbitrator's character was in doubt. The more he thought about Liu's crudeness, the worse it seemed. The man left a feeling of discomfort in him.

Could it be, then, that Lan and Zhan were heroes? For the first time, Taiming truly thought so. Full of energy, heedless of danger, above all firmly principled, they had an outlook that was not merely different from his but larger, higher. How pointless and contemptible his own life was, how like Liu's! The balance he was achieving on the farm returned to the same old tortuous questions. But they did not alter his day-to-day behavior: he continued to help Huang run the farm as his loyal right-hand man, and life went on, winter, the New Year, spring.

April was a time of reckoning. A disturbing piece of news reached Huang. Firmly convinced that the solution to the farm's problems was to expand its operations, he had requested several loans from the company, and his plan had worked in that the farm was still in business. When Huang said "the company," however, he meant the head of its agriculture section. The news was that he had been transferred back to Japan. As Huang feared, his replacement refused to lend him another yen. When Huang immediately contacted the former head, he was sympathetic but could not help. Only some time later did Huang learn that the decision had been handed down from higher up and that a mere section head, old or new, could do nothing about it. The company's conclusion was that the one-time schoolmaster did not have enough real estate to be asking for such loans.

That spring, Huang's farm lost more than six thousand yen. All that the two full months of concentrated work since the New Year had achieved was to meet the deadline; the harvest itself, due to the lack of rain on the high, arid land, was a mere 21,120 kilos per hectare. With the low price of rice having pushed that of sugarcane down to 43.6 yen, the loss per hectare amounted to a staggering 150 yen. Huang's unofficial debt to the company as of now exceeded 25,000 yen, which only reinforced his belief that he didn't have enough land. He meant to ask the company for more loans so that he could buy ten more hectares. Now, however, that seemed unlikely, and the end seemed near.

Feeling sorry for Huang and eager to return the favor he had never forgotten, Taiming offered to put his inheritance at his friend's disposal. It would just be to tide him over.

"Thanks, Hu," Huang said, "I appreciate your kindness. But in the name of friendship, I'll turn down your offer." He was not afraid of taking risks, but he was not going to take a chance with his friend's fortune. Taiming pleaded with him, but his friend's steadfast refusal actually seemed to suggest something else as well.

Taiming finally understood and also saw that Huang was trying to make it clear that his friend had no choice. "I guess you don't want me around anymore," Taiming said. "Well, I wish you the best of luck."

Another turning point came as he packed up and set off. As he looked back at the farm, his friend's farm, his beloved pupils, the farmhands, were following him. At the station, they waved their handkerchiefs until his train became a tiny speck in the distance. Bracing himself on the window sill, he waved back at the receding mass of women, "the women I worked with," he thought, "who taught me to teach them." He was feeling incredibly sentimental.

By the time the women, the station, the farm, and the town had dropped below the horizon, the train was thundering into a field of tall, waving trees of Australian origin. The distant sparkling sea, which he glimpsed now and then, seemed to be racing against the train.

9. The Call of the Continent

According to her brother Taiming, Hu Qiuyun was no more than a child, but while he was away, she had been happily engaged to a medical school graduate—a son of one of her father's friends—who intended to practice. The Hus were too busy preparing for her wedding to notice Taiming's arrival home.

The town geishas occupied the time and energy of Hu Zhigang, who argued with his wife when he was not neglecting her. Taiming did not feel strongly about his older brother's sudden need to sample women and to seek concubines; after all, Hu Zhigang was not the first man to use a comfortable inheritance for such antics. It was none of Taiming's business. Although he felt sorry for his sister-in-law, he did not consider making this known to his brother.

There was nobody to talk to in the village, so Taiming decided to dust his late grandfather's books. Sometimes, handling one of them pulled at the grandson's heart, and he then flipped through the book and read a page or two, then another, sometimes reading the whole thing in this unmethodical manner. Grandfather's spirit lived on in the pages. Gauging by the number of notes, his favorite had been, at least at one point in his life, Tao Yuanming. Guided by his grandfather's hand, as on that long-ago spring day, Taiming step by step reentered the world of the fifth-century poet and of classical verse and spent many hours there. Immersing himself in literature seemed to restore his balance. Irritating as it was that his parents—and sister—did not stop nagging him to find a wife, he had no difficulty ignoring them. The incident that disturbed his modest equilibrium was much more direct.

One day, shouting incoherently, Ah-Cha came running down the path from the hill. Construction workers were digging up a corner of the Hu graveyard. Fearing the ancestors' wrath, she had attempted womanishly, bodily, and futilely to stop the excavation. A muscular man, the supervisor, charged at her and hit her on the cheek. She argued with him, but he did not understand Taiwanese and hit her again. He seemed to be telling her, "Shut up!" Weeping like a banshee, she came scrambling down the path from the hill.

Sugarcane farming was spreading to Taiming's village. This crew was the vanguard.

Taiming flushed as he listened to his mother. When she started repeating herself, he interrupted her and rushed to the scene.

The supervisor snorted at his arguments. "I have a black belt in judo, so keep those hands off me," he recommended, though Taiming had not made any violent gestures. "Property? What do I care? Bring your complaints to the company and the three lawyers on our payroll! Ah, you want my name? Kitano's the name, remember it!" Further conversation was useless if the black belt was going to menace him in such a way. Taiming disliked violence.

He trudged home. So incessantly did Kitano's malicious comments haunt him that night that he had trouble falling asleep.

Sleep did not help him. His mother, meanwhile, was already resigned to the development. "Ah, we didn't need this," she said, but reluctantly ate eggs and somen noodles to defend against the encroaching ill luck.

Her son, schooled in the new ways, could not leave it there, however. He might bring the business to court, but when had Taiwanese won such cases? It was immaterial that his side was right. It did not improve his chances in the least. If his mother had been seriously wounded—only then would he have had a chance, but only to get Kitano jailed. The company, untouched, would quickly bail him out. In the first place, his mother had not been injured. The company's legal experts were undoubtedly experienced in maneuvering around the question of private property. Indeed, what counterattack would they not use? His thoughts were like salt in his wounds. His mother seemed to have escaped unscathed, and Taiming seemed to be the only one the incident had been able to hurt. Across the study flew the book he was reading, followed by the cry: "And Tao Yuanming doesn't help!" The questions that Taiming had pondered on and off since his earliest days, the questions that seemed to disappear when he could not answer them, were in fact always there, submerged in his memory, lying there calmly, waiting to be stirred up by fresh information, new turbulence. He began to dream of a place where he might breathe more freely: across the sea a continent beckoned wildly.

Qiuyun's wedding was approaching while Taiming fumed and dreamed. He had always advocated simplifying the marriage ceremony but gave in to his elders, as was customary. Qiuyun's opulent dowry, gathered with much hustle and bustle, included a dresser with three mirrors and a drawer in the modern style that she preferred.

On the day of the ceremony, the long procession of her possessions reminded relatives, friends, and local notables that the family's past was illustrious and its present state not so squalid after all.

At the hall, Opium Tong, representing the Hu clan, received the guests, while Taiming offered them drinks. The arbitrator Uncle Xu Xin—the one who asked the musicians to play "Tea Picking"—was present in a brand-new robe, his crest tacked on. As the guest of honor, flanked by other notables, he sat at the head of the table and drank heavily.

"They're fools," Uncle Xu Xin remarked, launching on a bout of criticism, loudly as was his custom, "fools swept up by the times—of which they haven't the faintest idea! Politics, society, nothing has changed. The terms for them have changed, oh yes, but they're no more than euphemisms for money. Things are the same as they were in the old days, but we were more direct then and said: 'Money talks.' Look at the lawyers, political movements, et cetera, of our days and times. Money is still justice, and I've known that for a dozen years. A schoolteacher is worth two thousand yen."

He paused and looked around triumphantly. Twirling his cup with one hand and stroking his goatee with all five fingers of the other, he continued, "You remember how I used to say what a waste of money school was. You also remember how people called me an old dotard for thinking so. Well, I guess I was tragically ahead of the times. Some fools haven't understood that yet. The other day, Dr. Hu's madam took a beating. Try and see what two thousand yen can't do: I say much more than what ten wise men who've studied overseas will ever do. Did I say two thousand? Five hundred's enough to get a head coolie fired. If you leave it to me, three hundred!"

Because he was the arbitrator, his audience had to listen to him and suffer through the alcohol-fueled polemic. Opium Tong alone was smiling.

Uncle Xu Xin was not finished yet. "But Taiming, you know your place and I respect you for that. I'll tell you what happened to one of my relatives, who graduated from law school. When he returned, he was persuaded to become honorary mayor. The position brought in no more than thirty or forty yen a month, which didn't even cover his 'expenses'—which, in plain language, was entertaining allies and befriending enemies. How his parents cried. They were nearly bankrupt by the end of his first term. Having been mayor, he could hardly become just a judge, and working for a wage was out of the question. That accursed little sinecure will force him to go around with a bowl for the rest of his life. But some fools have done worse, I mean the ones who joined political movements. For a while, they had a good time traveling and lecturing, but most of them are now languishing in prison—like your friend Lan, who came to speak here a while ago, and that other fellow Zhan. But I always knew regular public schooling was all one needed."

With this reassertion of prescience, his long speech finally came to a close. More saké was drunk, and everybody had a chance to impose his weaknesses on others. Opium Tong might have been expected to say a word or two, but the recession had gotten to him, and lately he had been quite subdued. Ah-San and Ah-Si likewise limited their participation to nods and ayes. Ever since they had fallen to the rank of day laborers, the duo had become self-effacing in the company of gentlefolk. The chief host, Taiming, disapproved of the silliness of it all but played his part.

Qiuyun's change of address having proceeded smoothly, Taiming was left alone with his mother who now, more than ever before, wanted a daughter-in-law but most of the time kept such thoughts to herself, knowing how little her son appreciated them. Bored, she visited her daughter often. Her son-in-law had just opened his own clinic and was friendly enough. Sometimes she came back with her daughter and the nice young man. Taiming disliked doctors, those sellers of distilled water, just as much as he disliked tax collectors, those pinchers of money, but he was forced to change his views the longer he chatted, and chuckled, with his sister's husband.

The latter once observed, "It's illness I'm after, not money. If I live long enough, I'll get to help, let's say, ten thousand people. Brother, I'm not trying to make ten thousand yen. But if I do help ten thousand people, I'll have made ten thousand yen." He was clever but not the way quacks were.

His sister happily married, Taiming sighed and settled back into his solitary life, or tried to. How could his grandfather have immersed himself in Tao Yuanming and ignored all else? Taiming envied him and fervently wished to turn into an old man. Why couldn't spring and summer and autumn and winter—all the seasons—disappear? He was still too young to immerse himself in Lao Zi and Zhuang Zi; his youth exuded hopes and ideals and made his idle existence into a titanic punishment. Cruel Lao Zi, whose idealistic teachings did not cool his rhetoric, stern Confucius, who spoke of a way but did not show him where it lay—whichever way Taiming turned, he was walking on a path of thorns.

Another New Year arrived. Under the evening moon, the tangerines in the backyard looked plump. Taiming wandered like a sleepwalker into the orchard. The new branch that had grown where he had snipped off one on another moonlit night bore a shining gold fruit much fuller than the preceding year's. He remembered and pondered the words he had spoken to the moon then.

His mother called to him. She said a man named Zeng had come to see him.

The rumor was that Instructor Zeng, who had given the overbearing Japanese faculty a lesson and resigned, had gone on to attend one of the imperial universities and was now living on the continent.

Taiming went in immediately, with surprise, awe, and expectation on his face. Zeng had returned to the island to attend his father's funeral. He now was a university professor in China, and what he said about the country, which he had been observing carefully from various angles, sent tremors of fascination through Taiming. Instructor Zeng had been an attractive fellow and an able conversationalist, whereas Professor Zeng was a man, seasoned, broad, and deep. For someone like Taiming, who lived in seclusion on a tiny island and never came into contact with great men, seeing Zeng face-to-face was a strain. The giant strongly recommended going to China. Taiming felt his youth course through his body and, for the first time in months, did not regret it.

Zeng soon left Taiwan, but about two months later, Taiming received a letter. He tore open the envelope, unfolded the letter with fumbling fingers, and devoured the words. No doubt thanks to Professor Zeng's recommendation, Taiming had been invited to teach mathematics at a Women's Exemplary National High School.

"His friendship was genuine!" He thought of Zeng with infinite gratitude and trust. Taiming's dream was coming true: nothing stood between him and the continent but the sea, and he was quite ready. It was about time he left Taiwan behind him.

The village absorbed good news as quickly as it had the bad. Taiming's presence emerged from communal oblivion and was in the spotlight once again.

"An invitation to teach at a vocational school is the modern equivalent of passing exams for interior service, a great honor," Taiming's father commented. Hu Wenqing felt he was being deprived of his son and secretly feared for him, too. But he hid his sorrow and anxiety because he knew his son's happiness was at stake.

Taiming was planning never to come back again. Full of joy, he packed his belongings and visited all his friends and relatives. As though he had been reborn, he reacquainted himself with his native land in order to bid it farewell.

It was his mother's idea that they visit the town temple to ask for divine assistance. To prepare, she fasted and carefully bathed. She was so eager that when the day arrived, she even put on shoes, which she rarely wore. They all were going to town: Hu Wenqing was in ceremonial attire; Ah-Yu, though no longer a young woman, still dressed like one; Zhigang had a new suit on; and his wife wore a *hakama* skirt that she believed to still be in fashion. Qiuyun and her doctor husband joined them, making a party of eight.

In the center of the temple, Taiming's mother knelt on a cushion and bowed reverently on her son's behalf while his father made the offerings and said a prayer. Taiming planted an incense stick and piously brought his palms together.

In the courtyard, his mother bought a sacred charm. "Very, very lucky," it said.

The doctor suggested that they have a group photo taken. By this time, no one believed that cameras stole souls.

The party proceeded to the best-known service in town. Photos were taken on the second floor, they were told; they should take off their shoes first. With Taiming at the head, the group filed upstairs.

When Ah-Cha had straggled about halfway up, a male voice thundered deafeningly, "Stop, you chink!"

A young woman in a beautiful red puffed-bow obi came running after Ah-Cha. With a scornful movement of her chin, she indicated, "You! No shoes!"

Ah-Cha hastily took off her shoes, which she rarely wore. It was the first time she had entered a building where shoes were not permitted. Taiming blushed beet red. He was embarrassed and mortified that he had gone upstairs first and had not made sure his mother obeyed the Japanese custom. He also was furious that the man had yelled at her so loudly and angrily. Taiming wanted to cancel the picture taking, but his father insisted, arguing that canceling it would bring bad luck. Bowing to his father's feelings more than to his authority or the superstition, Taiming stood in the center and tried not to look sullen.

No one mentioned the incident as they walked home. Qiuyun's husband chattered spiritedly; the shrewd doctor felt called upon to liven up the family. Taiming was the only one who remained silent all the way home. Mount Cigao was draped in dark gray clouds. It was going to rain.

Taiming was worried about his mother, but the doctor read his mind and offered to take her in. She had been wanting to live with her daughter, so she had no objection. Hu Wenqing had a mistress to look after him; if something happened, their elder son was there. The matter was settled that very day.

Taiming felt truly ready to go, possibly for good. His plan had been to see as many elders and older relatives as he could, to receive a lifetime's worth of advice, but the incident at the photo shop persuaded him to hurry. He decided to apply for his passport.

When he went to the district headquarters, a good-looking young policeman who stood guard bowed deeply to him. Taiming was taken aback; he must have been mistaken for someone else. But when the young officer addressed him as "Sensei," the face of a child surfaced from the depths of his memory and became the handsome one he was looking at now. The guard left his post to introduce his former teacher to the district headman.

Hearing the reason for his travel, the generous headman promised that the application process would be particularly quick.

Taiming thanked him. As he turned to leave, however, the headman said, "Allow me just one more question. You've been educated. Shouldn't young men like you stay in Taiwan and contribute to our island's culture? China isn't heaven, either—I hope you're aware of that." Taiwanese culture and youth: Taiming agreed to some extent and said so. But he had made up his mind. The headman nodded gravely.

The passport was issued with the promised haste, but Taiming still had to wait. The brave journey to the continent and to success should begin on one of those days that the traditional calendar called auspicious. When the lucky morning came, Taiming went to the temple to burn incense and to pray to his ancestors for help. Where the ceiling intersected with one of the walls there hung a frame that would have borne the word PROMOTION if some of the gold leaf had not peeled off, in such a time-worn manner that Taiming felt proud of his ancestry. In the patio, firecrackers were going off.

Inside, in the presence of all the Hus, Opium Tong assured him that his promotion to the bureaucracy guaranteed three generations' prosperity. Ah-San and Ah-Si congratulated Taiming and seemed to miss him already, more or less genuinely. Amid the magnificent send-off ceremony, attended by numerous relatives and dignitaries, Taiming realized that if he failed this time, he should die instead of return. That is, he had to be prepared never to come home again, whatever happened. As the firecrackers reached a crescendo, he silently started for the gate.

"Happy promotion! Happy promotion!" was the gauntlet of congratulation that he walked through.

At the gate, Opium Tong said, "Taiming, at the mouth of the Yangtze River, there's a mausoleum, our family's largest and richest. When you become an official, please visit it. It won't hurt your wallet."

The spring wind formed billows in the robe of his father, who stood proudly among the others, but his mother looked sad. As

Taiming walked toward the station, he stopped time and again to catch a glimpse of his house one last time. He felt in his heart that he would like to put up another frame like the one in the hall.

His brother Zhigang, his sister Qiuyun, and her doctor husband accompanied him to Chilung, the misty port where it lightly rained on and off. On the wharf, Taiming looked toward his destination. He remembered the previous occasion when the woman had secretly come to see him off. He had never seen her since then, but the story was that she was living happily as the mother of two—or was it three?—with a well-to-do doctor for a husband. Hu Taiming, however, was still a bachelor. If he had married her, he might have found satisfaction and happiness living in the country. But he had not, and his recollections made him sad.

The warning bell sounded through the misty harbor. Zhigang carefully summarized the main points of his big brother's advice. Today he was the earnest protector Taiming had known as a child. Qiuyun fluttered her eyelids as she said good-bye, while her husband laughed and pointed out unsentimentally that Shanghai, though on foreign soil, was really no farther away than Taitung; that at any rate, it was much closer than Japan.

Taiming, who also was aware of this geographical fact, did not share his brother's and sister's feeling that he was traveling to the end of the world. Something else worried him, though, and as Taiming boarded the three-thousand-ton steamer, he repeatedly pleaded with his siblings that they take good care of their parents.

Waving handkerchiefs immediately blossomed along the wharf when the vessel began to pull away from it. Colored a splendid blue, Mount Chilung inched across the horizon until a dusk-colored veil fell slowly over it like a blanket. The outer seas rocked the steamer, and Taiming went down to his cabin to lie down.

When he appeared on deck the next morning, a stunningly blue sky greeted him, but no trace of Mount Chilung. The weather was perfect for sailing. Flying fish jumped in and out of the powerful

Black Current that arches from the Philippines to the Hawaiian Islands. The fish sparkled in the sunlight.

Taiming felt as sunny as the skies, and his heart beat to a light-hearted tune. He had not heard it for so long that at first he did not recognize his desire to compose a poem. But a couple of quatrains came to him in a flash and seemed to require hardly any revision except for the last line, "A continent of kinsfolk nears." Officially, though, he was on his way to a foreign people. As his passport said, Hu Taiming was a citizen of the Japanese Empire.

Unable to come up with a satisfactory alternative, he was leaning toward keeping the last line when he remembered the chilling fate of Shen Deqian and ruled out that option. The eighteenth-century poet and critic was accused of criticizing the status quo in a verse about black peonies: "This breed bizarre usurped the throne / Rightly of the vermilion." Meant to be a clever allusion to a Confucian saying, the lines were interpreted as a jab at the reigning emperor: the Qing dynasty had ousted the Ming, which bore the appellation "vermilion." Treacherous though the lines may have been, the poet protested that his intentions were not. He was executed anyway.

One after another Taiming recalled many of the anecdotes his grandfather had related to him regarding fatal slips of the pen. When an unintended offense could cost a poet his life, why cling to a word susceptible to similar accusations? Changing the last line, Taiming wrote, in pencil, the final version in his notebook:

> O thoughts, I've aired you ten odd years
> Beneath unruly eastern skies;
> This fool so scoffed at all careers
> Till a nasty fall was no surprise.
> These waves that wash my wounded eyes
> Will likely drown my orphan tears
> Before we greet the paradise—
> A continent for pioneers.

He read it out loud. His heart was smiling triumphantly, he thought; it extended infinitely, like the ocean. The way he used to think suddenly struck him as being funny. An infantile disorder! Laughter slowly welled up from the bottom of his heart. Vainly trying to suppress the ungainly display, bending over with his hands on the railing, he raised his face toward the horizon. There was the first sign of the continent.

Chapter Three

· · ·

1. A Room with a View of Mount Zijin

To the east of Nanjing is a mountain that has, people say, a regal air. At sunset, the enshrouding purple mist seems indeed to be rising from the legendary gold that the king of Chu buried in these lands more than twenty centuries ago, to bring peace to his country. Come autumn, the mantle on Mount Zijin, or Purple Gold Mountain, is too gorgeous for words, and so too is the graceful line that links the peak to Lake Xuanwu.

Mandarin had gotten on Taiming's nerves, and he was gazing out the window on the second floor of the Zeng house. Taiwan's mountains were mere crags in light of this continental majesty.

Zeng and his family lived one flight above and never came down except at mealtime, so Taiming had the floor to himself after his teacher, who came for an hour every day, left. In the quiet, the lodger looked at Mount Zijin, and his mind wandered aimlessly. For almost a month, he had been living here—imprisoned, practically—because he did not understand Mandarin.

Zeng, who had invited him so enthusiastically and had even found a job for him, cautioned with curious persistence from the moment he met Taiming in Shanghai that their identity must be concealed: "People will look askance at us wherever we go, it's our fate. It's not about what we've done or haven't done. We're deformed—fate's monstrous children. Of course it's unfair, but we can't do much about it, and we mustn't behave like sulky foster children. We've got to prove ourselves through deeds, not words. The truth is that our passion is second to none when it comes to making sacrifices for China."

Taiming could understand this contorted position from his own experience at the China Association lecture in Tokyo, where revealing his identity had jeopardized his life. Still, he was depressed that he had to swallow such humiliation simply because he was born on an unpropitiously situated island.

At any rate, he was thoroughly fed up with this house arrest. How could he master the language speedily if he could not practice it in the streets? Did Zeng want an old man to be the girls' math teacher? To walk downtown, to breathe the air of China! "But nation building is a long and winding road," Zeng chided, "so calm down, Hu, and look at the Yangtze, which flows majestically but faster than you'd think. Let's be more like the great river."

What irritated Taiming was that the passion that the very word China could arouse in him was cooling with each day he wasted trying to learn a language in a vacuum.

He was at a loss. He was nostalgic for the days he spent in Shanghai. A piece of the real, living China, the city demolished the shallow, dated notions he had had of the country. The modern, Western atmosphere of its French settlement drove home to the young Taiwanese that he was, after all, a country bumpkin. The modern clothes of the quite visible young women did not succeed in concealing the aura of a mature culture, five thousand years old.

On the second deck of the bus he took from the French settlement were three schoolgirls who balanced on their laps foreign magazines with beautiful covers. Zeng explained that it was the fad among Shanghai's schoolgirls to travel with a book prominently displayed, and Taiming thought it was strangely feudal of the girls to glamorize reading. The trio's sophisticated dress duly impressed him: they all wore a blouse, a skirt, socks, and elegant Shanghai shoes and carried a handbag, but each girl's taste was distinct, shown by their impeccable color coordination. In comparison, Taiwanese girls, no matter how polished, were boorish. Finding the girls free of the spiritual conflicts typical of the mindless devourers of Western trends who abandon their own tradition entirely, Taiming noted to himself that they had already internalized the Chinese woman's sensibility and the Confucian principle of the Mean. Nor did he fail to notice their delicate manners, carefree eyes, and young skin, all of which he found mesmerizing. Were they perhaps aristocrats—ladies-in-waiting? Certainly not of the same world as he, for they seemed to embody the poetry of Chinese literature and to offer a history lesson, with a whiff of the *Analects*, a classical ghost living in modern times through them. And what did such creatures say to one another? Although they hardly spoke, they sometimes indulged softly in what must have been the most exquisite exchanges—why had he not learned Mandarin? Unable to make out a word of what they were saying, no matter how hard he tried, he sorely regretted having presumed that because Taiwanese were Chinese after all, he should be able to get by with the southern languages he already knew, those of Guangdong and Fujian. It was a mistake.

Although his tour of the great city lasted only a few days, he managed to see the cultural landmarks, to sample the international cuisine, to smell the back alleys, and to hear the wild fowl squawk, in other words, to meet the women of the street. Things Euro-American, Chinese, and even Japanese all coexisted chaotically in disharmonious harmony in the International Settlement. Tall buildings, those man-eating monsters of plutocracy, dominated the landscape while at their feet, people and automobiles formed a flood, so that one crossed the torrent at risk to one's life. When Taiming thought he had reached the opposite shore, he was drawn into an entertainment complex, a veritable whirlpool of human desires whose gaudy, artificial intensity gave him a headache in a matter of minutes. He escaped to the roof for fresh air, but there the darkness was thick with the murmurings of young couples, among whom alert women of the night kept an eye out for prospective customers. Even as Taiming watched, one was lured to some unknown place by a pitiless pro.

The other houses of amusement were no different, offering to souls paralysis rather than solace.

He hurried back to his inn. The next day, he went back out to chase the moving streets again. The city was diverse, with its fair share of beggars and those too weak even to beg, not to mention the thoroughly Westernized native girls, the arrogant pipe-toting Europeans, and those brainy Japanese who did not know about Li Bai's dreams. At the entrances of trading companies, banks, and factories stood armed Sikhs, whose size and attire were imposing but who seemed somehow emasculated, having lost all means and become obedient hounds. As gentle as they were, their glistening black steel weapons had the desired effect on Taiming. He had rarely seen guns.

He was quite willing to escape the monstrous city when the time came to depart for Nanjing.

He had looked forward to the view the rail journey would offer of Suzhou, where the hermit Han Shan used to live, but the bleak landscape did not appeal to him at all. The traveler recalled Zhang Ji's famous poem about the hermit's temple, and that was all. But just when the train was preparing to pull out of Suzhou station, a flower blossomed in full view.

The young woman who came on board may have still been a student, but her mature, sensual appearance attracted Taiming as never before. He laughed nervously at his heart, which did not respond as readily to landscapes as it did to women. He asked himself, "So is she what they call a Suzhou beauty?" When the train arrived at Nanjing, the Suzhou beauty, in order to retrieve her belongings from the rack where an attendant had placed them and which she could not reach, climbed onto her seat without taking off her shoes. She left with her baggage while Taiming sat pondering her unladylike manner. Two tiny indentations, left by her Shanghai shoes, remained where she had stood. So charmingly small were they that he forgave her lack of consideration, and his brain retained the imprints long after the velveteen surface had lost all trace of them.

Watching Taiming study around the clock, Zeng called him a Mandarin freak. But Taiming's efforts began to pay off in the form of an inordinate but unfulfilled desire to converse in the language. He took walks, venturing farther and farther each time, but never opened his mouth, still fearing what his speech would betray.

One evening, however, Zeng came to his room in a different mood. "Shall we?" he asked in Mandarin. They took the long moonlit path from the house to the closest street. Zeng looked at the crescent that was rising over Mount Zijin and remarked, "I've hardly taken walks since I came to Nanjing. You know, I'd forgotten how good it feels—nature, the evening, a friend, and all that."

Upon reaching the street, Zeng hailed a rickshaw, which carried the two to a restaurant called Dragon Gate. There, drink in hand, Zeng related to Taiming the recent developments in international affairs—how tense things were getting. A warm glow spread from Taiming's stomach to his extremities, partly due to the liquor and partly because his friend's enthusiasm was endearing. Taiming grew talkative, too, more than he had ever been with this friend, and after a few hours, when his voice started sounding strange to himself, his depression disappeared.

They stepped out for a walk and chose lonely alleys. By now, the moon of the lower Yangtze was shining at its zenith.

When they came to a street, a beggar appeared from the dark to ask Taiming for change. Finding only bills in his pockets, Taiming turned to his friend, but Zeng was pretending not to have seen the apparition. It refused to disappear, though, and followed them ten yards, twenty yards, pleading in a most pathetic tone, "Sirs, sirs . . ." At fifty yards, sensing that the sirs were not about to be forthcoming, the beggar switched to a louder, pushier "Sirs, sirs!" Mortified, Taiming dug into his pockets once more, but no change had materialized in the meantime. He did have several ten-yen bills, but in any event, he currently had no income. No one in his position would give so much to a beggar, right? And by the way, why was Zeng so opposed to parting with just a little change? Taiming began to find his friend very annoying but quickly grasped the contradiction and felt ashamed of himself.

The beggar now was crying. His pathetic wail ripped painfully through the dark. He showed no sign of relenting, perhaps having sensed that Taiming was debating whether he should part with one of his ten-yen bills.

"Here," Taiming finally said to the beggar, "don't be surprised."

But just as he was pulling the bill out of his pocket, Zeng slapped a coin on the beggar's hand and said, "Now get lost."

The beggar thanked them as melodramatically as he had pleaded, squatted down, and stopped bothering them. Taiming was baffled by Zeng's behavior. How could he walk on so coldly for so long if he were prepared to give, as he eventually did? There was something unfathomable about Zeng, or perhaps such behavior was the norm in China. Whatever the answer, the question restored Taiming to an undesired sobriety.

That night, he had trouble falling asleep. His mind, half awake, flitted from Shanghai to Taiwan to Japan, from places and times to people and ideas, mixing them all up. "Life," he thought, "provokes three kinds of tears: tears of poverty, tears of illness, and tears of parted lovers." But which were the worst? He fell asleep. It was morning when he opened his eyes.

There was one thing about life in the Zeng house that Taiming could not stand: he had to eat rice gruel every morning. He had never liked rice gruel, but a beggar had no choice but to keep his dislikes to himself. If he had to, he could stomach the Zeng family's notion of breakfast; what he really could not live with was that the Zengs ate frightfully little, satisfying themselves with a single bowl each. Taiming was humiliatingly hungry by lunchtime even if he had asked for seconds, thirds, even fourths—and that was easier said than done. No matter how quickly he ate, the Zengs were all done by the time he was finishing his second bowl. Taiming's first goal was to learn how to eat fast enough to be ready for a third bowl every morning. It was not a goal he could achieve without practice. Every morning, as he spooned the scalding pap down his throat, he tasted both the joys and sorrows of a beggar. To be liberated from such a predicament, he had to find a place of his own. He vowed to leave as soon as possible.

As autumn deepened in the lower Yangtze, the trees of the Pavilion of the North Pole shed their scarlet leaves, and the people of Nanjing prepared for winter. A housewife was repairing a futon out in the empty alley and basking in the last warm rays of the year. Taiming had a winter robe made for himself. It was not until he snuggled into his brand-new traditional garment that he realized the discomfort of Western clothes, the perversity of collars and neckties. The Chinese robe, loose and free, felt better than it looked. One could wear any kind of garment underneath it, and as many as one liked, layer over layer if it was cold, and lie down without worrying about creases. A fresh convert to traditional attire, Taiming also felt as though his robe were turning him into a different man. No one stared at him when he went downtown; he was one of them. It did not hurt that his Mandarin now was nearly functional. He was dying to be at the front, that is, of the workforce, but Zeng, who did not believe in on-the-job training, ignored his pleas. In his free time, Taiming went to places of entertainment but soon got tired of them. He could not enjoy films and plays when leisure nauseated him.

Snow began to fall like willow leaves. The second floor of the Zeng house was empty and stoveless. Wrapped in his blanket, Taiming tried to read a book but could not, but not because of the cold. He was wondering what rumors people back home might be exchanging about him. Ah-San and Ah-Si were probably bragging about the adventures of Hu Taiming as though they were the heroes. Such imagined thoughts made Taiming restless—and less and less able to read. Shut in by the snow, which fell day after day, his irritation rose. Mount Zijin, enveloped by snowflakes, shone a bright white as far as he could see.

One afternoon, a young man with a large trunk arrived all alone at the Zeng house. He was of the same ethnic stock as Taiming but had grown up farther south in the Pacific Ocean, where many Chinese had emigrated. A graduate of the University of Fudan, he spoke perfect English and some Japanese and hoped to work (a letter of introduction from Zeng would be of great help) for the People's Government's Bureau of Propaganda. His father had pledged an enormous sum to the revolutionary movement.

The newcomer locked the door every time he left his room, even though it was on the second floor, whose only other resident was Taiming. But Lai—that was his name—was not suspicious; he was just being Chinese. In fact, he turned out to be a carefree, talkative, and fun-loving man or, rather, boy, given the way he unleashed peals of laughter about nothing in particular. By the evening, he was blissfully off guard and addressed Taiming as a friend. For better or worse, Taiming's lonely days were over.

During dinner, Lai implored Mrs. Zeng to give him saké as though she were his mother. The man's impudence shocked Taiming, but only him. Lai prattled on about mahjong, dancing, plays, and other trivial matters about which Taiming knew nothing.

The next day, Lai was already teasing Taiming: "But relax! You don't really understand society until you've enjoyed life, I mean, until you've played until you're half dead. And if you don't understand society, you don't know what good politics is. No dance, no mahjong? We can't talk then, you and I. You really must be a teacher!" Coming from Lai, who was utterly devoid of malice, this cajoling did not annoy Taiming. In fact, the pair decided to go to the bath house together that afternoon.

Beyond the filthy shop curtain was an otherworldly warmth: the room for undressing heated by several stoves. A few customers were dozing peacefully in large armchairs. Taiming sat by one of the stoves and felt his snow-chilled body thaw as though spring had come. Lai stuck out his legs playfully, one at a time, so the attendant could take off his shoes and socks for him. The monarch's clothes and underpants were removed by the same hands, which Taiming shooed off when they tried to undress him as well. Taking his clothes off by himself, he wrapped himself in a large towel and followed Lai into the steaming room. The bath itself was divided into three sections, and Taiming chose the least hot. After a while, coaxed by the attendant, he lay down on a long wooden board that extended over the lapping water, and there surrendered himself to a coarse-grained towel that scrubbed the grime off his body from the tip of his fingers to his toes. As the towel was run sometimes vigorously and sometimes lightly over his skin which, after having shriveled in the cold, had suddenly relaxed in the warm water, Taiming experienced a sensation almost like pain. Leaving the bath room, he sank into the chair in which he had sat previously. There, the attendant gave him a deeply satisfying foot massage. Lai first glanced through a porn newspaper while his attendant pounded his feet, but soon his eyelids began to droop. The rhythm of the massage had the same hypnotic effect on Taiming, who forgot his worries about mastering Mandarin, forgot the beggars and whores who wandered the streets, and those twits who knew the number and location of cannons but nothing else, that pest problem in the parks. In his corner of the room, he forgot everything little by little and slept like a prince who did not know about watchdogs or bad men. It was already dusk when he awoke from his dream.

Mahjong, the theater, or dinner? But Taiming rejected all of Lai's suggestions and insisted on returning to the second floor of the Zeng house. On the way home, Lai, who had no choice but to accompany Taiming, began, for no apparent reason, to talk about liberty and equality. His ideas were childish. Desperately wishing to be liberated from the iniquity of this situation, barely listening to his friend's inanities, Taiming sensed at the same time a vague contradiction in his own attitude. For had he not also been transfixed by the mysterious allure of the Chinese bath? Had he not sunk into a mood of happy stupefaction, immersed himself in an atmosphere that he had so recently considered unclean when Zeng had tried to introduce it to him for the first time? While Lai chattered on about liberty and equality, Taiming pondered the strange assimilative force of Chinese society, its ability to numb the nerves of newcomers. China itself—or at least the Chinese bath—was opium.

With the addition of Lai, the Zeng house became a merry place, and its master started to come straight home from work. They played mahjong every night at Lai's behest but also because, as it turned out, Mrs. Zeng had always had a place in her heart for the game. When Lai, Mrs. Zeng, and her husband could not find the necessary fourth party, they looked to Taiming. The game was not half as difficult as Mandarin; a cursory introduction to the rules was enough to start playing; and the sullen parasite really had no right to refuse. As a child, Taiming used to watch Opium Tong and his cohorts gamble at a similar game involving four colors, compared with which mahjong seemed easy, and in fact, in less than ten nights, his skill came to rival Mrs. Zeng's. The only problem was that he was forced to stay up late on some nights— those when Zeng did badly in the first round and requested a second and sometimes a third. Two rounds meant staying up till one or two in the morning and feeling tired and stupid the next day.

One night, while they were playing to the tune of Zeng's baby's wailing, uninterrupted except for an occasional sneeze—it had caught a bad cold—the wail began to drift toward them. The maid was bringing the little prince to the table.

"Your boy is hungry, missus," the hired woman ventured.

"You feed him some milk," replied Mrs. Zeng calmly, not even turning to see.

The fact was that she was just a step from gathering a hand consisting entirely of paulownia tiles, the devastating "All Qing," a secret she had been struggling to keep her face from divulging. Let alone taking a break at this crucial juncture, she was not even going to let the maid's interruption get on her nerves. An overeagerness to continue playing might tip off the others, especially her husband, to what she had coming to them all. She had been losing tonight, and this was the last stretch of the round. With an "All Qing" now, she would not only make up for her losses but end up above zero, two thousand above zero, as she had already silently computed. The maid took the baby back to the other room.

There, however, the baby cried as though it were on fire, and after some futile efforts, the maid came back rather alarmed.

"Missus, I'm afraid he has a fever."

This time, Mrs. Zeng pretended not to hear and perhaps did not hear. She was busy trying to figure out if there were still any "one paulownia" tiles in circulation. Seeing only one tile in the discard pile, she rejoiced in the depths of her heart. She had a pair of them herself, so whoever had the fourth had no use for it and would discard it sooner or later—and then—

"Missus, your son has a fever."

"Please put him to sleep," she replied, this time her voice slightly betraying impatience.

But her husband did not notice. For although he had been dealt a marvelous hand—"Triple Yuan"—almost from the outset and had been close to winning for a long time, the tile he needed was being very shy. The master of the house was yearning for the "white" tile to come out of hiding while his wife was hoping for "one paulownia" or, as she now understood, "three paulownias," which would serve her just as well.

"Mrs. Zeng, how about a short break, your baby isn't well," Taiming suggested. Mrs. Zeng merely pursed her lips and did not take her eyes from the table. The maid took the baby back to the adjacent room, where it redoubled its piercing cries.

Around the table reigned the tensest of silences, disturbed only by the clinking of tiles and, of course, the baby's pleas. As each player took his or her turn drawing from the central pile, either discarding the piece immediately or keeping it and removing another from his or her hand, the others awaited like sharp-eyed eagles, hungry vultures, wise owls. Zeng already had two open threesomes, green and red, laid out on the table, and it was clear that he either had a threesome of whites in his hand already or was waiting for the third tile. The utmost caution was called for, and this sense of danger clutched Taiming, too.

It was Zeng's turn to discard. The others gulped while he hesitated. Suddenly, Zeng's eyebrows drew closer, and with a sweep of his arm, he threw down a "three paulownias" tile on the game table. Nothing he had done in days pleased his wife as much as this move. The game was over.

"Pardon me, Mr. Zeng, but I think you're a fool," accused Lai. He stood up abruptly, stomped around to Zeng's side of the table, and examined the loser's hand. Indeed, what a bonehead, Zeng should have discarded his "one bird" instead. The game ruled in cases like these—in which Lai and Taiming were helpless victims whose hopes and dreams had been dashed by Zeng's stupidity—that only the offender must pay up. His wife's glorious hand of "All Qing" cost Zeng thirteen thousand points, or a penalty of thirteen yen, and what was worse, the round was over. The defeated man clutched the now useless threesomes of greens and reds and bowed his head like a bereaved father. The gleeful Lai and the others merrily analyzed the suspenseful bout.

"Another round!" Zeng demanded.

But neither Lai nor Taiming, let alone Mrs. Zeng, wanted to play again. Meanwhile the baby, apparently tired of screaming, had quieted down.

It was at this moment, however, that the maid burst back into the room to say that the baby was in some sort of crisis. More interested in nursing his own hurt, Zeng stubbornly mixed the tiles and started arranging them for a new round. But his wife seemed to register that there was a problem and hustled off to see her baby.

All set, Zeng turned to the crouching figure in the dimly lit chamber. "Will you hurry up?" he yelled, his voice amplified by a certain vindictiveness. There was no response.

"Mr. Zeng, your son seems quite sick. How about playing again tomorrow night?" Taiming offered appeasingly with a half smile. One had to be careful with Zeng.

"Hmm," the master grumbled and trudged into the bedroom.

He came back in a second with an expression that was hard to describe. "Hu," he said, "could you call Changchun Hospital in Taiping Street? We need a doctor."

It was past one in the morning, and it was hard to reach him. When the doctor finally arrived, it was half past two. According to his diagnosis, the baby was suffering from acute pneumonia, with a high fever, and required round-the-clock medical attention. Taiming's mood darkened: so mahjong was opium as well.

When the new year came, the children of Nanjing played with buzzing tops in the streets. Filling the crisp air with their white breath and tightly bundled up in thick cotton, they manipulated the pairs of sticks—to which the tops were attached by a string—and shouted with joy when the tops spun and buzzed. In the Zeng house, too, the children were making enough noise for a whole year. Taiming did not particularly care for the festivities but had been looking forward to the new year. He was to start teaching, the mere thought of which dispelled his damp winter mood.

But Lai insisted on taking things easy and extolled the virtues of sponging on others until a good opportunity came rolling in his general direction. He was eager to elaborate for Taiming's sake: "People who've studied abroad are in such a hurry—maybe too much pride?—but it's counterproductive, I'm sorry to say. If what you're interested in is improving this country, you won't be able to do it until everyone feels the need. 'Rome was not built in one day.' You've just returned, and you hardly know China, its affairs. Why, you hardly speak its language. Let's say you get a good job, but at this point, I'm afraid you'd do more harm than good. No, I'm all for taking a breather. It might seem as though I were missing something, but a year or two is nothing. Good opportunities aren't all that uncommon. If I get to head the Income Tax Section for a year, just one year, I'll be able to provide for you until you die. So take it easy."

Taiming was offended by this loosely veiled opportunism, according to which a bureaucratic career was nothing but a splendid way to make money. Lai had neither theory nor ideals, only shrewd self-interest. "An office produces wealth," as he summed it up. Still, Taiming was impressed by how up-to-date on the bureaucratic scene his possible future provider was.

"The Chinese bureaucratic system isn't a ladder, did you know that? The beauty of it is that a broker working for a foreign-owned trading firm can become minister of finance overnight. Opportunity is the name of the game. If you find a good boss, your current occupation is irrelevant.

"Let me tell you, too, that a year governing a province can be more lucrative than ten years at the head of a ministry. It all depends. You can't top heading some financial department, but the next best deal is probably mayor of Shanghai. I bet you can't tell me why."

2. Shuchun

As planned, Taiming was finally released from the confines of the Zeng house at the beginning of the new semester. His return to the more or less real world, in the form of a girls' high school, proceeded smoothly thanks to his hard-won facility with Mandarin, and it did not hurt that the academic level of the exemplary institution was in fact that of the highest class of a Taiwanese middle school.

By the time the spring breeze began to caress the new teacher and his students on their way home, they were quite familiar with each other. When the new season's grip on the lower Yangtze seemed firm, Taiming invited some of the girls on a Sunday outing to the nearby tombs dating from the Ming period.

The landscape there was in full bloom, and his students, dressed prettily for the occasion and with delightfully open minds, reminded him of what the word *fulfillment* meant. These future mothers hanging on his every word, pliantly, sensibly delighting in every drop of his wisdom, were not bad at all. What a service he must be doing for China's future in thus guiding the girls to intellectual womanhood! The business of educating had its own rich returns—he had almost forgotten.

Taking in the panorama of spring from an ancient tomb and pointing things out to his eager disciples, who clustered closely around him, he barely noticed the other female voices coming from somewhere behind him. He turned around casually to find a European man leading a group like his own. When Taiming caught sight of the face of one of the women, however, he almost unintentionally exclaimed, "Ahh."

For who was it but the woman who had brightened his dreary train journey from Shanghai to Nanjing, the Suzhou beauty whose shoeprints on the velveteen seat still lingered in his mind? But the glance she cast toward Taiming was indifferent. She walked away without a trace of recognition when the other women did. Taiming's students informed him that the women were from Jinling University and that the European was their professor. This bouquet of flowers disappeared as quickly as it had appeared. After that, his words were incoherent, and the future mothers made fun of him.

Ever since that afternoon at the tomb, he was aware of a thread linking his destiny to that of—but what was her name? He spent every minute of his free time tugging at this thread, roaming the streets and neighborhoods in search of her shadow. Sometimes, he tired of all the people and chose the most desolate paths he could find. He visited one historical site after another.

The area around the Temple of the Crowing Cock was famous for monuments.

The Six Dynasties, whose resplendent capital had been Nanjing, were indeed dead. Walls that, though crumbling, had fared better than whatever they had enclosed meekly asked of the living, "Splendor?" The Rouge Well that people liked to mention did not hint at its past glory. Taiming left the abandoned shaft and trekked to the imperial palace.

One did not have to be a poet to shed tears on its ruins, the most renowned of those of the Six Dynasties. The palace did not live up to its reputation unless its fame could be based on the increasing disappointment that Taiming was feeling. The poet Weizhuang, traveling a century after Li Bai, had sung:

> It rains
> Upon the river.
> The banks are greener;
> Remains
> Of lines of sovereigns,
> However,
> A cipher.
> The grief a birdcall feigns!
> The willows don't remember,
> But perfect lanes
> Leagues long maintaining, shiver
> On misty plains.

As Taiming recited the lines to himself, he was struck, as by a blow, by the utter futility of all human endeavor. The absence of meaning made him stagger. The willows, sole evidence of the Six Dynasties culture, were in fact not related to the original trees, which had perished long ago at the hands of various armies. The ones he was looking at now had been planted much more recently—the vanity of it all! Throughout time, only nature lasted, sometimes chaining man to its endless needs. Why had he worried about Society and fretted about Nation? Because like most people, he was conceited. He felt foolish. How vain Confucius and Mencius were, who clung to their theories and preached to lords! Regarded as wise while they were alive, after they died, they found numerous adherents, who for more than twenty centuries vainly tried to build a path of virtue. It had not existed for a single day. Equally vain were Buddha and Christ. People shed tears for them, that was true, but no flesh-and-blood human had ever been saved by either one, though they had been fooled by them. Doubting even that which most people do not, Taiming felt an urge to give up everything, to abandon his current life. Was there any reason that humans shouldn't lead appropriately human lives? No, and he concluded a few hours later that "happiness for man means living peacefully with a lovely and healthy woman who shares his interests." What had taken him so long? Vanity, of course. He was a nobody who had been acting shamelessly out of turn. He felt stupid, but now, at last, he had an idea, and it seemed revolutionary to him.

Memories suggesting love came back to him, of Ruie, Naito Hisako, and the widow's daughter, Tsuruko. He admitted, not without pain, that none of these memories deserved to be called "love" now that they were as faint as illusions, if they had ever been anything more.

The figure of the Jinling University student came to him like a religious vision. "This must be love," Taiming said to himself. "The Bible (if one were to believe it) says, 'Seek and ye shall find.' But was Jesus also thinking about romantic love?" At any rate, Taiming already was seeking, and he wished to expand his search.

One day, returning late to the Zeng house after one of his endless strolls, he saw Zeng gesture to him: they needed to talk. In addition to his day job as a professor, Zeng taught Japanese at a private institution. Now, however, the Diplomacy Department was asking for his help, and he had to give up his language teaching. "The question, Taiming, is this: will you be my replacement?"

Taiming hesitated. Zeng strongly recommended the job. The place was a small, privately run center of learning, and he would not have to teach more than three hours a week. Eventually Taiming gave in, and Zeng said with a grin, "If my replacement were to be anybody else, I would have felt really guilty. Well, great! Please go introduce yourself—tomorrow." He might have told him this last bit a little sooner, but Taiming didn't have a good reason to refuse, anyway.

After school the next day, with Zeng's recommendation in hand, Taiming went to the private center of learning. The principal, beaming, said, "Ah, I didn't expect such an excellent replacement so soon! We have such difficulty finding suitable persons." He introduced Taiming to the other instructors. The school had three levels: beginning, intermediate, and advanced, and Taiming was to teach at the second, the very next evening.

Thus, only two days after Zeng's friendly request, Taiming stood at the head of a class that for some reason consisted entirely of women, both students and nonstudents. After the principal's brief introduction, Taiming started to take attendance. It was a lively place, and he was somewhat flustered by the atmosphere, but calling off the names on the roster alleviated his nervousness. By the middle of the list, his teacher persona had taken over, and he could look up and coolly scan the faces in his classroom. But wait, whose face was that over there in the corner?

"Ah!" his heart seemed to exclaim, skipping a beat at the coincidence. She had first come into his life at Suzhou station. She had visited him at a Ming tomb. She attended Jinling University but lived in his soul and appeared in his dreams.

Taking attendance had never been so thrilling or rewarding for him. She answered to the name "Shuchun."

That day, his teacher persona was particularly passionate, if not feverish. On his way home and at home, he trembled with gratitude: "Shuchun—a name I'll never forget." Whom should he thank for the coincidence? He had looked for and found "gentle," *shu*, and "spring," *chun*. There was a reason for his life now. For what else but destiny could have occasioned the encounter?

But for the next few weeks, their relationship did not advance a step beyond the ordinary closeness of a teacher and student. As a teacher, of course, he could easily manufacture excuses to talk to her, but that was something he would not, and could not, do, given the other students. His passion, meanwhile, grew with every lesson.

It was luck that came to his aid once again. Reading in the local paper one morning that the Sino-German Cultural Association was hosting an art exhibition, Taiming immediately thought of Shuchun. With a lover's instinct, he had discovered her inclinations and exquisite learning; "lover's instinct" were his words. With a confidence unusual for him, he made a mental note to ask her out on a date.

After class that day, the perfect situation presented itself. Among the students busily packing up, one was taking slightly longer than usual and had to give up the race to the door. While she resigned herself to sitting out the rush, Taiming felt the warm smile of the goddess of opportunity on his back. He sidled over to the lone figure and said:

"Shuchun."

He was amazed at the naturalness of his own voice. All teachers like some students more than others, and the reverse also is true. Wasn't it normal, then, for a teacher to gravitate more easily to a particular student in this way right after class?

"Yes," Shuchun responded to the unassuming utterance of her name; the normality seemed to have rubbed off on her. In an offhanded manner, she stopped packing up and looked him straight in the face.

"We could talk about anything at this point," Taiming thought. With the ease brought by his initial success, he mentioned the exhibition and said that he would be delighted to accompany her. She readily accepted. Her response seemed to confirm his instincts.

The woman of exquisite inclinations had promised to see him on Sunday. The roses that filled the air on his way home followed him to the second floor of the Zeng house and floated in the purple mist that enveloped Mount Zijin. Before the longed-for day of rest, he would see her in class once more.

The lesson turned out to be delightful. It was as though an invisible thread linked the man at the lectern to the woman at the student's desk. Shuchun's gaze contained a familiarity that had not been there earlier and that seemed to say, "This Sunday, remember, Sensei?" He responded by encoding a message in a glance he cast toward her. Throughout the lesson, their looks conveyed and deepened a secret inaccessible to the other pairs of eyes that, unbeknown to Taiming, expressed annoyance that he was misreading the text and blushing now and then.

On the morning of the Sunday in question, Taiming was suddenly seized by the fear that she might not appear at the meeting place, for reasons he would never know. Although this seemed unlikely, the incredible happiness of his past few days fueled his suspicion that there must be a catch.

Driven by his anxiety, he left the Zeng house long before the appointed time and arrived at the meeting place an hour early, despite a roundabout route.

He went into a bookstore to kill time. He flipped through many pages without reading even one line. "No art is so profound and no philosophy so elevated as to rival Shuchun's slightest smile," he concluded and left the store smiling.

It was now close enough to the appointed hour for him to enter the restaurant he had chosen as their meeting place. He sat down at a table in the corner. The wait was long and nerve-racking.

Shuchun arrived only a few minutes late. Although these few minutes were unspeakably tortuous, Taiming's face regained its color as soon as he caught sight of her. Shuchun's face was red and her breathing rapid; she had had to run. She apologized for being late. The beauty of her eyes, aglitter with life, stunned Taiming, and he duly noted that her blouse was indigo and that her skirt was a fresh field of flowers, some of which were hiding in the folds. A sour but sweet taste filled his mouth. She had come not as his student but as a member of the opposite sex.

They ate lightly and walked over to Shanghai Street where the Sino-German Cultural Association was holding its exhibition of calligraphic and pictorial art. The calligraphy section featured old and well-known manuscripts as well as the work of contemporary masters. In regard to a particularly famous book of history on display, Taiming wondered whether the country's proud heritage was visible in the edges of the ink. Although some of the items from the Jin era were copies, even they outshone the best modern efforts. The Tang and Song works were a marvel, needless to say, but it was a shame that not everybody was knowledgeable enough to pause before the Qing masters Shi An, Banqiao, and Bao Shichen. Almost all the paintings, on the other hand, were disappointing. Whatever it was that modern Chinese artists thought they were doing, nothing at the exhibition was worth seeing, Taiming concluded, except for a handful of works executed in the late impressionist style.

Shuchun seemed to have a deep respect for his critical eye. She was just as he had imagined, then. Though learned in artistic matters, her own comments included questions of form within a broader critique of civilizations. She seemed inordinately smart; and so their contemplation of beauty catalyzed the fusion of their souls.

This wholesome intellectual arousal followed them out of the exhibition, and they talked and talked, surrendering themselves to the workings of their hearts, consciously and unconsciously trying to learn more about each other. They seemed ready to talk through the night. Time passed without their knowledge, and dusk fell. Neither of them wanted the splendid day to end, so they had dinner together at a restaurant with delicious vegetable dishes. While he ate, Taiming decided that they must part after dinner. His pedagogic self was telling him that he should not detain her long after dark. But when Shuchun suggested that they go to the theater afterward, his pedagogic self determined that the experience might be educational.

The traditional opera at the Morning Star Theater was less absorbing than the woman who sat next to Taiming. Nonetheless, she herself followed the events on stage as though they mattered. A suspicion disturbed him: "She doesn't care for me as much as I do for her."

The lover's anxiety remained with him after they said good night. In the darkness of his room, at the edges of his growing happiness, shadows still danced.

3. That Which Follows

Although that Sunday, which brought them rapidly closer, was not their last —they went on to enjoy each other's presence almost every week—none of the later dates added as much to their affair as the first one had. Taiming was frustrated that their relationship was not progressing. It was already summer.

He wanted to verify her love, marry her, and sleep with her, the sooner the better.

Spring had its attractions, but so did summer. The change in season was as visible in Shuchun as it was in the landscape. Her shirt was a light blue like the sky, and the youth of her sensuous arms, flowing white out of her short sleeves, vied with the bright leaves. Just as a dying man thirsts for water, so Taiming craved her flesh and yearned for the day when her youth would be his to devour.

They never tired of walking, from the hills to Lake Xuanwu to the neighborhood of crooked alleys across Taizhun Creek.

One Sunday, on their second trip to Lake Xuanwu, Taiming was suffering from a kind of heartache. Since early morning that day, he had yearned for irrefutable proof of her love.

The place was crowded. Under a willow tree on the long embankment, he saw two charming young girls, sisters perhaps. The view was a ready-made embroidery. Taiming, who was feeling generally sentimental, now felt a surge of poetic emotion and came up with this:

> Notice the detail at the seam
> Below the thousand tendrils green:
> How sage the sisters seem,
> Doubting the slender form that willows preen.

Not dissatisfied, he handed the piece of paper to Shuchun.

After a minute of silent appreciation, she said, "It's not bad," but added, "I don't think their waists are so slender that they should be envying the willow."

It was a gentle jab, not so much at Taiming as at the sisters portrayed in his verse, a clear expression of Shuchun's own jealousy. A certain openness that their first Sunday lacked was now routine in their exchanges.

They walked from the embankment to the Five Islets Park. He waited for the right time. But the crowded area was not suitable for declarations.

At the place on the shore where boats, all painted in bright colors, were docked and boat attendants were waiting for customers, Shuchun suggested that they rent a boat. It was the opportunity Taiming had been waiting for, and the boat glided slowly toward the center of the lake.

As the girl attendant maneuvered the vessel skillfully with the single oar at the stern, Taiming and Shuchun sank back deeply in their seats and dropped softly into a contemplative mood. There was no one else on the boat.

Taiming waited patiently. The shore was far away, and no other boats were visible. Perhaps this was the moment.

"Shuchun . . ." he said, and the splashing water filled the pause. Against the boat, the lake lightly lapped.

"Shuchun . . ." he asked gently, "What do you think about us?"

He peered into her face. She looked back at him but did not speak. She glanced sideward at the wobbly dance of the lake's surface. Taiming studied the same mesmerizing play of water on her somewhat nervous face, which reflected the sparkling.

He had not forgotten his bitter experience with Naito Hisako and had vowed not to be too aggressive. A confession of love had to be cautious, in fact needed to be a gentle form of reasoning. Leaning back against the cradling boat and using its rhythm, he described his feelings, from those at the Suzhou station to this pleasure ride and this confession itself—a gentle, almost impassive confession.

This description of his feelings was followed by a long pause and some lapping of the water.

Then she said, "I was aware of Sensei's feelings, but may I tell you what I've been thinking? I have a particular idea, and I want to live by it. You might think me silly, but I have a very high regard for marriage—please don't mistake my meaning when I say that." It was her turn to talk, and what she told him was a theory. She was very idealistic about marriage; she would not be able to find her ideal partner if she did not go about it methodically. And the method? She had to go out with at least thirty boyfriends, fall in love with the three she liked best, and only then, from among the trio, choose a husband. She spent almost half an hour expounding this idea with perfect grace and ended by repeating her plea that Taiming not misunderstand her. "Everything I've just said is unrelated to the fact that . . . Sensei, I love you, too."

During her speech, from the moment he could tell that her idea was typical of the new woman—formulaic and superficial but strangely eager at the same time—Taiming began to sink into something very different from the seat, from which he felt suddenly ejected, thrown against the ground, as by the water buffalo on that far-off meadow. Because his situation physically was still so sweet—in nature with the woman he loved—he sank, all the more stupefied, into his darkness, his old despair.

"Brava, a courteous rejection!" he thought. "In the guise of a newfangled theory of ideal marriage! Well expressed!" He was struggling to hold back his tears.

But he thought about her words a bit longer. Was she asking to be thrown into the lake? Perhaps she wanted him to take the plunge? What an unforgivable woman, to escape into such a heartless formula, to reject him from on high! If she had an ounce of kindness in her, she wouldn't have resorted to such defenses. Why, she'd just seek his embrace, wouldn't she?

He recalled something a jaded playboy had told him back in Taiwan: "Hu, there are some formidable women in Shanghai who say that love is like candy. They get bored if they have to eat chocolate all the time, so they change snacks now and then. They aren't trying to shock you or anything. They mean it, and they practice it. Real women of the future! I wouldn't mind being one of their snacks. In fact, I'd love it. There's a real toast, eh?"

If that was the new woman, wasn't Shuchun a new woman? But he had felt so close to her! Now, suddenly, she seemed beyond his reach.

The boat had passed the Temple of the Crowing Cock and was now by the foot of Mount Zijin. Taiming maintained a gruff silence.

Shuchun said, "I'm sorry, Sensei. I know I'm being very difficult." She sounded less sorry than adamant.

Taiming nodded gravely a couple of times. He was too sick and tired to speak.

4. That Which Returns

Day after day, Hu Taiming took pleasure in nothing. He kept away from her after that Sunday, and seeing her in class was painful. Since he was not going to win her over, he wanted to stop teaching Japanese. But unbeknown to him, the affair was taking an unexpected turn.

Strange are the movements of the heart. Shuchun was beginning to learn that her theory was much easier to preach than to practice. It would be difficult to find thirty boyfriends without becoming something less than a new woman. The idea of choosing the best three from the thirty, and her husband from the three, was looking less and less realistic. With her plan crumbling in her hands like old parchment, she began to appreciate Taiming more. After all, just as she had a place in his heart, he had a place in hers. Her rejection had been nothing more than a passing burst of pride.

It was already late autumn when Shuchun came to the Zeng house one afternoon asking for Taiming. The visit surprised him, as they had not seen or spoken to each other outside class since that early summer day.

"Sensei, would you take a walk with me?" Her eyes glittered strangely as she offered this invitation.

Taiming did not turn her down. The aspen trees by the road-side had shed all their leaves, and in the chilly wind, the light gray trunks looked especially naked. The two entered a park, and as they walked in silence over the chicken feed, a pecking rooster flapped out of their way.

The grass was good to sit on in a soulless region of the park. Almost as soon as they sat down, Shuchun buried her face in Taiming's lap and exclaimed, "Forgive me about then!" Her body twisting, she spat out the words, "I've been so difficult. . . . I'm sorry."

Learning that she had come to accept his love, Taiming became a furnace. He roughly seized her chin, turned up her face, and stared into her wet eyes.

"Forgive you?" he said in a low but firm voice, "There is nothing to forgive. I was just . . . waiting."

That last word and her bursting into tears came almost simultaneously. Taiming's passion overwhelmed both him and her weeping. Her lips held up to his, he devoured them as his right and duty as a lover. He no longer hesitated, she no longer forbade, and their flaming lips came together, a seal on their joined hearts. They married a month later and took up residence on a block near Taiping Street.

5. Friction

Their married life began with the new year. Shuchun, who was to graduate in March, still had some course work and continued to attend Jinling University. Taiming went on teaching, now as a means rather than an end. A maid whom they hired managed the household.

Taiming was quite satisfied. Up to his neck in married happiness, as if in a tub of water at just the right temperature, he asked nothing more: Shuchun was the answer to all his problems. Although he finally seemed to have kicked his old habit of endlessly cogitating and brooding, this happy state did not last long.

After Shuchun graduated, the couple discovered that they held contradictory views regarding her future. The man wanted his wife to settle down and become a good housewife, whereas the woman insisted on pursuing a career.

She said, "When it comes to crucial matters, you're as feudal as a grandpa. I didn't intend to give up my freedom when I married, and I don't want to be tied to the hearth. Marriage isn't a business contract, you know. Or by any chance do you believe, like most men, that a wife is just a prostitute with a long-term contract?"

Taiming found such radical assertions very depressing.

Unyielding, Shuchun ignored all his suggestions, decided to go into politics, and landed a job in the Diplomatic Bureau with the help of her university. Taiming feared such a path was especially inimical to a happy home life, and his fears were borne out. Little by little, Shuchun's tastes and lifestyle began to diverge from his. In vain he recited his favorite lines from the *Romance of the Western Chamber* and *Dreams of the Red Chamber*, but she didn't want to discuss them anymore. The countryside ceased to appeal to her, and she did not want to take walks with him, not even on Sundays. Her new pleasures were dancing, playing mahjong, and going to the theater.

She was always surrounded by her favorite colleagues, all of them young men. One of them was Lai, who had entered the Bureau of Propaganda, just as he had wished. Shuchun's colleagues met in Taiming's own house, which, before he could do anything about it, had become a sort of club for them. Shuchun flourished, so aware was she now of her beauty, and she behaved like a queen. Mahjong tiles clinked night after night in the Hu Club. At first, the proprietor participated in the gambling, too, but only because he had to, for he actually hated the opiate. The more accustomed the clubmen grew to the place, the less gentlemanly they became. At one point, they began to exchange obscenities, and the queen did not stop them, for her religious faith in liberty and equality did not permit intolerance of any kind. Moreover, the absolute equality of the sexes in all matters meant that she did not care what her husband thought or felt. Because her minions were always ready to pay tribute to her—mostly cosmetics and ornaments—the principle visibly enriched her everyday life.

One evening, when her admirers were assembled in the guest room as usual, Lai, who had just returned from Shanghai, presented her with a gift from the city. With great delight, she opened the box and took out a pair of Shanghai shoes—of the latest style and very fashionable, according to Lai. Targeted at women who fell for the newfangled, the gaudy design was exactly what Shuchun liked. Taiming did not say anything but saw the smug expression on Lai's face and wanted to kill him. Lai's vulgar intentions showed through his filthy, lecherous grin. How dare he be on such intimate terms with Shuchun and completely ignore her husband? Didn't he know that the master of the house was displeased?

They played mahjong late into the night. Taiming hung around for a while, but finally, being too upset, he withdrew into the bedroom. The sound of the tiles and the men's coarse laughter still in his ears, he tossed and turned. His father, Hu Wenqing, always spoke of thieves, whores, and gamblers in the same breath and hated all three passionately. Taiming trembled with a premonition. But then, he realized with a start, wasn't his house already their temple? A high-pitched shriek of laughter reached his bedroom; his wife was having one of her dissolute fits of glee. This could not go on, he thought, as her lascivious burst subsided. Something had to be done, for his wife's sake, for his own, for the children to come. But the mere idea of having to ask Shuchun for her cooperation plunged him into despair. Not only would she refuse, but if pressed, she would demand a divorce on the grounds of "incompatibility," a sufficient reason in China. Given her character, he bet that she would advertise the breakup in the local papers. His courage wilted.

It was past three in the morning when the guests departed. Taiming had not fallen asleep for a second. He listened as his wife's dainty feet approached the bedroom. She opened the door, flicked on the light, and saw that Taiming lay wide awake.

Bubbling with joy, she said, "You're still up? You know, tonight we made two hundred yen just from the banker's fee!"

Something about her voice made him lose control of himself.

"Filthy lucre," he spat out, more vehemently than he meant to.

Shuchun froze and gazed at him, frightened. She threw down the money and said, "You . . . I don't believe it! You're telling me I'm a whore!"

She began to sob, angry as much as hurt. So helpless did she seem that Taiming felt sorry and consoled her: It was OK; he should not have said that; she should stop crying and get some sleep.

She did not change her ways, however, and to compensate for her late nights, got up late. Taiming had lived such a regulated life since his childhood that no matter how hard he tried, he could not stay asleep long after sunrise. Sometimes he lay awake till his body ached, and still she did not open her eyes. Thus every morning, he got up alone and waited pathetically for his wife to rise. Sundays were the worst. If he needed Shuchun for some reason and tried to wake her up, she was irritable for the rest of the day. But waiting for her to wake up was not good for his mental health either.

When she did wake up, the maid was summoned to bring water to her and to help her wash her sleepy face. Gargling, eating, drinking coffee—Shuchun never did anything without the maid's help. On Sundays, when the maid was out, she did not wash her face until she returned. And that was not all. Once, leaning back in her rocking chair and reading the paper, she started to ring vigorously for the maid, who lived downstairs. Taiming wondered what she wanted but did not ask. It turned out that some pages of the newspaper had slid out of her hands. She did not want to pick them up herself, since that would have required getting out of her chair. Taiming did not know what to say.

Meanwhile, Shuchun always had a lot to say, about the equality of the sexes, the liberation of women, the improvement of everyday life, the new domesticity. There was not a fashionable movement that she did not support, of which she did not want to become the spokeswoman, and that she did not try to push on everybody. But practice was apparently a different matter, for she did not seem to sense any contradiction. On this point, Taiming considered his wife to be a mysterious creature, an inexhaustible fountain of surprises, an everlasting source of wonderment.

Her passion for mahjong finally began to abate. It was just a game, and she was tired of it. She much preferred dancing now and rarely came home from the downtown dance hall before midnight. Her dance partners were culled mainly from her loyal entourage of young bureaucrats. Taiming, who could not stand mahjong, hardly knew what dancing was and never went with her to such places. This arrangement suited Shuchun, who did not care what he thought or, for that matter, what anyone thought. She was free, and her freedom was her only pride in life. Taiming told himself that all this was just a sign of a dawn, of new times, but he lost weight anyway. Every evening, he sat alone waiting for his wife to return. Some nights, when he had trouble falling asleep, he fantasized about his wife and how she must be dancing arm-in-arm with young men to the jazzy tunes that probably filled the dance hall. Such images aroused in him an obscene resentment. He remembered Tsuruko and wondered how free of ordeals his life would have been, how much happier, if he had married her instead.

One evening, Shuchun invited her husband to come with her. He had trouble reading her intentions, but she was so insistent, and he was so curious, that they met at an international restaurant downtown. Four or five members of the usual crowd, including Lai, were there as well.

What was pressed upon Taiming that night was, for someone with his ethics, an unforgivably extreme form of decadence. In tune with the salacious melodies, men and women contorted their bodies like insane people and showed no trace of shame. When the dancing reached a climax and the lights were momentarily turned off, noisy kissing was heard from everywhere in the darkness. If Taiming could have observed this scene as something unrelated to him, he might have been able to bear it. But shoved in his face were the dissolute limbs of his own wife, who changed partners now and then. Why, for what reason, was Shuchun so eager to show herself in this way to her husband? Was this what they called modernity?

Taiming could not sit through it. He left early, caught a terrible cold, and ended up spending an entire month in bed. It was as though he had met a demon on a mountain path. In bed for a month, he wrestled with the question of whether it was his duty, as Shuchun's husband, to rescue her from such a life. It was possible that the antiquated remnants of feudalism in him, which he had not been able to erase entirely, were hampering his understanding of modernity. Consciously or unconsciously, those who judged by past standards were always negative, defensive, reactive to the newness of the present, which deserved to be judged by new moral principles and a new cultural sense. Shuchun's deeds, grotesque at first sight, were perhaps one of those phenomena that inevitably accompanied social progress. In this sense, she was a victim, and the thought helped him forgive her somewhat. Still, he could not convince himself emotionally of the theory that he managed to accept intellectually. Even though he might allow his wife to carry on in this way, he feared that in the near future, her restraint might be tested and fail. Taiming could reconcile himself to the idea that the process of social transformation entailed sacrifices, but did that include an adulterous wife? Perhaps he should begin planning for this eventuality and prepare to be cuckolded. Here ended his reason; the rest was nothing but emotion.

When he finally recovered from his sickness, he had also arrived at a kind of resignation, as one sometimes does after a lengthy psychological struggle. "My wife is my wife, and I am I," he concluded. "I must recover the old self that I gave up when I married."

For the first time in months, he enjoyed the company of books. He became reacquainted with thinkers from Confucius's times and with the *Spring and Autumn Annals*, the classic history of that era. With his growing familiarity came the feeling that his worries were no more than the petty complaints of a petty man, and he welcomed the feeling.

No longer harassed by her husband, Shuchun experimented with one pleasure after another. Not until the end of winter did she begin to show signs of fatigue, which, however, suggested that she was quite ill.

One evening, Shuchun told Taiming what her problem was. There was an unusual feminine tenderness in her voice, a desire to be protected by her husband, when she told him, "Five months." An aspect of her personality that he had not appreciated was revealed. That evening, they talked late into the night and felt like a couple again. Taiming secretly hoped that motherhood would transform his wife into a different sort of woman.

The baby, born that summer, was a girl. Borrowing the character for "purple" from the mountain, they named her Ziyuan.

Little by little, it became clear that the baby was not fulfilling the task that her father had entrusted to her. As Shuchun convalesced, she left her baby more and more to the maid. In no time, Shuchun had fully recovered her old self as a new woman.

Her husband no longer expected any surprises from her. "What will be, will be," he decided.

Dissatisfied with family life, he channeled his passions into reading and teaching. His part-time job he found especially rewarding because learning Japanese had now become a fad. Not only were his students more enthusiastic, but they also were more diverse, bureaucrats and businessmen as well as college women. By now one of the institute's senior instructors, Taiming felt respected and needed and gladly agreed to double his teaching load to six hours a week.

The student with whom he spent the most time was of the same southern stock as he was, a diplomatic councillor named Zhang whose analysis of social phenomena his teacher found most entertaining. One day, over tea, Zhang asked Taiming detailed questions about the situation in Japan and paid for the favor by leaking some news from the bureau. He related the juicy gossip in the winning manner of a young and able diplomat.

"Let me tell you something that happened recently. The press club was grilling us with aggressive questions about our pro-Japanese policy. Huang, who's from our bureau, answered them right back, a really good answer, in my opinion. He said, 'China is about to fall. Let's all make as much money as we can from it!' This shut everybody up. Don't you see? Sure, his cynicism meant that he was angry about our sad state of affairs, but to think that he had to speak in such a self-deprecating way to drive home the brutality of historical change! The sorrow of China is that when Huang said this, all the reporters could do was feel sorry."

Zhang sighed. Taiming thought gloomily about this story. Like these foreign reporters, he had some rethinking to do. He and Zhang became good friends and saw each other often.

The coming Sunday was the Feast of the Chrysanthemum, and Nanjing's literati assembled at the Pavilion of the North Pole to compose poetry. Taiming set out to attend but decided not to go alone. He made a detour to Zhang's place to see whether his friend was interested. He was not; he didn't like Chinese verse and would much prefer going to the festival at the Temple of the Crowing Cock. Taiming, who did not want to push poetry on an unwilling person, agreed to this alternative.

To approach the temple, one had to walk past numerous beggars who begged in various ways under the scarlet leaves framing the Hall of Civil Examinations. A gray-haired old man, so sunburned that his face looked like tanned paper, kept banging his forehead on a brick so as to beg with a bloodied face whenever someone passed by. There was another whose legs were rotting, another who wailed with a baby in her arms, another apparently still a child but more like a moving pile of rags. Men and women, young and old, it was as though the harrowing paintings of the eighteen hells, which Taiming's mother had taken him to see when he was little, had come to life. He left small coins in his wake, but Zhang walked on as if he had not seen anything.

The two reached the top of the hill, where there was a pavilion from which to admire the sunset. At a nearby teahouse, they rested their feet, drank the sweet-tasting water from the waterfall, and gazed at Lake Xuanwu. Autumn had put on a good show.

Taiming fondly recalled his Sundays while courting. Not much time had gone by since then. Yet now, and despite their child, Shuchun was hopelessly far away. What if they hadn't married? While Taiming indulged in bittersweet grief, Zhang did not dwell on the sentimental. He lunged forth with ideas and swung them around as spiritedly as a lunatic with a knife.

Sipping the water, he remarked, "Sensei, the issue of treason is becoming popular among the intellectuals of this city. They like to criticize Qin Hui of the Southern Song dynasty for having persecuted the prowar faction in those days. What do you think?"

He was not really asking for Taiming's opinion; the solicitation was only a sort of preface to the exposition of his own views. This was fine with Taiming, who listened with greater and greater interest to what Zhang had to say with such passion.

"All acts that benefit the enemy merit the label of treason. There are many kinds, but I think historical traitors can be divided into roughly three types. The first are the ignorant and incompetent who are interested only in making a living and commit what amounts to treason without knowing it. The second are the more aggressively greedy who are very clever when it comes to satisfying their greed. Middle-class and intellectual traitors belong to this category; they like to think they have a theory, but in fact, they don't. They're feeble men, unprincipled opportunists. The third type has loads of talent and intellect but gives up on their country, forgets its history, and sets out to shake hands with the enemy—in short, sells out their country. The first two are lightweights. Only the third is committing treason in the full sense.

"Who or what can save China from them? My answer is youth and youth only—the feverish rectitude of youth. Just recently, the head of the Diplomatic Bureau had to cancel his train trip to a round of negotiations. This was because a university student who disagreed with our foreign policy lay down in front of the locomotive just as it started to pull out. Literally, the thing was going to happen over his dead body. The blood he was ready to shed is what can save China."

Zhang's last words were hoarse with emotion, and he was not the only one to be moved by the lecture. Indeed, Taiming felt ashamed of himself for being preoccupied with merely private matters. Equally regrettable was the way he had sought and found refuge in the classics. The friends continued to see each other frequently.

The young diplomat's earnestness was contagious. Gradually, the high school teacher adopted the same urgent style. What he thought was in his power, he acted on. Through his students, he tried to fuel the patriotism of the Nanjing people.

Zhang's ideas about classical education were revolutionary. He believed that Chinese culture had to be abandoned altogether, for even though it was immensely rich, it had an equal number of liabilities. Like the river Yangtze, which flowed faster than one might think, Chinese culture was indeed great in the present as well as in the past but did not consider human intervention and was impossible to purify. The result was that the culture could be appreciated only by aristocrats. Adapted to the few, it was undemocratic. The main problem was that the difficult writing required at least ten years to learn and thus effectively precluded the dissemination of culture. The masses had to make a living, which, of course, was not easy, and they didn't have time to master a complicated language. As long as characters were used, the masses would be illiterate. An ideographic language was protection for any autocratic polity and ensured an uneducated population. China could not compete with more civilized nations as long as it took half a lifetime to learn how to read. With such a handicap, how could a nation absorb the science and culture of other nations? The only solution was to adopt a phonetic writing system. Although the transition would be inconvenient for their own generation, for the sake of future ones, it had to be begun, now. Inconvenience for Zhang and Taiming meant convenience for their descendants.

Another absurd thing about Chinese culture was the literature it produced using that writing system. Sophisticated, abstruse, it was purposely beyond the apprehension of ordinary people. In China, the ability to read was sufficient for one to be deemed extraordinary. In this way, the literati had ruled China for many centuries. The common people could not even correspond with one another. Without a phonetic writing system, Chinese culture could not be reconstructed, and without a new Chinese culture, China could not become independent. Thus Zhang had decided.

Though hesitant to follow Zhang on this logical journey, Taiming had to admit that his friend was at least partly right. But granting that he was right, were his opinions practicable? Taiming doubted the wisdom of destroying an entire heritage that had lasted for aeons and had formed the nation's character, which foreigners admired. Was Zhang saying that what it had produced was opium? Taiming, who was not courageous, asserted that if this were the case, the classics should be preserved out of scientific interest. As a scholar and then as a specialist, Taiming would study this curiosity that did bring pleasure to a few. He was always ready to compromise.

6. One Night

The young men at the diplomacy bureau knew how to hold their liquor. Under Zhang's influence, Taiming was beginning to learn the joy of drinking for its own sake. Zhang took him to various gatherings, at all of which, however, the talk centered on politics.

According to Zhang, ever since China lost Manchuria, it was clear that sooner or later, it had to take a final stand. The steadily mounting pressure already was apparent in the rush to learn Japanese, which could not be dismissed as a mere fad. Those who had any feelings were worried about China's future. To be sure, some students at the Japanese Institute said in a casually self-hating tone that made one cry: "Since China is bound to perish, I'm learning Japanese to earn my daily bread tomorrow." But not everyone spoke that way. Others gave as their purpose of study, "Japanese culture is a culture of translation," "and their language is a gateway to sources from around the world." It was with discomfort and a sigh that Zhang added that some radicals were learning Japanese in order to fight the enemy. As much as Zhang wanted a diplomatic solution to the whole affair, he admitted that cruel destiny was perhaps impervious to human desire. Taiming shivered when he remembered that early in the twentieth century, when what came to be known as the Russo-Japanese War seemed imminent, people in Japan scrambled to learn Russian. If his students' interest in Japanese also was a forewarning of a storm, he was not going to participate quietly in such a tremendous misfortune of history.

Only a few days later, the bureau had good news for Zhang: he would be stationed in Japan. Taiming, who was invited to the farewell party, an intimate affair for close friends only, cut through the quarter where the cram schools for passing civil exams were clustered, went down a more verdant block, and, as he had been instructed, knocked on the door of house number twelve. He was shown to the second floor. There, in a room with several large chairs surrounding an equally large table with four vases of pretty flowers set on it, a number of young men sat waiting for the main guest to arrive. Not recognizing any of them, Taiming crept in but did not know how to introduce himself. After a while, an older man came in, spoke to Taiming, and introduced him by name to the others: four young diplomats and an instructor from the Shanghai School of Arts. The older man was accompanied by two women, beautiful entertainers, who briefly greeted Taiming and smiled broadly.

A car horn beeped out on the street, an engine was turned off, and footsteps came briskly upstairs. It was Zhang. A rose-colored silk handkerchief peeked out of his breast pocket. His suit clearly was new, and his shoes were shining. He shook hands with each of the guests, and they all congratulated him. Zhang, who was being overly modest, had to be forced to the place of honor. Taiming sat down across him, but when the other guests discovered that it was this quiet person who had taught Zhang his Japanese, they would not let him sit anywhere but beside the guest of honor. As soon as they were all arranged, Zhang was on his feet again, officially thanking his friends for coming.

Once they had had enough to drink, the celebration turned into a spirited debate. Eventually, the two art professors deadlocked over some minute point of aesthetics. One of them had studied in France, the other in Japan. The one with the degree from France got emotional and ended the academic disagreement rather abruptly:

"Anyway, you people will be ruling China. The people of France are not likely to take over this country." Spat out bitterly through pursed lips, these words silenced his opponent and everybody else at the table.

An awkward, oppressive silence threatened to spoil the whole evening. It was at this point that the two women revealed their reason for coming. Could they sing a song or two? But of course, none of the gentlemen had the heart to refuse them. The duo's rendition of "Tianshui Checkpoint" restored the gentlemen to their former high spirits. Now, in Tokyo, what should Zhang do first?

He had been handpicked from a large pool of young talented men. A lot was expected of him, and the gravity of the mission was crushing. A man bracing for a storm during the preceding quiet probably would have reacted in the same way.

He asked Taiming for advice, and the gist of the response was preparation and preemption. The young diplomat had to make sure that China did not always react too late to others' initiatives.

"I understand what you're saying. I'll try my best not to disappoint you," said Zhang, squeezing Taiming's hands in his. Zhang was going to Tokyo on an impossible errand, and Taiming prayed for his friend with all his heart.

Taiming was so drunk that he couldn't remember how he managed to make his way home that night. Someone had driven him home in an automobile, he was told later. That night, for a change, Shuchun came home earlier than he did.

It was she who opened the door. The virile political atmosphere of house number twelve was still with him, and he ordered his wife, "You! Bring me some tea!"

Curiously enough, Shuchun obeyed him.

Frightened, she peered into his face. "You've been drinking!" she observed, her voice slightly tinged with fear.

Her husband fixed her with dull eyes. Her rosy lips aroused in him an unusually imperious urge. "Hey, come here!" he commanded, throwing an arm around her and pulling her to his chest.

Interestingly enough, Shuchun did not complain. It was with a fawning look that she said, "Oh, you."

That night, forgetting everything as he did the night itself, her husband feasted on her flesh like a healthy beast.

7. Before the Tempest

The café on the sixth floor of the Fuchang Restaurant, though furbished in no particular way, played only tasteful music records. Intellectuals, finding the place relaxing, frequented it. The view to the east was magnificent, and on sunny days, Mount Zijin seemed to be within arm's reach. Looking down, one could see the city's bustling streets stretching all the way to the entertainment district.

When Taiming grew stiff from wandering aimlessly through the streets, he came up here to listen absently to the records and to enjoy his solitude. His married life had not improved.

His ideas about family life, with which his wife did not agree, instead were fulfilled by his daughter. Not receiving much love from her mother, Ziyuan became attached to Taiming. She added flavor to his otherwise vapid life, and the time he spent with her—teaching her new words, for instance—was certainly his most satisfying. Yet this, too, was marred by a certain anxiety.

The ubiquity of politics was threatening to destroy what remained of his conviction regarding the true happiness of man. The news from Shanghai that a people's front had been formed and that grisly acts of terror had become commonplace divided Taiming's workplace into two factions, for and against war. The atmosphere was electric, and animosities grew personal.

In an attempt to escape that turmoil, Taiming was killing time again at the sixth-floor café, when loud chanting and trumpet blasts coming from the world below drowned out the tasteful record music. His reverie interrupted, he walked to the window, and saw that the students were demonstrating.

The trumpeters were playing the national anthem, and the chanting that punctuated its phrases consisted of prowar slogans like "Down with imperialism" and "Fight for the nation." The demonstrators were marching, and as they approached in perfect unison, the noise of their orchestrated steps grew to an earth-shaking rumble.

Taiming lost his hold on the precious calm he had been nurturing that afternoon. Since his earliest days, scenes like these had always thrown him off balance. He felt irritated and restless.

Leaving the café like a hounded man, he marched down the main street in the opposite direction toward the new quarter, as if to counteract the students, only to discover that the vortex of frenzy had swallowed up the less excitable people as well. In the new quarter, masses of ordinary people had assembled at the traffic circle, and in their midst, agitators were speaking to them.

"Here, too?" Taiming wondered, but stopped. Standing up on his toes at the outermost of the concentric walls of people, he tried to find out what was being said and by whom.

Various speakers of both sexes were taking turns at the podium, all of them young and sharing a curious enthusiasm for clichés. But their passionate tone—tearful or irate or both—appealed to the crowd, and a round of applause followed every platitude that they fervently uttered.

The audience cheered loudly when a pretty woman came to the podium. Wasn't her figure vaguely familiar? Taiming squinted. It was his wife.

With a certain disdainful curiosity, a stranger's cool interest, he wondered what she had to say.

"My brothers, my sisters," she began. What followed was in the irate style. Like the other agitators, she spoke like a sentimentalist who had nothing to say but who knew how to string together the relevant phrases. Impressed that she had had to absorb so much hostility, the audience clapped sympathetically.

It was too ridiculous for words. As Shuchun went on, Taiming instead began to feel a quiet hatred. If she were his daughter rather than his wife, he would have dragged her away and given her a thorough spanking for being so irresponsible. He would have done the same to the other speakers for propagating theoretically groundless opinions that were not even theirs, leaping to conclusions, and promising the impossible. Political frauds had been common throughout history because the people were stupid. As Zeng once put it, they understood "phenomena but not reality—and in this regard, nine-tenths of intellectuals can claim close ties with the people." Taiming seemed to have found the perfect example of Zeng's view. Rant about the inevitability of war but say nothing about the armaments of the parties concerned. Say nothing? See nothing! For Taiming knew how little his wife knew about China's military, let alone military affairs in general. Should we fight anyway? It was depressing. These irresponsible political brokers who were urging the masses to take up arms that they did not have, the absurdity of someone like his wife advocating war, made his skin prickle. To defeat the Kingdom of Wu, Goujian of Yue waited twenty years, spending a decade on production and another on spying. Unless victory was almost certain, war had to be avoided. A wise man did not draw his sword if he could bear the indignity. The fact that one's arrogance was unmatched was not a sound basis for declaring war. But whether or not China should go to war and how it could win was not his point, he remembered. What annoyed him was that Shuchun—wasn't she supposed to be a diplomat?—was advocating war when she didn't even know how many cannons China had. Although Shuchun was not so meek a woman as to follow her husband's advice, what sort of a man was he to allow her to be like this? Maybe his silence was to be pitied. He sighed.

Meanwhile, Shuchun's speech was becoming more heated, and the audience egged her on with more and more applause. Taiming could not stand it any longer and fled the circle, his hurried steps a plea for escape. He was hurt beyond words by the idea that his and Shuchun's married life had been such a disaster.

So the fevered air of the lower Yangtze—and the politics of summer—did not subside but continued and even intensified. In August, the political parties became even more active. The "Society for National Salvation" was formed and immediately issued 200,000 copies of its organ, *Mass*, which shook the Shanghai publishing world. September came but did not cool the sweltering heat. Nanjing's pavements were still hot.

Though highly sensitive to this gathering of energy, Taiming refused to consider what had caused it. Readjusting his interpretation of the matter each day to suit himself, he struggled to find whatever peace he could in his own rationalizations. If the crisis had a mind, however, it did not agree that he was a bystander and proceeded to draw him in.

One night in the middle of September, a hot night that brought Taiming out to his yard, he received a visit from a messenger: Master Zeng wanted his former lodger to come to see him as quickly as possible. Such a call was without precedent. Speculating wildly, he tagged behind the messenger. One look at the house, however, exceeded all his expectations.

The house had the peculiar hushed air of an abandoned building. But it had not been abandoned, at least not entirely, for a solitary lamp shone through the window of what was or used to be Zeng's study. The messenger left. Taiming entered the house and then the room, on the bare floor of which Zeng sat doing nothing other than wait for his friend—who exclaimed upon seeing the state of the study, "What happened?"

The room was nearly empty except for the bookshelves, themselves empty as well. In a corner, three large suitcases lay on top of each other in a neat pile.

Zeng was laughing. "The time has come!" he declared. "I am leaving tonight!" he announced. "You don't need any more explanation, do you? We should have a few more drinks together, though. True, it's unusual for the person leaving to be hosting the farewell party, but I didn't think you'd be surprised. Please, drink up."

Indeed, a modest banquet had been prepared on a low table that had not been stored. So that was it! Taiming did not have to ask where Zeng was going and why; it was to the northwest according to an escape plan Zeng had ready for some time. It was finally being carried out, and his wife and children had, no doubt, been sent ahead. Matters were coming to a head, then! Taiming, who had had no clue, stood speechless.

That night they drank silently. There was not much that they needed to say, although each felt feelings and thought thoughts. The fact that Zeng was leaving everything behind—and that the other, who was not, had been invited to drink with him—was an eloquent expression of Zeng's philosophy. Although it had never been a secret that Zeng avidly studied political affairs in order to decide whether or not to pursue a certain goal, nor hard to guess that the physics professor's frequent trips to Shanghai were a way of staying in touch with members of the allied front, still, for Zeng to act so soon and so decisively came as a great surprise to Taiming. His own behavior, on the contrary, was probably indistinguishable from sitting on the fence. Zeng's silence seemed disapproving, and Taiming could not look at him.

When the time came to part, they shook hands firmly. Without letting go of Taiming's hand, Zeng said, "We've come to a point where abstract reasoning won't help. There's only one thing that can save China now. That, of course, is action. I don't know what direction your path will take, but I just hope you find one. Permit me to give you some advice, though: at least give up all your ideas. What's going on now isn't just other people's business. It's your own, Hu, and it eventually will affect you."

This advice, characteristic of a man of principle and action, also was a senior compatriot's farewell, but Taiming could say nothing in return. As the other left, Taiming bitterly deplored that he didn't share the strength of Zeng's convictions.

8. Another Room of Captivity

The fast-moving times brought resistance in their wake. The Communists joined the Nationalists after the Xian incident. The dark clouds that covered the continent rolled over Mount Zijin, too, and spring and its flowers could not dispel the anxiety or the turmoil.

One night, just as Taiming was falling asleep, he felt as though somebody were shaking him. When he opened his eyes, a few strangers were standing by his bed. Panicked, he was about to yell and ask them to identify themselves when he was interrupted by a low, confident male voice.

"Metropolitan Police. We're sorry to disturb you at this late hour. Just a couple of questions—please come with us." The man's epaulettes gleamed coldly, intimidatingly, on his shoulders. His name card identified him as no less than the head of the Secret Service Division.

"It's happened at last," Taiming realized, and this put him strangely at ease. "All right," he answered, "but could you wait while I get ready? In fact, my wife hasn't even come home yet . . ."

"Your wife, is that so? Certainly we can wait," the secret person replied. His smooth manner was unspeakably oppressive in its very gentlemanliness.

"It might take a long time," Taiming added.

Fortunately, Shuchun returned while he was packing. She understood the situation immediately but kept quiet. Husband and wife conferred for a couple of minutes to arrange for her to handle matters on her own while he was away.

Then Taiming said to the officers, "Sorry to keep you waiting. Let's go."

Nanjing was dark. The automobile took them down Taiping and Jiankang Streets before turning off on to narrower streets. A long trip on a one-way ticket, Taiming thought. He shut his eyes and sank into the darkness, like a lost man wandering deeper and deeper into a maze, but his mind felt unusually alert. The uniformed bodies that sandwiched him in were warm and elicited a bizarre longing for human company.

The automobile stopped on an unknown block somewhere in the city. The shabby building was probably a special, isolated facility; it certainly was not the police headquarters.

The house's interior was forbidding. The entrance hallway, lighted by a single bulb, stretched deep into the shadows like a road to hell, down which, guarded at the front and the back, Taiming proceeded. They walked through a number of rooms. They finally stopped in a makeshift interrogation room with an imposingly large desk, behind which the head of the secret police sat down. There was a chair in front for Taiming. The questioning began immediately.

From the moment Taiming saw the police in his bedroom, he figured out why he was being arrested. The purpose of the interrogation, which concerned his background, proved him right. So be it, he decided; from his first day in China until now, he had never really wanted to lie about his status. Openly admitting that he was a citizen of the Japanese Empire, he explained his genuine affection for the Chinese nation.

The interrogator extended his sympathies. He said he was impressed but that "the administration's policy" was a different matter, that pleading with him was futile. "Mr. Hu, you've convinced me—thoroughly, I might add—that you're not capable of espionage. I wish it were within my power to release you. Unfortunately, by order of the government, I am to limit your freedom."

The questioning over for the time being, Taiming's freedom was limited to horribly dilapidated confines behind a locked door. Left among cobwebs, he understood quickly and viscerally that he had been cut off from the rest of the world and could do nothing about it. The weak electric light source of the closetlike room revealed an old desk and what appeared to be a bed. Sitting on the latter, Taiming heaved a huge sigh and contemplated the sudden change of scenery.

Many other civil servants of Taiwanese origin must have been suffering the same fate. Why this persecution, Taiming wanted to ask. Was being Taiwanese so bad? He remembered Zeng's parting words that "it isn't other people's business." Zeng had been right. Still, who would have expected this business to affect Taiming so soon? And who was it who revealed that he was Taiwanese—his own wife, perhaps? That was impossible—but then, who? The more he thought about it, the more the mystery deepened. In the first place, how, when, and from where did the police sneak into his bedroom? What, could they turn into smoke? The more he thought about it, the more confused he became.

He thought some more between the filthy, stinking sheets. When he got used to the stench, he turned off the light to get some sleep. But his eyes grew accustomed to the dark, and his overworked brain could not rest. He started worrying about his daughter, Ziyuan. Now four years old, she had been raised by him and the maid and hardly knew a mother's love but still was getting to like Taiming's wife well enough. Shuchun returned her affection and sometimes played with her now that her daughter required less care. But surely little Ziyuan missed her father? His daughter's affection made his heart ache.

How interesting that the Japanese word for bedbugs is "Nanjing bugs." In any case, the itching was severe. The absolute silence of the room was broken only by his occasional twisting and turning until the sun streamed in through the bars of the tiny skylight. He examined the bite. It was a red circle the size of a large coin.

All day he waited for the second round of interrogations, but his captor was not obliging. Apart from the times the guard brought him his meals, Taiming could not even hear footsteps. The room was dank and chilly. He wanted to read, but there were no books. He wanted to write, but there was no paper. He thought some more, but no new thoughts came to him, and night fell again. Even though Taiming enjoyed peace and quiet, this hush, this desperate loneliness of solitary confinement, was too much. Was he imagining it, or was he actually trembling? He lay down to get some rest, but his overtaxed mind kept working aimlessly.

Little by little, the mountains and rivers of his homeland appeared to him. Behind his grandfather, who led him by the hand, he was hiking to the Ladder to the Clouds. Such happy days, when in the fields and hills wild pomegranates awaited anyone with a basket, which could be filled in no time. The rivers teemed with fish. A pound or two was easy catch for anyone with a rod and a free afternoon. In those days, there were no bad people, and people did not mind missing a couple of tangerines or persimmons from their orchards—provided it was just a couple. The villagers hardly ever studied but did not doubt that greatness was in store for anyone who did. Taiming shared this belief and, as a child, vowed to study hard and become great. He studied hard but did not become great. . . . Grandfather's tomb lay on the hilltop. The view was good from there: far away was the Central Mountain range, and close by was a tea field surrounded by acacia trees. Before leaving his village, Taiming burned five incense sticks there and prayed to his grandfather. Pledging to become the first of many generations of Hus in the Yangtze delta—where *his* bones would be buried—he sought his ancestors' protection. Though not as strong willed as Zeng, Taiming now vaguely wanted to go home. The mountains and rivers of his homeland were exquisite songs and poems compared with which the continent's peaks were prosaic. He choked on his emotions at this thought. The snowless country was green, green with banana and palm trees. . . . His mother's face appeared before him. How was she? But he had not written to her for a long time, and her careworn face, or its apparition, faded. Other faces came and went: his father's, his brother's, and, one by one, those of neighbors whom he had never thought about in his entire life. If and when he was cleared of suspicion and released from this cell, he would go home. Anything about his dear homeland he was ready to suffer, everything about it would endure. . . .

But he did not know whether he could go home again. Exhausted, he finally fell asleep. There were many more red coins on his skin when he woke up.

The wretched days and lonely nights merged into a span of gray time as his body and mind wilted into one. At least two weeks of anguish and tribulation passed with no calls from the interrogator. Three times a day, the prison guard brought his food. Taiming looked forward to the taciturn man's visits.

One night, around midnight, he thought he heard someone knock at the door. Though suspicious that he was imagining things, he pricked up his ears and peered through the darkness. In a moment, he heard more tapping. It certainly came from the door, which he rushed forward to open, even though it was locked from the outside. Something was slid under the door. It felt like a piece of paper.

Instinctively, Taiming asked, "Who's there?"

There was no response. Whoever it was tiptoed away, and the silence resumed its reign. Fearfully, Taiming turned on the light to examine the piece of paper. On it was a poem, written in a clear and slender script:

> Remember how a sparrow found
> A farmer's hut could be its nest?
> Remember having by a mound
> Intoned, "A life is but a guest"?
> Remember always, Yue or Wu,
> We're kin and kind, as heaven knows.
> Master, remember that, and do
> With harsher chants this shame oppose.

At the end of the poem were a couple of characters that Taiming at first took to be the signature. He could not recall anyone with such a name but in a moment realized that "bingding," an ancient synonym for "fire," was an instruction to destroy the piece of paper once he had figured out its meaning.

But what was it? He read the poem over and over again to try to understand the message—not the superficial one but the one underneath, its hidden meaning. To begin with, who was the eccentric who wanted to play such games after midnight? The script looked female. Who was the difficult woman?

Just then it occurred to him that it had to be her, that clever girl who was among those he had taken to the Ming tomb. He remembered the lines he had composed in the garden by the mound; that she had quickly grasped their meaning and that her own poems had been precocious. Her name was Suzhu, and when Taiming saw that its first character had been worked into the poem, he was convinced that it was she. Suzhu had gone on to marry a detective. "Ah ha," he thought. The entire puzzle finally seemed to be coming together. What a novel-like coincidence! He was trapped in a house whose mistress was his former student. Suzhu, she was the author of the letter, and the reader's heart beat fast.

9. Flight

The novel did not have any more installments. The time without day or night resumed, marked only by the meals that the prison guard, Taiming's sole contact with humanity, brought three times a day with mechanical regularity. The miracle of Suzhu did not recur.

The days were somewhat brighter than the nights. When the dark grew thick and sticky, it was night.

One night—was it a dream?—he thought he heard footsteps. It appeared that the faint noise had waked him up, though he did not remember falling asleep. He strained his ears, and the footsteps ceased. He was sure he was not hearing things. Somebody was there (somebody other than himself) listening just as hard on the other side of the door; somebody was breathing as quietly as he was. There was a rustling and the sound of a key being inserted into a keyhole—the one to his cell. Taiming held his breath.

The door opened slowly, seemingly by itself, and without so much as a creak. Something like a shadow slipped in and drew close.

It said in a breathless whisper, "Teacher, it's me, Suzhu." He was right, then. The odor of a young woman wafted over him. The person of Suzhu was there. Was it a dream? But in a moment, they were hugging tight.

They compared notes in the dark, in hushed voices, her bosom against his, but this was no time for talk. She had not come to renew old ties; she had come to free him from his present bondage, and the first step was out of this closet. She left a twisted wire in the lock to indicate the prisoner's resourcefulness. She seemed well prepared.

"Quick, this way," she said, leading him. Tonight, her husband—the head of the Metropolitan Secret Police—was out. He was attending a banquet. The prison guard she had sent out on a complicated errand.

Everything proceeded as planned, and the final step of the deception was to bind and gag her. There was not a moment to be spared now. Her eyes begged him to be off. Former teacher and student exchanged parting looks full of emotion.

He slinked out of the house and ran west down a dingy alley. The soles of his shoes rang loudly in his ears. Across the deep night, he ran as fast as he could, at one point knocking over something that he later realized was a person.

A taxi, barely fitting into the alley, awaited him at an intersection. On the window of the rear left door was draped a large white handkerchief that seemed to shine in the dark. He tumbled into the back seat. Soaked in sweat, he was too breathless to notice that he was not alone, but the car accelerated with a roar and sped down the alley.

"Teacher, it's me." Taiming recognized the voice, which was low for a young woman's. He could not see her face in the dark, but it was no doubt Youxiang, whom Suzhu said she had contacted. Youxiang had also come on that Sunday outing and had admired the garden by the tomb. A wise girl, with a broad forehead, she had been one of his favorites, attending his special math sessions after school and, like Suzhu, giving him poems to read and revise. The three of them were aficionados of poetry as well as teacher and students. After graduation, the girls returned to Shanghai, where both of them had grown up, and corresponded with their favorite teacher for a couple of years before losing touch with him. Taiming did not know that they were in Nanjing—a dramatic, even melodramatic encounter.

The taxi drove down Taiping Street and turned at Central Mountain West. The police sergeant at the intersection momentarily frightened Taiming, but he let the car pass. The fugitive wanted to stop by at his house but thought the better of it: the person he had knocked over in the alley may have been the prison guard, in which case his homecoming would quickly end in his being rearrested. Youxiang agreed and promised she would put him in touch with his wife. The taxi whizzed past another policeman. Why were the nights of Nanjing being so carefully patrolled? Youxiang asked the cab driver to take Main Avenue, which was not so prosperous as it sounded and was free of police after dark. The car passed through Yijiang Gate, turned right, and skidded to a halt. They were on the Lower Piers, where the *Hankou* was moored, flying a Japanese flag.

The escape was three-quarters complete. All that remained was for Taiming to board the *Hankou*. If the captain refused to grant him illegal passage, then that was that. He was ready.

10. So Long

Youxiang handed him some money and gave him the address of a man named Li, to be contacted in Shanghai. Their good-byes were short.

Facing the captain, Taiming gambled by telling him the truth and pleaded in Japanese for special passage. The *Hankou*'s skipper was an odd sort. He nodded and even echoed his words amiably throughout Taiming's story but, as soon as it ended, said cuttingly, "I think I get it, mister. When you're in trouble, you folks become Japanese citizens. Ha, how convenient!" Then contradicting this, he spat out, "Falling onto my boat. . . . Take the berth next to mine. I can't refuse, can I?"

Not for nothing had the man sailed up and down the Yangtze in these tense times. He may have been prickly, but he was broad-minded and trustworthy. Taiming came to agree with the captain that the *Hankou* was the mother ship of the Yangtze fleet and that there was no safer place.

Taiming's landing in Shanghai required some playacting on his and the captain's part, but the show was an easy success.

He had made it. The escape from the cell to the boat to Shanghai could not have worked out more elegantly. It was a miracle.

He found an inn in an abandoned quarter and registered as "Huang Taiming." Once he had calmed down, he went out to meet Li.

Li, a broker now but formerly an official in the People's Government, had married Youxiang's older sister, Taitai, a graduate of Beijing University. She loved debating and welcomed him as a comrade, Taiming soon found.

In Shanghai, the rush of history was gathering speed as in no other place. The overpowering current easily carried off mere individuals without even allowing them to take a breath. Prominently active was the Society for National Salvation, whose anti-Japanese operations steadily intensified the general anxiety. The foreign settlements served as a superb hiding place, but there, too, the talk centered on war. Sensuous melodies were no longer heard in the cafés, bars, and dance halls. Instead, people sang stirring songs by a native composer about the vanguard as society at large silently inched toward war.

United under the slogans of the allied front, the people rose all at once; the curtain rose on the historic strikes against Japan's textile interests. Day after day, students, even those still in high school, demonstrated in the streets. It was rumored that the Koreans had also risen and that their independence movement was under way. But the Taiwanese were mysteriously disappearing every day. Caught in the vicissitudes of history, divided internally—exactly as Japanese "higher politics" had envisioned (which saddened Taiming more than anything else)—Taiwanese were facing the their greatest crisis in modern times.

One evening, Li said to Taiming in a sarcastic tone that was only slightly playful, "You must feel pretty lonely watching things from on high. It breaks my heart, really. You see the forces of history carrying away everything, and you can't join any of them. Let's say you manage to convince yourself one way or the other. You won't convince anyone else; everyone'll think you're a spy. Come to think of it, you're a sort of misfit, aren't you?" Li had been infected. He had given up his job and was now feverish from political activity.

Taiming was afraid that the ex-broker wanted to use him in some kind of covert operation. When Li offered to take him in, however, he left his inn, for the Japanese settlement was now being searched for dissenters and was no longer a safe haven. In the bloodthirsty eyes of the Japanese authorities, who at that moment did not have time to ferret out subtle differences, all natives from the province of Taiwan were suspect. The fact that one was innocent was not a good reason not to be terrified.

About that time, three letters from Nanjing arrived at Taiming's new address. The first two were from Suzhu and Youxiang. Taiming gobbled up his former students' reports; braver than he, they cheered him on and promised to remain in touch with his wife. He opened the third letter, and Shuchun's handwriting—he had not seen so much of it in a long time—conjured up warm feelings he had not felt toward her for ages. Back when they lived together, her ways offended him more often than not, but now that he was underground in a stranger's house, her spiritedness was a relief. There was absolutely nothing to worry about, she wrote, except that Ziyuan's ability to make mischief was improving. Enclosed was a photograph of Ziyuan and her mother. The younger lady was laughing. But wait—it wasn't possible—how could his daughter become even more adorable than she already was?—and Shuchun looked good. Their future had been weighing on Taiming, and he felt relieved. The idea he had been mulling over in his mind was beginning to look more and more practicable. Li agreed that it was probably necessary for Taiming to seek refuge. His wish to sail home thus became a plan to do so.

One day toward the end of May, Taiming boarded the *Mount Song* from a pier on Yangshu Bay. It was a lonely departure. Only Li was there to wave to him as the propeller churned the muddy waters of the Huangpu, shortly to flow into the great river and out into the ocean.

Watching the city by the river recede, Taiming tried to sort out his feelings. He could not decide how he felt when he thought, "So long, continent—will I see you again . . . ?"

The ship was heading for the river delta. But it was going against the current, for the tide was rising and the water was flowing upstream, washing the ship on the way.

The water brought with it a man floating facedown. He neared the ship and rubbed against it. Nobody clamored to lift him out of the water; the continent was a cold place. In the timeless flow of history, he was worth no more than a handful of dust, no more than a corpse.

But wasn't the magisterial river flowing backward? So it was, carrying the nameless man toward—Shanghai.

"So long, continent," Taiming said once more. Dusk was setting on the international city.

Chapter Four

. . .

1. The Gloomy Homeland

Looking back on them from his homeland, the years Taiming had spent on the continent were but a passing dream. He was relieved to be back in Taiwan, but at the same time, from the moment he got off the ferry in Chilung, a burdensome feeling weighed on him wherever he went.

The excessive, meticulous inspection by the harbor police and customs surprised him. Although he had nothing on his conscience, he cringed in their fine net. He actually trembled when he faced the detective on duty.

Because Taiming had become accustomed to the continent's freeness and openness, its happy-go-lucky atmosphere, it was as though he had suddenly wandered from a wider place into a dank, narrow alley. It was suffocating.

This feeling boarded the train with him at Chilung station. In Taipei, where he got off, he noticed a swarthy man with razor-sharp eyes. The man followed Taiming like a shadow to the bus, to the coffee house, wherever he strolled. The shadow came along to the Ximen market when he went shopping. Was he being followed? There was no other explanation. Discomfited, he cut short his stay and decided to head straight home.

Since he had not sent word of his homecoming, there was no greeting party at the beloved old station. When he dropped by the luggage area to pick up his belongings, however, the station-master had an unpleasant message waiting for him. Taiming had to visit the police before going home. There was a branch office at the station.

Troubled, he did as he was told and identified himself to a uniformed officer. Apparently, he had nothing to fear. Treating Taiming with the utmost courtesy, the officer asked him a host of questions regarding China, but hardly any about himself. After the interrogation, Taiming was allowed to leave for home.

The villagers were aware of the turmoil on the continent and were especially pleased to welcome back their native son. He was the only person from the village ever to have crossed the strait. The mere fact of his safely making the round trip excited the villagers and generated a lot of admiration. It only added to their enthusiasm that Taiming had been an instructor at an advanced school, which is to say that he had held a high post in the civil service. The next day, starting in the morning, an endless stream of friends and relatives came by to his house to hear him talk about China.

He was already getting tired of receiving these guests when the local police officer came by in the early afternoon. They had lunch together. The visit made the heavy feeling that he had had since Chilung—the sense that he was being hounded—even less bearable. Everything seemed to be closing in on him, blocking his way out, depriving him of air. Had his country in fact become a less comfortable place? The policeman nattered on until he was satisfied, apparently not noticing Taiming's anxiousness, and then left.

Thus, not everything was as Taiming would have liked it in the countryside, which now was his again. But his village had changed a lot and felt new and more alive. The main street was much wider and flanked by full-grown eucalyptus trees. Down this avenue, a bus—a beaten-down old model but nevertheless a bus—bumped along four or five times a day, leaving the scent of civilization in its wake. There also seemed to be more young people, none of whom Taiming recognized by face. But when he asked who their parents were, he remembered.

Each of the members of the Hu clan had had ups and downs marking the passing of half a generation's worth of years. Opium Tong had been dead for three years now, and Ah-San had been alive until just a year ago. Ah-Si had kicked his opium habit and had moved away with his son-in-law. Cousin Zhida no longer could make a living as a lawyer's interpreter and had become a perennial idler; nobody paid any attention to him anymore. Strangely enough, Taiming's father's medical practice was thriving. Hu Wenqing was old but healthy, and with fewer and fewer doctors practicing traditional medicine, the demand for his services had risen proportionately. Doctor Hu's second wife, Ah-Yu, for whom the insecure status of mistress was in the past, now seemed every bit the brave woman that a mother ought to be; at least, she no longer wore gaudy makeup. And some people in the village had persuaded Taiming's older brother to become the local arbitrator. Hu Zhigang was now a busy man of influence.

The village's inhabitants had changed in accordance with the divine providence that replaces the old with the new. Only the main hall of the Hu house was still unchanged in all its timeworn splendor. Taiming entered the shrine for the first time in many years, offered incense sticks to his ancestors, and prayed for the repose of his grandfather. His heart was full. Cobwebs now covered the gilded letters that had always been peeling off, and the metal sections of the memorial tablet shone with a sad pallor. The last time he had been in the hall, he had been preparing to leave for Jiangnan, China, ready to die there, and praying to his ancestors to watch over him. He felt remorseful and guilty that he had had to give up the idea.

It was in this remote village and under such circumstances that Taiming wondered what step he should take next. Hu Wenqing warned his son not to take his credentials as a bureaucrat too seriously, prestigious though they were. But what was tormenting Taiming was simply that he did not have anything to do from day to day. After a few days spent at home, dissatisfaction, emptiness, and loneliness made him restless.

He had not yet seen his mother because she now was living at her son-in-law's with her daughter, Qiuyun. Before he came home, his plan had been to ask his mother to live with him and to remain with her in peace and happiness, but now that he was back, he realized that perhaps she might be better off with his sister. Before arriving at a decision, he had to see how Ah-Cha, his mother, was faring. Although Taiming knew full well that he soon had to pay his regards, he was unable to muster the will to go out, and finally, while he was delaying, his mother and his sister came to see him themselves.

"Mother was waiting for you, didn't you know?" Qiuyun reprimanded Taiming when she saw him, forgetting to welcome him home. "You take it too easy, brother. That goes for the rest of you, too."

Ah-Cha was staring at her son's face so hard she could have bored a hole in it. "Taiming is back? This must be a dream. . . . Ah, I'm glad we made that trip to the temple," she said. Then she rubbed her teary eyes over and over.

Taiming noticed that his mother had brought a basket with her which contained a chicken and some incense sticks. A guardian deity or the clan's ancestors were about to receive word that her son had returned safely. Meanwhile, Qiuyun had arrived with a carrying cloth in which was wrapped a jar of peanuts. Taiming could not observe all this without feeling a lump in his throat: his mother's sweetness touched him deeply. He wanted to bury his face on her lap and weep his heart out there forever. Seeing how much sadness his endless traveling had inflicted on her, he was full of contrition.

That evening, Hu Wenqing and Zhigang were present as well in what they told him was the first family feast in a long time. Until then, Ah-Cha had been careful not to cross the threshold of the former concubine's section of the house, but that night became the exception, so badly did she want to be with her returned son. Although Hu Wenqing was visibly satisfied with the family reunion, Ah-Yu, considerately, did not sit at the table. Even though she and Ah-Cha were not enemies, there was inevitably some awkwardness between them. Taiming thought of the understanding his mother had shown for so many years and found her a bit pitiful.

The banquet was merry. His beloved peanuts in hand, Taiming spoke of the continent's scenery and manners. When the others demanded to hear about places he had not been to, such as Suzhou and West Lake, he could not paint the pictures to their satisfaction. But when the talk turned to Shanghai or to Nanjing, his eloquence entertained them greatly. Hu Wenqing, in high spirits, remarked that he would give anything to see all that for himself. Ah-Cha was brimming with joy seeing everyone trying to speak at once.

When Zhigang began to brag about his renovated room with Japanese tatami, Qiuyun, a mother now but no less mischievous, interrupted, "Brother, promise to go with me wherever I go."

"Why?" asked Zhigang.

"Aren't you an arbitrator? They say trains stop just for you."

The sarcastic remark drew a mild chastising glance from her mother. Zhigang, laughing embarrassedly, said, "Don't be silly, all that is history; we don't enjoy such privileges nowadays. Well,

I guess people do let me get on first when the bus is crowded. But that isn't granting too much to a holder of public office, is it?" This restrained answer silenced his little sister.

In any event, for the first time in a long time, merry laughter was heard from the Hus, who put aside all grudges that day, late into the night.

It was decided that for the time being, Taiming should live at his sister's husband's Extended Benevolence Medical Clinic. Qiuyun's husband, Dr. Lin Yuedong, was a young idealist, and his charitable, affordable practice was popular with the area's peasants, who called it simply "the new clinic."

After settling in, Taiming began to help him out on the administrative side so as to have something to do. Most of his work turned out to be playing host to the many guests, perfectly healthy, who came by to visit. Taiming finally realized that there was something suspicious about the visits. For indeed, the Extended Benevolence was being visited by the police—the local officer, sometimes even a special agent—who found a reason to pop in almost daily. Only after some time did Taiming see that their business was with neither the clinic nor its doctor but with Taiming himself. The casual visitors from the police would be inordinately curious, for instance, about a letter sent to Taiming from China.

So frequent were these visits that eventually he and the officers assigned to him took to chatting with the ease of friends, though they did stop short of sharing their innermost feelings.

"If you ever go on a trip, you have to notify us, OK?" the special agent requested, always incidentally.

One day, Taiming did have a reason to travel, to the southern reaches of the island. Recalling the agent's warning and assuring himself that his conscience was clean, Taiming resolved to report to him first as requested. But when he found the familiar face at the special service bureau, he was told that the brief trip was of no concern, that in fact, he would not have had to come in at all. Cracking jokes all the while, the agent showed barely any interest in the itinerary.

Taiming could only laugh at himself then. But once he had left, he realized that the agent was quite serious about keeping him under surveillance. While he was waiting for the train that would take him farther south—he was already as far down as Pingtung, having changed at Kaohsiung to the Pingtung Line—he left the station for a brief stroll, to kill time. As he was looking at the tropical plants in the town's park, he felt for an instant a burning gaze on his back. Startled, he turned around and saw a man quickly hide behind a tree. Taiming's heart leaped in his chest. The man looked exactly like the one he had shared a compartment with that morning. Suddenly anxious, Taiming hurried back to the station and was the first to board when the train arrived. The man he had recognized also climbed into his carriage. In fact, everywhere Taiming went, the man followed tirelessly like a shadow.

He was being tailed after all. The special agent had pretended not to care about Taiming's travel plans and had responded to his visit with small talk, but he had also sent this man to watch him. It would pay to be careful.

Taiming made a mental note to himself: "From now on I will have to try to live inconspicuously." After returning home from his trip, he stopped going out, and, almost always staying inside, became a reclusive bookworm. When the world finally seemed to start forgetting about Taiming's existence, the annoying visits from the special agent also became less and less frequent. "Good, I can relax a little now," thought Taiming. But it was around this time that he heard talk of young Taiwanese men on the continent being deported one after the other back to Taiwan and being swiftly imprisoned. The ominous atmosphere of the time was like a harbinger of war.

2. In the Shadow of War

Finally, what had to come had come. The crack of a single gun-shot at Marco Polo Bridge ignited the smoldering coals that had gradually been burning brighter.

There was a welter of opinions concerning the implications of the event, including the optimistic view: "It's no different from the Manchurian Incident; it won't develop into an all-out war." People tried to remain unconcerned, an outlook that was more prevalent in the elderly. As the fighting progressed from northern China to Shanghai, this optimistic theory lost adherents. While people held their breath waiting, a full-scale war unfolded as Japan and China collided again and again. And now it was about to spread like wildfire. Taiming, meanwhile, absentmind-edly observed this historical about-face.

As the war progressed, Taiwan also was quickly designated for fighting.

In both the countryside and the towns, talk of the war was on everybody's lips, and raised flags seeing off soldiers going to the front and departing civilian military-workers were everywhere. Community-spirit mobilization movements had begun, and lectures on these movements were being held in every corner of the countryside. Not only the heads of households but also house-wives and even sons and daughters were mobilized for each of these meetings, where they were required to listen to lectures given by village heads, school headmasters, arbitrators, and others.

One afternoon, Taiming left for a meeting with the owner of the rice dealership next door. The meeting that day was about rais-ing money, and everyone was called on to hand over every cent they had to "scourge the atrocious enemy, China." The speakers, including the village head, denounced as unpatriotic all those who were hoarding gold. Although their arguments threatened those not handing over their gold, the arbitrators knew exactly who had it anyway.

After the meeting, Taiming started home with the rice dealer from next door. As the two slowly made their way, groups of three or four people poured out of the meeting hall and walked in front of and behind them. They could hear the animated conversation between two ladies walking in front of them. What appeared to be a middle-aged woman was cautioning a young bride.

"My ring? I have never worn it, so I will be all right. . . ."

"Oh no, the arbitrator was at the wedding."

"But won't it be spared as a wedding memento?"

". . . If they find out, you're in trouble."

They noticed Taiming approaching them from behind and, surprised, stopped talking and, suddenly lengthening their strides, started walking as fast as they could. It seemed they had mistaken Taiming for a civil servant. Taiming felt rather miserable, and the rice dealer murmured to him in Taiwanese:

"Developing new mountains and selling old fields."

This was a saying that warned against selling good paddies for new ones when they haven't been cultivated yet. Taiming only nodded gently, remaining silent, but the rice dealer continued with another:

"Long whips don't reach the stomach or back."

This meant that whips that were too long were useless. Taiming caught the meaning and asked, "Not worth the effort?"

The rice dealer, noticing that Taiming had grasped the meaning, said, "So, Master Hu, you *do* speak the language well, as I suspected. China is a vast land with more than four hundred provinces. Even if each region resisted for only a year, the war would last for eighteen years. It can be aptly compared to chasing a rat around a large room: if you aren't efficient, you will tire in the process of chasing and never catch it." He continued talking, expounding on the rise and fall of China. He seemed to have an education in the classics and enjoyed using words rich with connotation hinting at this education.

"The third arbitrator was arrogant, calling this a holy war and labeling people as unpatriotic, but where exactly is the justice in Japan's actions?" he said, venting his daily frustration.

Taiming, having nothing to say in reply, walked silently.

The demand to hand over precious metals had given rise to an untimely panic among the women. Even Taiming's younger sister, Qiuyun, and elder brother, Zhigang, argued over whether or not to hand over some earrings. Since becoming an arbitrator, Zhigang had been an avid war supporter and so was very enthusiastic about handing them over. Also upon becoming an arbitrator, Zhigang had remodeled his house into a Japanese-style abode, constructing a household Shinto altar, and even a tatami-mat room, which was very unusual in the countryside. Such devotion was also evident in his visits to the shrines with his wife, both of them in Japanese dress. When the Manchurian Incident broke out, as if driven to a frenzy by the war sentiments in town, he made a fool of himself by becoming a pawn of the Japanese. Because he wanted to improve his record as an arbitrator, when it came to handing over precious metals, he urged his entire family to give theirs up. When his sister hesitated in handing over her last remaining earrings, he crushed her youthful feminine feelings by coercing her with threats like "What if the police search the house?" and "I'm going to tell them!"

At no point in the argument were there any feelings of affection or family bonds on display. In the end, Qiuyun, in tears, had to hand over the earrings.

One day, when Taiming and the rice dealer were chatting at the rice shop, three Japanese wearing government-clerk hats strutted in. Two or three peasants, who had been taking a break, stood up, saying to the Japanese, "Please, take our seats," and then disappeared quietly.

The three Japanese were obviously rice inspectors. The peasants had just been decrying the "heartlessness" of the rice directives. The dealer of the store was flustered in greeting the untimely and unwelcome guests. His son, who spoke Japanese very well, could usually be counted on to attend to the guests, but today, of all days, he was out, and the inspectors were visibly displeased by his absence. The son always knew what to do, so when he was there to welcome them, things went smoothly with the officers. The rice dealer apologized to the officers in his rudimentary Japanese for his son's absence.

The inspectors turned on him angrily. "What? He's not here? But you knew that today was inspection day!" They burst out forcefully, "We'll inspect anyway!"

Panicking, the rice dealer followed after them. Bags of rice were lined up in four or five rows and piled high in the rice storage container. Leaning against them, the officers looked from the bags to the rice dealer's face and back again, pointing the sharp end of the rice-sampling implement into the bags with malice in their movements. Finishing this, they then moved off into a corner of the storeroom and began muttering quietly to one another.

Suddenly, facing the entrance, they yelled for their coolie, "Hey, come here!"

Their coolie approached, bringing a bamboo sieve. One of the inspectors suddenly thrust the rice scoop into a bag nearby and then poured out what he had scooped into his palm, proceeding to inspect it. He then purposely threw the rice violently back into the sieve so that it would end up scattered around the place. The rice bounced off the edge of the sieve and landed all over the ground. Trampling the rice with the soles of their shoes, they continued their inspection, plunging their scoop into every single bag.

"Hey, there's stone in this one—you've failed the inspection. Wash it all again!" With this parting shot, the inspectors headed swiftly toward the front of the shop without even attempting to inspect the remaining bags. Ashen faced, the rice dealer followed them and argued earnestly about something or other. He was expecting a loading boat soon, so if the rice didn't pass, he would be in serious trouble.

Taiming watched this unfold, his chest burning with righteous indignation. It was barbaric to order someone to rewash all the rice—of which there were more than a thousand bags—after having inspected only around ten and finding only one containing, by chance, a measly pebble. Now, having decided to call it a day, the inspectors did not go home but remained seated in the shop and drank their tea, which had gotten cold, with apparent distaste. They obviously had an ulterior motive. One of the inspectors caught sight of a wooden mortar lying in the garden and went over to have a look at it.

"It's camphor—good quality," he said, and, with a greedy look in his eyes, started stroking it with his hands.

"Camphor?" his superior officer echoed. With an effort, he stood up and went over to look at the mortar. Laughing, he returned and said to the rice dealer, "Can we have that mortar?" He narrowed his eyes.

"Can we have it?" meant, of course, for free. Taiming felt sick watching this but thought that if the rice could be saved with just one mortar, then it was best to hand it over. He whispered into the rice dealer's ear that he should part with it. The rice dealer did not understand Japanese as well as his son did and was a rather inflexible fellow, but he finally agreed after hearing Taiming's advice.

The mortar changed hands, and the superior's face suddenly broke into a smile. "Hey, Pops, you're smarter than I thought," he said. With a complete about-face, he added, "But you'll have to wash your rice better from now on." He signaled with his eyes to his subordinates that the rice should pass the inspection.

The subordinates complied and went around stamping the second-class mark on all the rice bags without even inspecting them.

After this, the rice dealer entertained his guests with saké. Taiming tried to leave, but the rice dealer stopped him, and he ended up reluctantly joining them as an interpreter.

When the inspectors became drunk, one of them observed, "The worst beat is vegetables, and the best's sugar. Those sugar guys are not only treated to a feast, they can take home some sugar as well!"

"That's right. By the way, I like beer more than saké." The rice dealer had neither beer nor sugar. The inspectors were behaving as though they were at some bar café.

Taiming thought to himself, "How awful can these men be?" But they were the type who, even if Taiming had voiced his thoughts, would not simply leave. In the end, the inspectors found what they wanted at a place in town, where they drank themselves into a stupor, and went home on the last train.

Later that night, as Taiming lay in bed at home trying to fall asleep, he was kept awake brooding over the incident. If this really was a holy war, what were those inspectors up to, anyway?

3. Calls from the War Front

After a long absence, Taiming left his sister's house and returned home. His brother Zhigang was still thoroughly infatuated with the new regime and was assiduously trying to upgrade his lifestyle. For him the new regime meant installing a new bathroom containing a bathtub made of cedar that emanated a strong woody smell. Furthermore, because the interior of the house had been the traditionally deep Chinese red, he even had it repainted in more typically Japanese colors. The toilet had also been remodeled into a Japanese-style one.

Because Zhigang had not seen Taiming for a long time, he proudly asked him, "So, what do you think of my home?" Taiming thought back about the time when his sister, Qiuyun, had angered Zhigang by harshly disparaging his assimilationist life-style and thus decided not to say anything particularly critical. Zhigang's pride became even more evident as he started giving Taiming an account of the pains he had endured to improve his way of life, as though he were delivering a lecture.

"Let's have something Japanese for lunch today," he said and served udon noodles. As he drank the soup, he asked Taiming, "What do you think of this soup? You lived in Japan, so you will have a discerning palate for this. Is it all right?"

Taiming considered recklessly hurting Zhigang's feelings but maintained his brother's mood by saying simply, "I've already forgotten what it should taste like, but this seems to be all right."

"It is, isn't it?" Zhigang responded, all the more satisfied. Observing his brother's simplicity, Taiming was filled by an indefinable sense of pity.

Taiming had not been home in some time, so he went for a stroll in the garden and walked to the public office. There now was a Shinto altar outside the hall as well as a Japanese scroll hanging there. However, the scroll somehow looked skimpy, unsuited to the large building. Taiming left the area and wandered aimlessly down the country roads, going wherever his feet led him, until he reached the town.

He noticed that as though by agreement, the women wore one-piece dresses and the young men were in the national uniforms. Taiwanese attire was considered, along with Chinese styles, to be "of inimical character." Drapers and tailors were doing a profitable business.

Whether he was at home or walking around, Taiming felt somehow empty. The enthusiasm of the zealous crowds in which he found himself failed to rub off on him, and eventually, his feelings of alienation spiraled into great loneliness. The look of hopelessness and apathy so apparent on his face was a cause for concern to his family, particularly his mother. But he could not hide his feelings. When Taiming mulled over his private thoughts alone in his room, his mother would often slip in as silent as a shadow, speak his name in a voice full of kindness and warmth, and smile almost shyly. At times like these, Taiming knew what his mother wanted to say. She had recently begun to bring up a particular subject from time to time—a subject she had previously pressed Taiming about before he had gone to the continent. Concealing her motive behind a weak smile, she would chat with him, and after some hesitation, she would bring up, once again, the same old topic:

"Taiming . . ." and then nervously, "Have your thoughts still not changed? Why don't you take another wife?"

Taiming's mother knew about Shuchun and Ziyuan. But in her thinking, they were beyond saving because the war had spread throughout the entire mainland. Even if they were still alive and Taiming were reunited with them, it would not be shameful to have a concubine as well as a wife.

Taiming, however, felt an indescribable sense of resistance to his mother's tone when she suggested that he "take another." He did not doubt her genuine compassion, but she was just a foolish elderly woman adhering to the old customs. Taiming could not accept such out-of-date ideas. He had decided that until he knew his wife's whereabouts, he would not remarry. The decision was based on a sense of responsibility rather than love for his wife.

Thoughts of his wife frequently tormented him at night, but there was nothing he could do. He would tell himself that he could do nothing but wait, and attempting to alleviate his pain, he would pick up the Mo Zi he was reading. Mo Zi was much more actively antiwar than the pacifist Mencius; his arguments were extremely clear, and reading them gave Taiming a sense of contentment. Mo Zi opposed the tragic path of history and tried to stop it, but in times of war, his theories were little more than a single drop—an unpolluted drop—in the murky, torrential flow of history. No matter how passionately Mo Zi asserted his views, by themselves they were powerless.

Closing the book of essays, Taiming thought about the common tragedy of all intellectuals. Mo Zi was present in the heart of all feeling people. However, the intellectuals of the past, no matter what the period, were always left behind by the passage of time as they helplessly flailed around. Perhaps they were no more than rootless floating weeds in the current. In the past, to avoid being swept along by the torrent of history, subscribing to the beliefs of Lao Zi and Zhuang Zi or perhaps Tao Yuanming was an option, but this was no longer practical. In the current climate of total war, an individual was powerless. Whether or not he liked it, everyone was destined to be drawn into the vortex of war, under the supreme injunction of the state. The wisdom of Lao Zi and Zhuang Zi, the thoughts of Tao Yuanming—they had not the power to regulate modernity.

Taiming lay awake for almost the entire night, turning over these ideas in his mind.

The next day something terrible happened that changed Taiming's circumstances. An order that arrived out of the blue demanded that Taiming join the civil naval force and be posted at the war front. This was not entirely unexpected; by then, young Taiwanese men were being heavily conscripted for support units. Even so, holding the order, Taiming had no control over the complex emotions welling up inside him and making him tremble.

Feigning composure as best he could, Taiming entered his mother's room and explained the turn of events in a way so as to avoid frightening her. After circling around the issue, he told her the truth.

His mother's face suddenly changed color, and for a short time she said nothing. Then suddenly, at the top of her voice, she wailed: "Are there no laws in heaven?" She then began to weep loudly. Taiming did not know how to comfort his mother. All he could do to ease her state of mind was to tell her that all the people who had landed at Bias Bay were still alive.

The date for his departure to the front finally arrived. A send-off party was held by the head of the town hall. Two other young men who had also been conscripted attended the function as well. All three were promising young native Taiwanese with exemplary academic backgrounds.

The proceedings started with the village head mounting the platform and giving a conventional send-off speech. Then it was the turn for the summoned to give their greetings. The other two took turns on the podium and told the crowd with great vigor and enthusiasm of their resolve to fight. But their words seemed forced and pitiful. Taiming shut his eyes and listened to them unfeelingly, as if he had nothing to do with it. Soon enough it was his turn to take the stage. He had wanted to avoid speaking, but the atmosphere in that hall did not offer this option.

So Taiming headed toward the podium with heavy feet. He thought he had nothing to say. But when he looked out from the podium at the audience, the countless faces crammed into the hall, he felt pressured to address them and mechanically opened his mouth to speak.

"Ladies and gentlemen." His gaze surveyed the hall and stopped when it reached his mother sitting at the back, crying. The sight pained him greatly, but he managed to continue speaking calmly. "Ladies and gentlemen, I am very grateful to you all for this wonderful farewell. Forever in your gratitude, I will do my utmost at the front." With this he bowed and left the podium.

He felt it would have been dishonest to say anything more. The audience, expecting a longer, more rousing speech, were surprised by his brevity. The hall was momentarily silent and nobody clapped. Recovering, the crowd came to life and filled the hall with applause.

4. Tragedy

No matter how much he wiped it away, sweat kept seeping onto his skin. The dull roar of the airplanes in the dazzling blue sky above made the heat even more unbearable.

Taiming had arrived in Guangdong as a civilian employee. Although it was a reasonably calm town, the residents seemed to be frightened of something, and their days were filled with fear. Not yet used to the weight of the sword he was forced to carry, Taiming uncomfortably wandered around the town and, when meeting with the townspeople, would feel an indefinable, speechless resistance from them. Underneath the residents' veneer of dutiful respect, Taiming sensed a hidden animosity. He wanted to break down the barrier somehow and be honest with these people, but with his halfhearted attitude, it would not be possible. So instead, he withdrew even further into himself, thus fortifying the barrier of oppressive silence.

One day, walking across town, Taiming saw, at the foot of a bridge glistening under the ferocious sun, a well-built man who was tied up with thick wire. At the time, while order was certainly being returned to the town, there still were frequent cases of arson, robberies, and acts of terror. The man at the bridge was probably a perpetrator of such a crime. In the scorching heat, he fixed his imploring eyes on the passersby. There were marks on his skin, obvious evidence of a painful struggle to free himself. The Chinese people passing by pretended not to see him. Next to the man stood a notice on which was written an indictment charging him with robbery. The sign was in Chinese and in stark black ink and included the threat that all those who carried out evil acts would meet the same fate. Sadly, the indictment reflected none of the goodness in the man's face. Taiming felt sorry for him.

"Poor man . . . if he stays like this, he'll dry up and turn into a mummy," he thought, unable to look into the man's eyes.

The man happened to notice the sympathy in Taiming's eyes and started moving his mouth in an attempt to say something. His words were almost incomprehensible, probably because he had little strength remaining: "You must be from Hubei or Shandong. You're not from here, at any rate."

From the accent, Taiming could guess where the man was from. He was overcome with pity, and, looking around to make sure there was no one in sight, he quickly unfastened his drinking flask and poured some water into the man's mouth. With a look of infinite gratitude, the man gulped down the water noisily, relishing every drop. There was no time for words.

At that instant, they heard a voice yell suddenly. It was a Japanese soldier. Taiming thought he was in for it, so, flustered, he grabbed the flask and began to run away. He could not, however, bear to leave the man as he was. After making a quick decision, he took out of his pocket a container with mouth refreshers in it, emptied it, and stuffed them all into the man's mouth. He then walked away.

Taiming realized that the man would probably die of starvation, thirst, and heat and that his own small act of kindness would not save the man in the end. Yet the water and mouth refreshers had enabled the man to enjoy a little respite before his imminent death. If there was any comfort at all for Taiming, it was in these thoughts. Even after returning to his lodgings that evening, the man's look of utter gratitude remained fixed in Taiming's mind.

The next evening, Taiming decided to take a walk outside by the river to get away from the oppressive heat. Three soldiers having a drink on the grass invited him to join them, asking him if he were in the civil force. They were a friendly group, so Taiming joined them, taking a seat on the grass. As the alcohol began to take effect, the talk turned to women.

"The women around here are so chaste," remarked a middle-aged soldier. He continued, talking about his unsuccessful attempts to rape the women in rural Guangdong on his way home from fighting. "She wouldn't do as I said, so I had to pull out my sword and wave it around. She fell to the floor when she saw that! I thought, 'Got you now,' and as I was about to go about my business, the damn bitch ran away. She was so fast! One minute my catch was there, the next it was gone." He still looked quite disappointed.

Another soldier, licking his lips enthusiastically, now started giving an account of his own experience. "Well, *I* was successful. It was during a patrol mission in central China. We heard a rustling in a cornfield, so we went to see what it was. Thinking it suspicious, we went slowly and quietly. We heard voices. The voices of young women. Immediately my heart started racing. We jumped out to see more than thirty women and children. Upon seeing us, they quickly scattered like birds. Two young ones didn't get away. They were shivering with fear, and we made them, you know . . . aah, my best experience ever. Afterward, though, my buddy thought we might get in trouble, and so, bang! He shot them from behind. It was cruel and heartless, you know, after they had given us so much pleasure."

Taiming felt himself sobering up as he listened. Even these soldiers, who were easygoing and amicable, had a barbaric side to them. Although he thought he had figured them out, Taiming revised his opinion of them.

Unaware of what was going through Taiming's head, another younger soldier, not to be outdone by the middle-aged men, responded to the previous story. "When we entered Nanjing triumphantly, the refugee shelters were swarming with girls from Jinling University. We had our pick. They were all so white and succulent, much better than the women from around here. But all of us in my battalion, which arrived first, were young, and we didn't touch them. The battalion that arrived afterward, though, had many older men in it, and apparently they had a feast on the girls. We were so foolish to let that chance get away!"

"Oh well, first in best dressed. For three days after the city fell, we were up to our eyes in it, but it all ended when the MPs arrived. Honest men will always be fools."

Taiming had heard enough. "Thank you for the drinks," he said, and made a hasty exit. Walking away, he thought, "What on earth is war? What is it for?" Conjuring up images of the numerous incidents like the soldiers' stories—inhumane incidents concealed by the shadow of war—Taiming was driven to frenzied distraction.

A few days later, Taiming's battalion arrested eight men on suspicion of anti-Japanese terrorism. This was a mere formality, however, because once they were arrested, their fates were sealed. Nonetheless, the men were interrogated, and Taiming's job was to interpret. They seemed valiant men of unfailing conviction. No matter how much they were threatened, they remained undaunted as if they had already accepted their death sentences.

The cross-examinations yielded no hard evidence. The interrogating officer became increasingly impatient and, rather than sticking to facts, was swayed by his emotions. The principal reason for the men's arrests was merely that they had been found with oil on their hands. The interrogating officer asserted that the oil must have come from a gun. Taiming, however, argued that it may have been machine oil and that therefore another detailed investigation was necessary. To no avail.

"Shut up! This comes from higher up." The officer desperately wanted to execute the men on the grounds that they were anti-Japanese terrorists. There was no longer any point in Taiming's stating his personal opinion, so he was silent. The officer then bubbled over: "Right, the interrogation is complete. I announce the death penalty." Taiming listened to the sentence in despair, stricken with grief.

The arrests of "anti-Japanese terrorists" continued, and the path to execution remained unchanged. After routine interrogations, the death penalty would be announced. In effect, an arrest meant execution. Taiming interpreted for all the interrogations, and gradually, he began to feel immensely burdened. The convicted were composed in death, and Taiming felt oppressed by the noble courage they displayed as martyrs for their country. Whereas these men faced death unperturbed, Taiming was anguished, his conscience wracked by guilt.

Then one day, something happened that truly had an impact on him. Ten terrorists belonging to the Volunteers for National Salvation were arrested. The commanding officer was a handsome, fair-skinned youth who could have been only eighteen or nineteen.

His attitude during the interrogations was even more exemplary than the others.

"Affiliation?"

"Volunteers for National Salvation."

"Who is your leader?"

"I don't have to tell."

"What are you?"

"Company commander."

"What's your rank?"

"Major."

"Your academic background?"

"Normal school."

"How many subordinates do you have?"

" . . . "

"Where are your headquarters?"

"You won't get anywhere with this. Go ahead and kill me."

With that, the commander grinned. His attitude was remarkable for its fearlessness.

It was finally decided that the executions would be performed that afternoon. A total now of eighteen prisoners, including those who had been sentenced the day before, were put on a truck. Another truck containing armed troops followed. With their black barrels gleaming eerily in the sun, six submachine guns were pointed at the prisoners at close range.

Taiming rode with the executing officer in a separate passenger vehicle, following them to the execution grounds on the outskirts of town. The midsummer sun beat down on the asphalt, making the road to the execution ground shimmer. At last, the convoy arrived at the site. The prisoners were pulled off the truck one after another and lined up. A large ditch had been dug beforehand: it would become the prisoners' grave. Presently the prisoners were made to kneel in front of the hole.

The time for execution had come. The prisoners looked into the face of death calmly, not even fidgeting. Extending their necks, they awaited the moment in silence.

"Hie!" came the sharp cry, slicing the surrounding air.

Reflecting the shine of the midsummer sun, the blade of a Japanese sword glistened as it danced in midair. At that instant, a sharp thud was heard; a head came off a body and tumbled into the pit. The decapitated body then crumpled and followed the severed head into the hole. A gurgling noise came from the point where the head was severed, and dark red blood spurted out, staining the ground a deep red. As the executions continued, Taiming started getting the chills and had to struggle not to pass out. By the end, his entire body was shivering relentlessly.

The last prisoner to be executed was the commanding officer.

"Hey, you, the civilian!" he called to Taiming sharply.

He wanted to be shot rather than beheaded, so Taiming translated his wish. The request was rejected on the grounds that it would be a waste of ammunition.

"I see," the prisoner said simply, and let it drop. Then, undaunted: "This is my last request. Let me have a cigarette."

This wish was granted. Taiming lighted a cigarette and held it in the prisoner's mouth, and the prisoner took a deep drag, exhaling the white smoke.

When he had finished the cigarette, he said decisively, "I don't want a blindfold—I'm a soldier." He then intoned, "Man conceives the deed and heaven sees it through; in eighteen years another decent man—"

"Hie!" a cry reverberated before the prisoner could finish. His head was separated from his body and rolled into the ditch with a thud. His body then collapsed. At that instant, Taiming became dizzy. He thought he felt a gust of cold wind across his face, and he could feel himself faint.

"What a weakling," somebody jeered from somewhere behind Taiming. He could remember nothing after that.

That evening, he went to bed with a high temperature of 104 degrees, incessantly murmuring some kind of nonsense and slipping in and out of consciousness. A week passed and he did not recover. Finally, he was sent to the army hospital.

A severe psychological shock was the trigger for Taiming's collapse. A succession of unfamiliar experiences in the region to which he had been deployed, plus severe mental anguish compounded by physical fatigue, had already strained Taiming's mind and body. The executions he witnessed were too much for his already weakened state, and once he collapsed, he could not get back up. Seeing that his condition was not improving, the doctor gave up and decided Taiming's fate with a simple pronouncement: "He must be sent home. He is no longer of use here."

So one day, Taiming was sent back to Taiwan. The boat home traveled noiselessly down the Zhu River on a quiet, windless day. Taiming, now a bit better, gazed at the city of Guangzhou as it disappeared out of view. In reality, his stay at the front had been brief, but to Taiming, it had felt like ages. Peaceful days lay ahead for him, but the clouds of war still loomed over the world. His own peace would not be real, since he could be easily drawn back into the vortex of war. He was worried.

5. Convalescence

After returning to Taiwan, Taiming initially sought refuge at the Extended Benevolence Medical Clinic, which was run by his sister's husband, Lin Yuedong. Having been medically discharged from the army, he felt somewhat reticent about returning to his homeland, where he had many acquaintances, and preferred to spend some time quietly convalescing alone.

His spirit ravaged and exhausted by his unusual experiences, Taiming gradually began to improve amid the sights and sounds of his tranquil homeland. Physically, however, he was still not himself, nor could he decide what he wanted to do. Besides, even though the Extended Benevolence Medical Clinic was quiet, with the comings and goings of its many visitors and patients, it could hardly be considered repose for one's nerves. After a short stay at the clinic, Taiming returned home to his village.

The person who rejoiced most at his homecoming was his mother, Ah-Cha. Having regained the son whom she had given up for dead, she swore that come what may, she would never part with him again. She also resolved that once he recovered, she would follow through with her previously aborted plan to see him wed. Her one and only hope was to have her son get married so that she could spend her twilight years in happiness and peace.

For some time after his return, Taiming savored the atmosphere of his village and the affection of his family, but as his condition improved, he gradually became bored.

One day, he made a visit to Zhigang's arbitration office. As it happened, Azuma, the deputy village headmaster, and several others deemed to be local intellectuals had stopped by and were deep in conversation. All of them, including Azuma, had taken Japanese surnames. Azuma's name had originally been "Chen," but he had removed the left part of the Chinese character, leaving the Japanese-sounding "Azuma."

Taiming's brother, Zhigang, had similarly changed his surname to the Japanese-sounding "Furutsuki" by dividing the Chinese character "Hu" into its two components and reading them separately. By addressing one another as "Mr. Azuma," "Mr. Furutsuki," and so forth, the men indulged their pride in being citizens of the Japanese Empire. At the same time, this move was another expedient way to advance their careers.

When Azuma spotted Taiming, he began to extol in his inherently affable manner the distinguished accomplishments of the Hu clan and of Taiming himself.

"By the way, Taiming," he ventured, "why don't you follow your brother's example and change your name, too?"

Taiming did not respond.

"I must admit," Azuma continued, "that after changing my name, there have been some inconveniences. For example, when we go out to the provinces, I've sometimes had the unpleasant experience of having some obtuse department head introduce me to the governor by saying, 'This is Mr. Azuma, formerly Mr. Chen.' But if you consider the matter calmly, you'll see that this is just an unavoidable consequence of our being in a transitional period. It is by passing through this painful transition for our descendants that we'll become distinguished Japanese."

"I don't think Mr. Hu fully grasps the urgency of the problem," chimed in one of the men there, discerning that Taiming gave little sign of being persuaded. "But think about how it will be when your child enters middle school. Then you'll see the reason for the urgency. Even the most conservative among us then can see the necessity of changing our name."

The man was alluding to the fact that on the entrance examination, the number of passing students who had not changed their name was very low and that even if they did manage to pass, the school would eventually force them to change their names anyway.

As Taiming listened to their discussion about changing names, he suddenly remembered what had happened to Sorai, an eighteenth-century Japanese Confucian. Inordinately enamored of Chinese culture, Sorai had changed his name to a Chinese one, only to be censured by a later generation of Japanese scholars. If one can never be anything other than oneself, then one can hardly expect a name change to yield a new personality. In the case of the group here, who were motivated by expediency and self-interest, Taiming sensed in their taking new names an ulterior motive that revolted him.

At the time, a ditty ridiculing name changing was popular among the lower-grade students at the public elementary schools.

> Flies in the outhouse and red sea bream
> Red sea bream done change their name
> The arbitrators think they're the same
> Flies in the outhouse and red sea bream
> Flies in the outhouse and red sea bream
> Red sea bream, red sea bream

Chanted in a singsong manner, the ditty mocked the fact that during rationing, families with Japanese names or who spoke Japanese were granted special favors, including rations of red sea bream.

Taiming could not bring himself to laugh at the satirical spirit that had reached even the children's hearts, and whenever he heard these mocking words, his face stiffened with a mixed feeling resembling a tearful smile. He also remembered the sight of Zhigang's wife trying to greet guests with the inept Japanese she had learned at the district school, before scurrying off with embarrassment to her inner sanctum.

"Flies in the outhouse and red sea bream," Taiming muttered to himself. "Then our efforts to become loyal Japanese citizens are nothing more than a cartoon?" It all disgusted him.

This reminded him of another intolerable situation. His mother, Ah-Cha, had recently started raising vegetables near their house in an attempt to become more self-sufficient. Elated by her initial attempts, she extended her plot, with Taiming's help, to the adjoining area. In addition to the vegetables, she also planted about thirty banana saplings, which took root in the newly cultivated earth and flourished with each passing day.

One day, Taiming was gazing untiringly at the banana trees, whose growth he had so painstakingly nurtured, when a threatening voice summoned him from behind.

"Hey, you! Did you plant those?!"

He turned around to find an inspector from the Irrigation Association, the same man who used to be a police sergeant. When Taiming answered in the affirmative, the man replied in a dictatorial tone that the valley was under the administration of the Irrigation Association and that any unauthorized cultivation or planting was prohibited. The valley in question was indisputably the Hu clan's property, and Taiming calmly pointed this out. The inspector, however, obstinately insisted that the Irrigation Association naturally had control over all waterways, which would include any water flowing in the valley. He also insisted that even the trees along levees were its property.

At the time, the association's general method, which was to claim that anything related to water could be taxed, had become the target of intense public criticism, and this tendency had become even more pronounced with this man's arrival. Armed with this pretense, the man was trying to tax Taiming's bananas. In order to rationalize his own unjust demands, he brandished his duplicitous legal knowledge in an attempt to coerce Taiming into submission. That was the association's favorite trick. Listening to him, Taiming became incensed and launched into a sharply worded counterattack. Faced with the well-reasoned rebuttal, the inspector seemed to think, "Good heavens! This one's more formidable than an ordinary farmer!" and muttering to himself, he retreated for the day.

A notice from the Irrigation Association, however, arrived some days later. Concerning the abolishment of the pond and a special water tax, the notice demanded that in order to increase production, the pond had to be filled in and turned into a rice field. The designated special water tax would be seventeen and a half yen. Taiming let out a groan. If he had to pay the special water tax twice a year, it would amount to thirty-five yen! It was doubtful whether the plot would yield even a thousand pounds of unhusked rice per year, which would bring in only 92.53 yen at the official price. When he considered that in addition to the regular water tax, more than a third of it would be subject to the special water tax, he couldn't see the point: after adding in the cultivation costs and land taxes, it would be cheaper to purchase a new field altogether. Moreover, the pond was not merely a fishpond but was built because they needed a reservoir to supplement the irrigation.

If he eliminated the pond, four or five acres of the lower fields would be turned into parched earth at the mercy of the weather. The directive was an unjust demand that clearly ignored the circumstances of the concerned party. Taiming resolved to go to the Irrigation Association to get to the bottom of the issue.

The Irrigation Association occupied a majestic two-story building, more splendid than the local district headquarters. The entire facility had undoubtedly been funded with the unjust taxes exacted from the sweat and blood of the masses. With trepidation, Taiming pushed open the door and entered. A young Taiwanese clerk approached him, and Taiming briefly explained the situation. The clerk took a high-handed attitude from the outset, asserting that increasing production was a matter of great national urgency and that they could not afford to make allowances for individuals' circumstances. He added that those failing to cooperate were traitors. The words were different, but the peremptory tone that Taiming had grown to abhor was the same. Pawns of the Japanese, Taiwanese were extorting exorbitant taxes from other Taiwanese, all under the guise of a national emergency. As things stood, Taiming didn't think he could afford to leave, but he could see that he wouldn't get anywhere with the clerk, so he mustered up his courage and requested an interview with the director.

A discarded provincial district headman, the director was a genial, hearty gentleman, slightly over fifty. In contrast to the young clerk, he appeared to be a man of some understanding. Taiming turned to him and explained in detail how matters stood with the land and the pond. His argument unfolded in a logical elucidation that would have gained anyone's assent. The director nodded along as he listened and showed some signs of compromising: the program for increasing production, he said, had an eye to the future, so that even if the pond currently could not be converted owing to the conditions of the land, Taiming still had an obligation to pay the water tax. Taiming, however, extended his criticism to the crucial matter of the association's methods, which seemed to rub the director the wrong way, for his attitude suddenly hardened. When Taiming retracted the comment, the man then began to insist on eradicating the pond at any cost. Getting on the man's wrong side was a mistake, but Taiming didn't believe he had said anything wrong and preferred not to distort his beliefs just to placate the director.

In the end, the argument turned emotional.

The director went so far as to say that in order to implement their policies, they would be justified in turning the fields into a wasteland. Such a flagrantly outrageous remark left no leeway for negotiation. Taiming stood up and started to leave. Apparently pressured by such determination, the director called Taiming back and became conciliatory, saying that if only Taiming paid his water taxes, he could leave the pond as it was for another year or two. What cunning! If those were his demands, he could have said so from the beginning, but this must have been the bureaucratic mentality. Taiming was all the more disgusted.

When he left the Irrigation Association building, he noticed a row of seven or eight attractive apartment buildings at the back. They were the lodgings for the Irrigation Association employees. From the interior of the complex, a phonograph record was blaring a vulgar, Japanese pop song that was current in the cafés. So this was what became of the money culled from the blood and sweat of the people—all in the name of irrigation!

Taiming felt an undefined indignation well up in him with the thought, and when he raised his eyes, flaring with that indignation, he saw white clouds scudding to and fro across the peaks of Mount Cigao, which basked in the faint winter sunlight. The clouds appeared full of turbulence.

6. Mother's Death

One year of war was equivalent to a hundred years of peace. Everything continued to change at an intense pitch and pressure never encountered during peacetime, and the various Taiwanese customs that had taken root in history and tradition were no exception. The Yimin temple festivals, which fell on the twentieth day of the seventh month in the lunar calendar, were the first to change. Even the Fangliao Yimin Temple Festival, at which tens of thousands of frenzied participants from fourteen villages gathered each year to sacrifice well over a thousand pigs, was abandoned, and the Taiwanese theaters, no longer giving performances, were shut down as well. The old lunar calendar was replaced with the new solar one, and Taiming's family fell in step with the other villagers in welcoming a solar New Year that seemed more like a wretched state of emergency. The celebrations were mere formalities, devoid of emotion. Taiming's mother was dissatisfied, and when the old lunar New Year arrived, she furtively made her sweet cakes with lingering attachment, and worshiped anew her ancestors and the goddess of the sea.

Another change was that when the rice-planting season arrived, amid vociferous cries for increased production, the authorities' enforcement of programmed planting intensified. There seemed to be no end to the number of farmers who were called to the police department and raked over the coals for noncompliance. Those summoned were forced to kneel on a concrete floor for more than an hour or were slapped across the face. Even so, the problems between the farmers and the district patrollers and officials did not diminish, for even when a farmer strictly implemented the intensive planting methods, if the rice was not planted in the standard intervals of twenty-one centimeters by twenty centimeters, the officials would complain.

For instance, there was the case of an old farmer who had tilled the same fields from childhood until the age of seventy and who knew from experience the most appropriate planting methods for maximizing each field's harvest. The man continued with his methods, but then an inspector appeared, measured with his ruler, and reprimanded the man for being out of compliance.

Trying to make his point, the old farmer explained that his methods, deduced from experience, were sound; that because the conditions for higher and lower fields were different, you couldn't just plant by the manual; that if you planted too closely together in poorly ventilated hollows, you risked infecting the emerging rice plants with blight; and that the stalks wouldn't grow thick if the plants weren't spaced at the appropriate intervals. Taiming happened to be translating and felt that the farmer was making excellent points, but the officials turned a deaf ear to everything the old man had to say.

"Unacceptable!" one of them yelled. "You absolutely have to follow the regulations. Replant everything. If you don't like it, come to the district headquarters tomorrow."

His comment ended with a threat. Regulations were all they knew, and reality was irrelevant. They couldn't rest content until they forced everything into their mold of regulations, even if this lowered production.

"Son of a bitch!" muttered the old farmer, out of exasperation at their intransigence, and clicking his tongue in disgust, he tossed his spade aside, raised his whip, and drove on his oxen with a "giddyap!" The oxen cruelly trampled row after row of the painstakingly planted rice seedlings. Nothing could be done in the face of an official's order, but when Taiming considered how painful it must have been for the man to plow up the seedlings that he himself had taken the trouble to plant, he couldn't help feeling sorry for him. When the officials saw what the old farmer was doing, they finally were satisfied.

"OK, let's get going," they said, taking their leave. But even they seemed to feel ashamed of themselves. "Old people are so stubborn," they explained, trying to curry favor with Taiming. "You young folks are much more understanding."

The strict crackdown soon had every rice field in compliance with the vertical and horizontal standards of an orderly dissected *go* game board, and the authorities were pleased. Although the transformation did not seem to increase production, the authorities adhered to their theoretically projected production targets and blamed the farmers when the actual harvests did not reach those goals. Although the excessive demands were enough to overwhelm the farmers, an even more intense demand for increased production came crashing down on them: Taiwan was suddenly assigned a quota of five million bushels of rice, and a campaign to raise production commenced.

Farmers had a proverb that said, "April, May, and September, not one friend do we remember." This meant that in farming villages, the drain on the economy during those months precluded human kindness. After farmers planted their crops and paid the necessary expenses, the custom was to live frugally while irrigating and weeding the fields in anticipation of the harvest. During April and May, every field glittered with green as far as the eye could see, and those months were filled with the hopes of the impending blessings, but they also were a financial struggle. On top of that, good and poor harvests were at the whim of nature, so farmers were extraordinarily anxious about the weather. Constantly praying to be spared from storms, they eagerly awaited the harvest. These were the farmers who were suddenly struck with the demand for huge contributions of rice.

Before the official announcement, the towns were rife with rumors, but the details remained unknown in the concerned farming villages. For this reason, the farmers—who were certain to be the principal victims—remained in the dark. But as the various rumors filtered out of the towns, the sense of dread began to descend on the farming villages too.

One day, Taiming was weeding in a peanut field when several local farmers came up and started gossiping about the rice contribution campaign.

"You can't buy rice in town anymore," one of them said. "All the rice shops are empty."

Their opinions differed as to whether the supply would fall short or whether rice could be bought in other areas. That a crisis was imminent seemed inevitable. That evening, Taiming's mother told him about the recent outbreak of sweet potato thefts in their village, and convinced that this, too, had a connection to the rice shortage, Taiming related what he had heard in the field that day.

"That's bad news," replied his mother. "But listen, Taiming: when your grandfather was alive, he always used to say, 'Every year, prevent hunger; every night, prevent theft.' He hated leaving rice outside and always stowed it away. And in the evening, he always checked the outer gate. And most important, late in life, he always used to store away more than enough rice to see us through any emergencies. Your mother developed the same habits thanks to him, so we'll be fine."

Then she told him about the great famine that struck China during the life of his grandfather's grandfather. Riots had broken out, and wherever they saw smoke, the mobs were sure to attack. Taiming's great-great-grandfather, however, had anticipated the famine during that year's harvest and had made provisions for April, May, and September. He had cleverly warded off the danger by hiding the unhusked rice in clay bricks that he piled up against a wall, so that even the many marauders never found it. Even though Ah-Cha was talking about famines in the past, she seemed anxious about the present, and she broached the subject with her son.

"But Taiming," she said, lowering her voice, "I wonder how things really stand now."

Taiming tried to reassure her by explaining that although there were crop losses in Korea and northern Kyushu, the Japanese government would never invite famine in the way that ancient China had. This explanation did not seem to assuage her fears.

The next day, Zhigang, the arbitrator, returned from a meeting on the rice contribution quotas and communicated the results to the villagers: rice rations would be one-third pint, and all remaining rice and unhusked rice would have to be turned in. Those who refused were traitors and would be severely punished. The communiqué threw the village into a panic. After racking their brains, they decided to contribute some of the rice and hide the rest. Pandemonium broke out as some villagers ground their rice into powder, others made it into sweet cakes, others made steamed dumplings, others buried it in the ground, and still others hid it in ponds. Such behavior was necessary to ensure the security of one's family. Taiming did nothing, but Ah-Cha used various methods to hide unhusked rice just as the other villagers did.

A few days later, search parties finally started making their rounds to the various districts. Composed of police officers, district officials, and Youth Corps members, the parties searched house by house.

When the search parties arrived in Taiming's village, the villagers were filled with trepidation and silently prayed to the goddess Matsu and the Yimin spirits. The more brazen ones, however, moved their rice to the forest or a bamboo thicket, posted sentinels, and then feigned ignorance. Ironically, only those carrying out such large-scale plans of concealment managed to escape the snares of the search.

The search of Taiming's house didn't turn up anything at first, but just as they were about to leave, the district official stopped.

"That pile of sweet potatoes looks suspicious," he said.

When Ah-Cha turned pale, one of the Youth Corps members ran over and started rooting through the pile.

"I've got something! I've got something!" he yelled excitedly.

All eyes turned in his direction as he proudly raised high for all to see the gasoline can that he had ferreted out. The can swung heavily, and no one doubted what it contained.

"Damn traitor!" the official viciously cursed in local dialect. And with that, the party closed in triumphantly to claim the seized gasoline can. Having recovered from her initial fright, Ah-Cha suddenly became emboldened like a cornered animal.

"Bandits!" she sharply cursed in a soft but scornful voice.

The expression of the youth with the can underwent a sudden change, less from indignation than the momentary confusion of having been caught off guard.

Leaving things as they were, they carried off the gasoline can in silence, and the district official whispered a few words to Zhigang, the arbitrator.

That evening, Zhigang paid them a visit, and reprimanded his mother severely. Taiming couldn't bear to stand by and listen.

"Brother, it wasn't Mother who concealed the rice," he said, protecting her. "It was I. You shouldn't scold her." Nonetheless, Zhigang persisted in his tongue-lashing, so Taiming instinctively retaliated: "So how do things stand at your house? Haven't you concealed anything?" Zhigang was struck dumb by the question; obviously, he was hiding rice, too. As arbitrator, however, he had escaped being searched. His concealment of rice, which took advantage of his privileged position, was far more immoral than the actions of ordinary people. Muttering to himself, the exposed Zhigang beat a hasty retreat.

"You idiot! Pawn of the Japanese!" Ah-Cha scathingly cursed as she watched him go. Her eyes were filled with tears, for she had never used such invective toward her own son.

Beginning on the following day, Ah-Cha took to her bed. For a couple of days she still got up and around, but after that, despite having been such a hard worker, she spent most of her time lying down, saying that she didn't feel good. Unexplainable signs of decline became obvious. When the ears of rice began to hang heavy on the stalks, Qiuyun, the sister who had married into the Extended Benevolence Medical Clinic, paid a sympathy call, a mysteriously acquired sack of rice in her arms.

"Oh, you look so pale!" she said as soon as she saw her mother.

She was shocked at how emaciated her mother had become. Taiming had been by his mother's side constantly, so the change had not been so discernible to him, but to Qiuyun, who had not seen her for some time, the decline was obvious. In fact, Ah-Cha was soon only a shadow of her former self, and by the time the rice was ready to be harvested, she couldn't get out of bed; it was as if all the fatigue of her long life had hit her at once. Lin Yuedong, from the Extended Benevolence Medical Clinic, exhausted every means at his disposal, but even then, Ah-Cha did not improve.

One night, she called Taiming to her bedside.

"The harvest will begin soon, Taiming," she said, "I'm so relieved."

In a voice steadier than expected, she talked about how to secure provisions and other matters, but before long, her condition got worse, and she fell into a coma. Although she occasionally called her dearest son's name, she never fully regained consciousness. Yuedong attended her devotedly until the end, but there was nothing he could do. Her long life ended in the way a decayed old tree falls.

7. Persecuted Youth

The death of Taiming's mother further eroded his already dwindling zest for life. He had no desire to see anyone, and the pastoral lifestyle that had once been his soul's comfort now seemed enshrouded in a dreary hue of gray. Even after the hundredth-day memorial service, he was loath to leave his study. The lethargy persisted, and in due course, the old year passed into the new.

After Ah-Cha's death, Ah-Yu became increasingly attentive to Taiming's personal affairs. Her son, Zhinan, had already grown into a fine young man, worthy of joining the Youth Corps. Her unaffected goodwill eventually found its way to Taiming's heart, and he sometimes intervened on her behalf to resolve various disputes that arose between her and a tenant farmer, a man who took advantage of his landowner's weakness by inundating her with problems. In the man's defense, since the mandatory rice quotas were put in place, many tenants were insisting on lower taxes or were returning land to the owners. In general, everything had been turned on its head, so that now landowners were pleading with their tenants.

On the evening of the first full moon of the year, Ah-Yu said her prayers to Tian-gong and extended a dinner invitation to Taiming as an expression of gratitude for all his assistance. Taiming felt at ease with her and accepted without hesitation. Taiming's father, Hu Wenqing, also was there.

Hu Wenqing had aged noticeably, but he was as lively as ever, and once he had had a few drinks, he began arguing in favor of Japan's expansion into mainland China. Taiming could not agree with his father's argument: like many proponents of the policy, his father had fallen for the Japanese propaganda and assumed that such expansion meant reconstruction of the continent. Taiming, however, was keenly aware of how things stood in China and could not approve. Leaving that aside, he was nonetheless happy to see his father so full of vim and vigor in his old age.

As she served the meal, Ah-Yu gazed happily on the scene of father-son harmony, but before long, she became unusually agitated. When Taiming asked what the matter was, she answered that her son, Zhinan, had still not returned from a Youth Corps assembly. The assembly had taken place during that morning, and the other neighborhood boys had already come home; only Zhinan remained missing at this late hour. In particular, she was worried that something horrible might have happened to him, given the rumors circulating about the violent methods of the Youth Corps leaders.

At nine o'clock, Zhinan finally returned home, his face white as a sheet. When they asked what had happened, he explained that he had been urged to enlist in the army, had incurred the displeasure of his teacher by refusing, and had been kept in detention until now.

Because Zhinan had refused to volunteer for military service, the youth-training leader had become distraught, dragged him to a classroom, and abused him mercilessly. Zhinan was forced to kneel on a concrete floor and given a lashing, but he did not relent. When the cane cracked against his back a second time, Zhinan whirled around ferociously, wrenched the cane from the teacher's hands, and snapped it in two in front of his eyes, finally escaping through the window. That was all the resistance he could muster.

Zhinan's behavior, however, sent the entire school faculty into an uproar. The teachers turned out in full force to apprehend him, so even the obdurate Zhinan could not do anything but resign himself to his fate and meekly accompany them to the office.

In their fury, the teachers became emotional and cursed Zhinan with foul language, thereby throwing the office into chaos. Zhinan's pale face turned to stone as he endured the invective, and with a firmness surprising for a boy, he asked, "Could someone please explain to me why we call it *volunteering*?"

He spoke with composure, and not surprisingly, the words had the effect of dousing the incensed teachers with a barrel of cold water. At that point, the principal could no longer ignore the situation. He restrained the teachers and saying, "You can come with me," took Zhinan to his office. Then, after carefully trying to cajole him in honeyed tones, he finished with, "Well, think about it for a while," and walked out, leaving Zhinan by himself. In the principal's stead entered the headmaster, a Taiwanese who had been Zhinan's homeroom teacher.

"Zhinan," he said, "I'm not going to say that your idea is wrong, but the spirit of the times won't accept it. It would be better if you just gave in and signed the forms." He explained in detail the school's policy and the ways of the world: those who were working were forced to volunteer by their superiors; those who weren't working were rounded up by the local police; and Youth Corps members were handled by the schools. The world might look simple, but it wasn't. The government's policy was to promote conscription by manufacturing a groundswell of power, even if they had to use deception.

"I'd never tell you to do something that wasn't in your own best interest," he continued, with artful persuasion. "There's going to be a lot of trouble, so you'd be better off listening to what I'm telling you. After what happened today, even if you volunteered, you wouldn't necessarily be inducted. The school wouldn't have the courage to recommend you, and if you're not a first-rate model youth, well then . . ."

In the end, Zhinan trusted him and signed the application. When Hu Wenqing and Taiming heard the story, they were choked with anguish. Ah-Yu buried her face in her hands and sobbed with a mother's grief.

8. Reunion

For Taiming, all sights and sounds were depressing beyond words, and to escape from such stimuli, he became even more reclusive, seldom venturing from his study. But the tense developments of the times nonetheless reached his ears: first, when spring moved into summer, he was hit with the reports of the sudden outbreak of war between Germany and Russia. The German army had quickly conquered the Balkans and forced France to surrender and now was apparently pushing forward into Russia with unstoppable force, all the while expanding its previous operations against Britain. The world seemed to have entered an age of destruction.

For some reason, Taiming could not sit still and left his study in search of someone he could confide in, yet there was no one he could turn to. Every sight and sound was a reminder of wartime: the public elementary school students singing war songs as they gathered the hay; the rather forlorn-looking village, bereft of its young people off on voluntary labor, with only the elderly, women, and children left behind; and the topics of conversations on the street. People talked only about how with the rationing, one seldom ate pork nowadays; that Japanese or Japanese-speaking households received special rations of sugar and other sundries even when production was low; and of how incredibly tight things had become now that the government's list of rationed supplies had been extended to include more than twenty items, including pigs, ducks, geese, straw, jute, shell ginger, castor-oil plants, hay, bamboo, wood, chinaberries, handkerchief-tree fruit, cotton-rose bark, and scrap metal, to say nothing of sweet potatoes and rice.

"I guess everything belongs to the government," said one man, self-mockingly. "First, they take our children, and before long, they'll be coming for our wives."

Taiming again began to want time to think, and deciding that a change of mood required a change of scenery, he resolved to impose once more on the Extended Benevolence Medical Clinic. One day, he left.

It was his first trip by train in a long time. The bright coastal scenery was refreshing as if his eyes, having grown accustomed to the ubiquity of mountains, had been washed clean. Just as Taiming momentarily lost himself in the coastline landscape, a voice roused him.

"Hey, I thought it was you! It's been a long time."

Standing in front of him was a middle-aged man. It was Lan, the former classmate with whom he had stayed in Japan. All vestiges of his youth gone, Lan had the face of an established middle-aged gentleman. Taiming hadn't seen him since before leaving for China, so he invited Lan to the Extended Benevolence Medical Clinic.

Qiuyun welcomed her brother and his friend and was delighted to entertain them.

Lan had now settled down working as a lawyer after years of political activism, jail terms, and extended travel. Although the former acerbity was gone, glimpses of his wit still were apparent when the talk turned to politics.

"Did you know that nowadays the nonsense that it's preferable to live in idleness than to die with honor has become quite popular?"

Prefacing his argument in this way, Lan expounded his views on current affairs. He criticized the thinking of the Taiwanese in the pro-Japanization camp, saying that they had forsaken their own history and rejected their own traditions in their yearning to become Japanese, and were working only for the welfare of their offspring; consequently, little Japanese clones were sprouting up like mushrooms after a rain. Not only that, Japanized writers and critics were popping up, too. But even if Taiwan managed an external form of Japanization, what would be done about the lingering race question?

"Undoubtedly," Lan lamented, "politicians would say that if it comes to that, you can't become a true Japanese without a complete blood transfusion."

He then turned his lance on the state-controlled economy.

At the time, both Taiwan and the Japanese mainland had tightly managed economies, but in Taiwan, the policy was also a clever excuse for strengthening Japanese protectionism. The executives and high-level staff in regulated companies always were Japanese, and since most of them were bureaucratic old-timers, the companies seemed like nursing homes. Moreover, there was a theory that more and more Taiwanese were being sent farther south, to make room for Japanese to immigrate to Taiwan, where sanitary conditions had been established. The pro-Japanese camp took advantage of the trend and was on the rise. This was the so-called live-in-idleness doctrine, certainly one lamentable manifestation of a disappearing race.

Taiming, however, had a different view of the subject: admittedly, the Japanization movement was a policy that weakened the

Taiwanese, but although they appeared emasculated, such was not the case; only those blinded by the lure of fame and riches had been corrupted, and the majority of Taiwanese, especially the peasants, were as sound and uncorrupted as ever. Although they had neither knowledge nor learning, their lives were firmly rooted in the earth. The outlook on life that sprang from this experience had a healthy dimension not easily manipulated by propaganda, and as long as they had their feet on the ground, they would never waver. Conversely, those in the apathetic pro-Japanese camp were easily swayed, largely because their actions were driven by physical sensations. They were rootless weeds floating in the wind, and although they appeared powerful, they were not; the slightest breeze would sweep them away.

After going to bed late that night, Taiming's thoughts turned again to China. Opportunists were numerous on the continent, some recruited during the Sino-Japanese War and others voluntarily presenting themselves. They appealed to the people using every trick in the book, but the people were not fooled in the least; they astutely saw through their opportunistic leaders, who were betraying their comrades for the sake of fame and riches. At this point in his reflections, Taiming felt as if a ray of light had shone through the darkness. Although he could not define that light, he knew that it contained a promise of hope.

"The darkness of the present day is a predawn darkness," he said to himself, "and in due course, it will pass."

This was the conclusion that Taiming finally managed to reach. He felt an invigorating vitality permeate his body, and when he suddenly woke up, dawn had already broken with a streak of light in the sky.

Chapter Five

. . .

1. War Between Japan and the United States

They say that spiritual and physical well-being are closely linked, and this was certainly true of Taiming's health. Curiously enough, after his chance meeting with Lan, Taiming's ideological anxieties began to give way to growing hopes. It was a vague feeling, but it was as if a beam of light had penetrated his feelings of despair. The past was the past, but the anticipation of the unfolding future brought a bounce to Taiming's heart, and his health began to improve noticeably.

At the same time, the climate grew more and more oppressive for Taiwanese intellectuals and young people, and Taiming's immobility made him impatient. He dreamed of returning to the mainland, but this dream was thwarted by the troublesome process of obtaining a passport. Companies on the island were so constricted by regulations that they were virtually paralyzed, and conditions were such that even long-standing family businesses had to be abandoned because of the regulations. The heavy weight of the war made its presence felt more keenly every day.

At that time, Japanese public opinion regarding the United States had hardened to the point that war threatened to break out. Taiming had faith that the Japanese still had enough good sense to avoid such folly. But the time would come for him to be cruelly disabused of his optimism.

It happened on December 8. The owner of the rice shop next door burst excitedly into Taiming's room, clasping a newspaper extra. "Our boss (Japan) has finally gone and started a fight with the rich!" he exclaimed in a loud voice. Even though fighting with the rich implies the inevitability of losing, he actually seemed pleased by the prospect.

Taiming took the extra edition from the shopkeeper's hand and read the big, almost dancing, print that announced the military gains. The war seemed to be going surprisingly well for the Japanese. But deep down, Taiming thought, "This is really nothing more than a repeat of the Sino-Japanese War!" It was as if he could hear his last hopes draining away.

Despite this feeling, a new resolution grew in Taiming's heart. He promised himself to take this opportunity to cross back over to the mainland, where he could lead a life without contradictions.

The shopkeeper's attitude was, "No matter how the world changes, as long as we have two yen, we'll be all right." (Two yen could buy tall wooden clogs, meaning that one could straddle the fence and wait.)

Taiming, however, was unable to take such a detached outlook. In order to cross over to the mainland, he would need an invitation from his destination. But all Taiming's friends on the continent had fled into the interior as the invasion progressed, and none remained in Japan's occupied territories.

For the moment, there was no way even to obtain permission to board the ferry. Moreover, since the outbreak of the Pacific War, the ferry to Shanghai had been closed for three whole months, and there was no air traffic either. Even if he were able to figure out a way to obtain an invitation, there would be no way to get across. For the time being, Taiming had no choice but to give up the idea.

2. A New Workplace

The Pacific War spread and progressed with great speed. Hong Kong and Singapore fell in the blink of an eye. The news of the war victories excited Taiwan and delighted the boys in the street and educated youth alike. They dreamed of going to the South Pacific. But aside from the draft, there was no way to get there, so their dreams seemed unlikely to be realized.

With the rapid changes in international circumstances, Taiming's desire to return to the mainland grew even stronger, but there still was no way he could do it.

Taiming's aspirations were frustrated by a matter as mundane as obtaining a passport. He had no choice but to bury his pride and wait for the right moment. As before, he was reduced to biding his time, but a closer examination of his psychological state reveals that it was not entirely passive. Rather, he was crouching like a mongoose, calmly waiting to catch his prey off guard.

One day Taiming was in his garden enjoying some quiet thoughts when he happened to notice some figs growing. They were concealed by the shadows of the large leaves and hard to see at first glance, but the tree had produced quite a number of the plump fruit. Taiming plucked one and split it open to look inside. It was packed with deep red, juicy ripeness. As he gazed at it, Taiming was struck by an indescribable emotion. Basically, he thought, there were two ways to live life: like a flower that blossoms prettily and fades away without bearing fruit, or like the fig, which is not showy but inconspicuously produces fruit in unseen places. For Taiming, this seemed to contain a meaningful lesson. Something about the nature of the fig tree struck a chord in his heart.

Taiming walked along the hedge, still holding the fig. The hedge of Taiwanese lotus had been neatly pruned, its young leaves forming a thick, green wall. When examining its leaves, he saw that a large branch traversed the inside of the hedge, its limbs stretching out in all directions. He took another look at the branch, his eyes sparkling with wonder. He observed that while the branches that had tried to grow upward or toward the sides had been chopped off, this one alone had grown unchecked, willfully expanding its life force, and he was deeply impressed.

"Even the Taiwanese lotus has found a way to survive without compromising its own individuality!"

He felt as if his eyes had finally been opened to the depth of nature's wisdom. Reflecting on his own conduct, he felt ashamed of himself in the face of the Taiwanese lotus.

"I, too, must live boldly, like the Taiwanese lotus," he resolved.

By this, he meant that he would emerge from his passivity and take as active a stance as possible within the existing circumstances. He proceeded to throw himself into dealing with reality. He took a job with the X Association, an auxiliary organization of the X Bureau.

The association was actually a false front that had been created in the wake of the rice regulations. Superficially, it appeared to be a subsidiary organization that worked for the bureau, but its real purpose was to make money. Taiming's job was accounting. One or two accountants shared the workload for each item on the budget, and Taiming belonged to the general accounting section. His work consisted mainly of managing the payroll, and on average his work took up only a half hour each day.

Taiming worked under the chairman of accounting, who was overseen by the chief clerk, who was in turn supervised by the director. The director's superior was the branch chief, who also served as the head officer of the bureau. This was because they needed to use the power of the bureau, which supervised the rice industry, to have their authority respected by the rice dealers. Consequently, the branch chief served as an important business facade, even though his work consisted of little more than blindly stamping documents with his seal. As remuneration for this task, the association provided him with travel expenses, a stipend, and bonuses.

Because of side benefits like these, most of the officials in the bureau had similar double roles. In fact, this was the association's actual function. Taiming had held higher expectations of his new job, and when he learned about the machinations of this bureaucratic structure, he was very disappointed.

Neither the chairman nor the chief clerk did any real work either. They behaved more like guests, spending hours engaged in meaningless small talk. With the higher-ups behaving in this manner, the clerks and employees who were waiting for their decisions naturally fell idle as well. To combat their boredom, they passed the time industriously opening and closing meaningless files and proposals and pretending to work.

All of this was new to Taiming, even though anyone who worked at a public office or association had to resign himself to these fundamental principles. For Taiming, however, this was difficult to accept.

One day, rather than simply wasting time, he began to read a book. It was a literary work that had nothing to do with the job. As he read, he became completely immersed in it, and the hours passed by without his notice. Suddenly, Taiming felt the clerk next to him elbowing him. Startled, he looked up in time to see the director looking down at him sternly before walking off. Since the people around him were doing nothing but killing time anyway, Taiming turned back to his desk and continued reading his book.

After a short while, the office boy approached him. "Mr. Hu, the director wants to see you." He gave Taiming a meaningful look. Taiming supposed that it was a work matter and reported to the director immediately.

"You think it's acceptable to read the literature of an enemy nation at a time like this?" the director shouted when he saw Taiming. Oh, so that's it, thought Taiming.

"No, sir, that was *Faust*," he replied.

"I don't care whether it was *Faust* or Jesus Christ! All horizontal writing is the writing of the enemy!"

"But *Faust* was written by Goethe, a German like Hitler. Is Germany an enemy, even though it's Japan's ally?"

"Germany? What are you talking about?"

Consternation seized the director's face at having revealed his own ignorance, but he quickly changed tack. "What kind of idiot reads books during work hours?"

"Yes, sir." Defeated, Taiming returned to his seat.

Working under such a boss was depressing, and Taiming felt enveloped by an environment of pointlessness, with everyone opening and closing meaningless documents and pretending to work, all the while thinking only of quitting time. Many of the director's underlings were natives who were much more educated, cultured, and respectable than the director himself. But islanders were only islanders, and they were not eligible for official appointments. Working at a place like this, Taiming became acutely aware of the miserable lot of the Taiwanese.

The next day when Taiming came to work, his fellow Taiwanese workers said sympathetically, "You got chewed out yesterday, huh?"

They all harbored an unspoken animosity toward the director, and they commiserated with Taiming. Among them, a young worker named Fan warned Taiming, "Hu, you should especially watch out for Lackey." "Lackey" was the nickname for the chairman of accounting. Taiming did not feel guilty, so he did not feel a particular need to be wary of anyone. Still, he appreciated the goodwill behind everyone's warnings.

That day, during the lunch hour, Taiming took a walk near the office. The same Fan who had cautioned him earlier caught up with him and, grinning, suddenly spoke to Taiming in fluent Beijing dialect. Taiming realized immediately that the young man had been to the mainland. It made him nostalgic, as if he had bumped into an old friend in a foreign country.

After further conversation, Taiming learned that Fan had graduated from high school in Xiamen and had spent five or six years on the mainland before returning to Taiwan after the Sino-Japanese War. He was the son of a rich family and did not need to work for a living, but just before the national mobilization, he had joined the association because it was awkward to be at loose ends. He was a cheerful, friendly youth, well liked by the islanders at the office. Fan told Taiming a lot about the association's internal workings. In this way, Taiming learned about the factions, sycophancy, informing, and other complex, swirling currents that existed in the office.

Among the islanders, too, were those who had accepted imperialism. A typical example was an employee of the bureau who went by the Japanese name of Nakajima.

For twenty years, he had been a dutiful assimilationist and led a life of miso soup and plain clothes. Impressively enough, he had passed the exam immediately after graduating from private middle school to become a regular civil official and was a good worker who was passionately devoted to the assimilationist cause. But he was an eternal drudge: for some reason his career had failed to advance during his twenty-year stint. Rather, only his salary was raised, and this kept him from moving up in the company because his salary was already equivalent to that of a top-level chief clerk. Thus, if he received an official appointment, the lowest rank to which he could be assigned would be that of director, which would put him in a superior position to a number of Japanese employees. Owing to these circumstances, even after twenty years, he remained ineligible for an official appointment, but unfortunately, the pitiful assimilationist himself was ignorant of these forces. Rather, he believed that his failure to receive an official appointment was due to a lack of assimilation, so he applied himself even more assiduously. Like the other assimilating lackeys, he treated his fellow islanders with an attitude of pompous superiority while assuming an attitude of abject servility toward the Japanese. He even emulated the Japanese in his thinking, parroting unbearably childish criticisms of the Chinese that he had heard somewhere. Once he announced to everyone: "The Chinese are famous for being lying megalomaniacs. They're a hopeless race who love to talk absurd nonsense like having white hair 'thirty thousand feet' long."

Fan, as well as others who had previously borne Nakajima no ill will, now wanted to put him in his place, and they appealed to Taiming for his help.

Taiming thought that it was childish, but he confronted Nakajima, speaking softly. "Mr. Nakajima, both Fan and I have spent time in China. It's an incredibly vast country, and it is genuinely hard to understand, especially for someone with as mediocre an intellect as I have. Now, the phrase that you mentioned about the thirty-thousand-foot-long white hair is often used as an example of Chinese hyperbole, but would you happen to know the rest of the verse, Mr. Nakajima?"

Nakajima did not.

Taiming continued, mixing humor into his explanation: "Most five-word verses cannot be understood without the second line that accompanies them. Some of them even require four to complete their meaning. The phrase about the thirty-thousand-foot white hair is no different: without its other half, its meaning is unclear. It sounds hyperbolic only when taken out of context. It was not with affectation that Li Bai wrote, 'My white hair grew to thirty thousand feet; such was the depth of my sorrow.' This sounds affected only if one is not aware of Li Bai's sadness.

Even a poet like Du Fu, with his solid literary style, could be interpreted as hyperbolic. He penned the phrase 'A letter from home is worth ten thousand gold pieces.' To a modern man, who can communicate with any far-off place as long as he has two bits, this sentiment may seem incomprehensible. But even today, if you were to go into the interior of the mainland or to New Guinea, you would probably understand what Du Fu meant. Li Bai is probably laughing bitterly in his grave at Japanese people's self-serving interpretations of his phrase about thirty-thousand-foot-long hair."

Nakajima found himself unable to say anything in response. The other onlookers were gratified, and they regarded Taiming's erudition with renewed respect.

3. Fools on the Home Front

The longer Taiming stayed at the association, the more he learned about the details of its internal workings. Business trips were the perfect opportunity for officials to line their pockets. Taiming once accompanied his boss on a business trip that was ostensibly a survey of inspection fees. From start to finish, they were wined and dined by the dealers. When an inspector from the association went to a rice warehouse to inspect it, he could check three thousand or four thousand bags in one day. The fee per bag was three *sen*, which ended up amounting to quite a sum. Because the net output of the entire island totaled nine million bags of rice, the inspection fees alone amounted to hundreds of thousands of yen. There also were profits to be reaped from the jute bags and rice fragments. Moreover, the association's inspection was only preliminary, with an additional inspection carried out by the bureau itself. In other words, the association borrowed the authority of the bureau to conduct a completely meaningless procedure so that its officials could profit from its intermediary role.

In addition, the association absorbed personnel who were too old to work for the bureau. That was why the bureau sanctioned its profiteering. Both parties colluded in this system. The manager who accompanied Taiming on the business trip was a reticent man who had lived for twenty years flicking the beads of his abacus, but the relaxed atmosphere of being on the road loosened his tongue.

"The association is a difficult place to work in, but it's worth being patient. If you stick it out for twelve years, you'll receive a forty-month pension, as well as a large bonus. Once you reach the management level, even if you quit, you'll be taken care of for the rest of your life."

Finally, both the association and the bureau had the same organizational structure and goals as the Taiwan Electric Company and the Taiwan Development Company.

The branch chief had come alone to Taiwan, leaving his wife and children home in Japan, and he frequented the entertainment quarters. Once, Taiming noticed a suspicious-looking woman coming to visit the branch chief.

Cautiously, Taiming asked his boss about the woman. His boss held up his pinky to signify a girlfriend, and told Taiming, "the Cow's."

"Cow" was the branch chief's nickname. Taiming's boss explained that the woman often stayed overnight with the branch chief in the night duty room. Taiming was disgusted with this indecency.

"Take a look at these," the boss said, showing Taiming several receipts from a certain restaurant. All the receipts belonged to the branch chief and were to be reimbursed as miscellaneous expenses. Surprisingly, they constituted a mixture of public and private expenditures. That was not all.

"We received several thousand yen from business associates when we celebrated the completion of the new office. The Cow has poured all that money into this same restaurant." The more he listened, the more surprising things Taiming learned.

Before long, however, the branch chief was drafted. The association and the bureau collaborated to throw him a lavish farewell banquet, and that was the last of it. The day he left, the crew who had flattered him in his presence did an about-face and began to complain about his despotism. The branch chief had been fond of orchids, and the same people who previously had imitated his predilection and marveled over the flowers now would not so much as glance in their direction.

When word spread that the newly assigned branch chief was fond of fishing, the head of accounting brought in fishing line and everyone suddenly began to express an interest in fishing. Some went as far as to bring their rods and reels to the office.

The new branch chief was a young, serious engineer who had been educated in Taiwan. The rumor proved true; he was fond of fishing, and the fishing craze spread. The chief clerk of general affairs brought in a minnow creel that he had made himself and showed it to everyone during the lunch hour; the others showered him with insincere praise. Greatly pleased with himself, the chief clerk went on to give a lecture on how it was made. The expert sycophants fawned over him still more, asking questions to which they already knew the answers.

Elated, the chief clerk began to come to the association on all his days off to talk about fishing. The former orchid aficionados immediately sought the chief clerk's advice and became fishing fanatics, and not one of them would so much as turn his head to look at an orchid. Now and then, Taiming took care of the abandoned flowers. Unlike the others, he had never made a fuss over the orchids in a crude attempt to curry favor with the boss, but now he felt sorry for the forsaken blooms and made an effort to tend to them when he took his lunchtime walks with Fan.

Under the sponsorship of the new branch chief, a minnow-catching competition was held, and the fishing mania reached fever pitch. Everyone was completely obsessed. The same group of people who had been the favorites of the last chief won the favor of the new chief using the same old methods. Taiming alone resisted the changing currents, remaining detached and aloof. Something about this attitude managed to displease his superiors, and gradually his alienation grew.

A new fiscal year began, and the schedule for the bureau director's inspection tour was announced. The director of the bureau also served as the executive administrator of the association, so he was to be welcomed with great pomp and ceremony. In addition, a rumor circulated that on one of his business trips, the director had thrown a fit because the arrangements for his car had not been properly made. So the day before his arrival, the staff was in a frenzy of preparation, cleaning the office and stocking tea and sweets for his reception, despite the difficulty of obtaining such things.

When the big day came, the bureau staff as well as all the employees of the association waited breathlessly in front of the office to greet the bureau director. But the appointed time passed with no sign of the guest of honor. They all waited until they were completely exhausted. Eventually, in place of the director, the manager of general affairs came running up, out of breath, and informed them that because the director was tired from the train ride, he had gone to an inn to rest. Upon hearing this, the crowd was astonished.

Nobody said so out loud, but everyone was disappointed. Like schoolchildren, they fell out of line and began talking among themselves or kicking at pebbles. Two more hours passed. Then word came that the bureau director had left the inn, and everyone scrambled to get back into line.

Before long, the noisy rumble of a taxi reached their ears. The taxi stopped in front of the line of people. The director stepped out and nodded curtly to the crowd before turning straight into the office. He was a stereotypical midcareer bureaucrat. He spent only ten minutes in the branch chief's office, then made a tour of the building and came back out. The crowd reverently saw him off.

The bureau director completely ignored them. He said a few words to the chief and then climbed into the car and left. After having gone to such great pains, the workers were completely deflated by the anticlimax. In the end, they had hardly had the privilege of seeing the man's face. All told, the work at the association amounted to nothing more than one such folly after the other.

4. Fan's Resolution

As the resistance in the South Pacific grew stronger, the army finally noticed the enemy's seemingly bottomless reserve of material resources and frantically called on the populace for a drastic increase in production. In response, the public collection of metals went into high gear. Every metal object, even pots and pans, had to be surrendered. Based at the local police station, the collection drive was carried out by municipal workers, arbitrators, and the like. When a predetermined amount of metal was collected, it was gathered together, and a Patriotic Exhibition of Collected Metal was held in that neighborhood. This was meant to serve as a promotional device to accelerate the collection effort. Each time an exhibition was held, employees of the bureau had to show up, and they took turns attending when they had time.

One day, Taiming went to one of these exhibitions and invited Fan to accompany him. The site was packed with tin boilers, zinc plates, rusted old farm implements, metal furniture, iron window bars, metal bed frames, tanks, sheets of iron, rails, bells, gongs, and so on. Even the warehouse contained a veritable mountain of scrap metal. There also were special display rooms containing various metal products sorted by type: iron, aluminum, copper, silver, and so forth. Decorated with valuable pieces of art and old family heirlooms, these rooms almost resembled the showroom of an antique shop. Many items were worth anywhere from one hundred yen to several thousand yen apiece, including gold-copper alloy vases, ashtrays, statues of gods, buddhas, and various gold and silver ornaments. Valuables like these were labeled with a tag bearing the name of the person who had contributed them. They all had belonged to well-known people.

As Taiming took in all these items, a strange feeling came over him. These pieces of art, fashioned by master craftsmen, would soon become guns and artillery or sharp blades and be used for mass murder. It was a perfect symbol of peace and war. The same pieces of metal, shaped by different hands for different purposes, could be incarnated as either works of great beauty or deadly weapons. The painstaking work of the craftsmen would be completely transformed into tools for slaughter. How utterly senseless it was! As soon as this realization struck him, Taiming lost all interest in his surroundings, and the place itself felt oppressive to him. He called Fan and they left immediately.

As the war grew fiercer, the volunteer system gained force. In Taiwan, all men between the ages of eighteen and thirty-eight were eligible to serve. The association helped recruit applicants according to vocation. In reality, though, enrollment was not so much voluntary as obligatory. Unless someone had an acceptable excuse, he had to apply. Acceptable excuses included conditions like blindness and other disabilities that rendered one useless. Because Taiming was beyond the upper age limit, this did not present a problem for him.

In spite of this environment, Fan obstinately resisted volunteering. Repeated exhortations by the branch chief proved ineffective, and eventually Fan was dismissed from his job. The day he left the association, he whispered this conviction to Taiming:

"When the flow of history is perverted, it is not in the power of the individual to stem it. But I want to at least transcend it."

Taiming was heartened by the surprising strength of spirit evident in his young friend's attitude. "Let's both stand firm and remain true to ourselves," he replied in encouragement.

After Fan's departure, Taiming suddenly was lonely. The desire to quit his meaningless job at the association only grew stronger with each day. One day, after work, Taiming wandered aimlessly through town. With no particular destination in mind, he simply walked wherever his feet took him. But there was nothing in the town of any interest to him. Nothing that he might ever want was to be found in these deteriorating streets. Eventually, he got tired of walking and entered a café.

He ordered black tea, which he had not had in a long time. There were quite a few customers in the shop. Taiming scanned the room as he sipped his tea but found no familiar faces. He drained the rest of his cup in one gulp. The reddish color of the tea reminded him of the red beverage of the mainland. His thoughts drifted unconsciously to his wife and child there. "I suppose Ziyuan must be getting big by now. She probably can't study properly, moving from place to place, with Shuchun fighting for the resistance." When he thought of them, intense paternal feelings welled up in Taiming, and his longing to return to the mainland grew even stronger. He felt sure that his presence in Taiwan—not to mention at the association—was utterly meaningless.

Suddenly, Taiming noticed that the man sitting in the opposite corner of the café was staring at him. The man looked familiar somehow, but Taiming could not place him at first. Then the man got up from his chair and came over. "Well, if it isn't Hu!" he said in greeting. At that moment, the man's voice stirred up an old memory in Taiming, and he realized that it was Sato. Taiming had met him long ago on the ship returning to Taiwan after graduating from the physics school. Back then, Sato had still been a young man and quite a bit thinner than he was now. They had spent only a few days together, but for some reason the man had left a strong impression on Taiming, and for quite a long time afterward Sato's astute opinions remained chiseled into Taiming's brain.

The two men were delighted at the unexpected meeting. Taiming learned that Sato had just recently come to Taipei. Sato strongly urged Taiming to leave Taiwan, where he had no friends. Taiming intended to follow Sato's advice and quit his job at the association, but for various reasons he was unable to do so immediately. He continued to wait for the right time.

One day it came. The chief clerk plopped down a file on Taiming's desk. It was meant as a message to Taiming and had to do with an exchange that had taken place between them several days earlier. The chief clerk had asked Taiming to "assist" him with peanuts. In plain language, this meant that he wanted Taiming to get peanuts for him. This was a standard trick used by the higher-ranking officials to obtain rare goods, and even though Taiming knew this, he did not provide the peanuts. The consequences of this insubordination soon would be made evident. Taiming quietly opened the file. The draft inside was covered with red lines. Taiming strained to make out the lettering underneath the edited sections, but it was completely unreadable.

The chief clerk and the head of accounting both liked to have a hand in writing draft bills, perhaps because of their lack of actual work. It was a way for them to leave their mark and show that they had looked over the materials. What it amounted to was a sort of editing for editing's sake. For example, if the log said "Y examination," they might rewrite it to say "Y inspection tour" instead. This time, however, was different. Every line had been crossed out in bright red and rewritten. No matter how he tried, Taiming could not make sense of the edited version. If it were published as an official document, it would only cause confusion at all the branch offices. Of course, the document had been approved, so it was not really Taiming's responsibility, but he still did not have the courage to submit it. As a precaution, Taiming showed the draft to the branch chief and asked for his opinion. The branch chief appeared to be surprised by the jumbled text. He immediately called over the chief clerk and asked for an explanation. When the branch chief heard what he had to say, he understood the intention behind the corrections and, with a wry smile, ordered it to be revised again.

Although the branch chief could dismiss the incident with a wry smile, soon another problem occurred that could not be dismissed so easily. One day, Taiming's boss called him over and gave him a thorough tongue-lashing. His castigation was unreasonable and blatantly emotional, and when he was done, he told Taiming, "You had better watch out. Just remember that."

Taiming was not interested in remembering anything. At this point, he had already made up his mind. He could not stand to remain in this atmosphere any longer. That day, he turned in his letter of resignation and left his job at the association.

For the first time in a long while, Taiming returned to his hometown. His father, Hu Wenqing, seemed to have aged a decade in the year that Taiming had not seen him. The villagers showed definite signs of malnutrition. Their cheekbones protruded, their eyes were hollow, and their complexions were wan. Their tattered clothing made them look all the more haggard. The one-pieces that had been popular for a while when the economy was good had disappeared, and everyone had returned to wearing traditional Taiwanese clothes. Whenever he ran into someone he knew, he would complain about the lack of food. Taiming was struck by how swiftly the world around him had changed, though he supposed that that was the nature of war.

For his part, Hu Wenqing was extremely pleased at Taiming's homecoming, and they stayed up until late at night talking in Taiming's room. Hu Wenqing expressed his uneasiness about the times.

"Taiming, I think we're really in a tight corner. What will become of us if things go on like this?"

Taiming's father, a doctor of Chinese medicine, had anxieties related to his occupation. His supply of medicines had been completely cut off when transportation was suspended. Substitutes did not work. For this reason, he was unable to prevent the deaths of many patients with treatable illnesses. In fact, under the circumstances, he felt that he could no longer call himself a doctor. Still, many people came to him for help, and he did not know how to treat them. The rationing of rice, in particular, had led to a rise in illnesses. A month's ration of rice did not last ten days even when made into porridge and eaten sparingly. Besides the problem with substitute medicines, there also was no other food available to supplement the rice, so nutrition was steadily declining. While meals dwindled, workloads doubled. Added to the weakened bodies and immune systems, the heavy public service requirements were devastating.

Such were the causes of Hu Wenqing's discontent. Now that he was old, he felt a strong desire to seek support from Taiming, and his tears flowed freely. "Taiming, the situation these days is worse than during the Qin dynasty," he said with a sigh. "The first emperor of the Qin used Shang Yang's reforms to make the country prosperous and strengthen the military. To keep the people ignorant, he burned books and buried Confucian scholars alive. He used people mercilessly to build the Great Wall of China. He instituted the *bao jia* system, which was like binding the people in iron chains. They say that it was the most despotic government that the Chinese people have ever known. Hu Wenqing repeated to Taiming the story of the construction of the Great Wall of China as it had been passed down to him.

San ding chou yi, wu chou er, dan ding du ẓi ta ai xing, he chanted.

In other words, one member in a family of three, two members in a family of five, and even single people and only sons were required to go to work on the wall. Drafting the laborers was made the collective responsibility of the neighborhood administrators, so that not a single person could escape it. Hu Wenqing was trying to say that in terms of numbers, the draft for military service, civilian work for the military, manufacturing, and public service work now exceeded one in three and two in five. In addition, with the currently seamless rationing system, the arbitrators wielded more power than ever before.

Taiming could not find any words to assuage his aged father's grief. All he could say was that if they were patient for a little while longer, things were bound to get better. But even Taiming could not say how long "a little while" might be.

Taiming's father was also plagued by the fear that if he were to die, they would be unlikely to obtain a proper coffin. "Mother was lucky. Back then, we still had the resources for a fine coffin and funeral," he said. "Taiming, I'd like to go ahead and buy a coffin now, before it's too late . . ." he proposed haltingly. His father had always been so strong, and Taiming felt an indescribable sadness to see his spirit so weakened.

Still, Taiming's father forged on, pushing his weakening body to perform his duties as a doctor. Each morning, his examining room was crammed with patients, most of whose complaints were attributable to overwork and poor diet. Taiming peeked into the room and was astonished by the extent to which the tragedy of war was displayed before him.

One patient rambled on to nobody in particular, telling his story: "I went to the government lands at Qing Puxi to do my public service work, but the hygiene there was terrible. There was excrement everywhere. You'd step out of the dormitory, and the fields and the hills were all completely covered in feces. Whenever I think of it, I become unable to swallow my food. Just look at what's become of my skin." Here, he pinched the flesh of his arm so that everyone could see.

Then, the woman sitting next to him picked up where he had left off. "Doctor, will my illness get better? I've become so weak . . ." she asked Hu Wenqing in a anxious voice. She had been married for six years, and she had never before been sick. Ever since her husband had been drafted the year before, she found herself unable to sleep at night. She worried about her husband and children every night until dawn, and her body had gradually gotten weaker and she had developed a pain in her chest. Every doctor she had seen had told her that she must not worry. "But I simply cannot stop worrying," she said, sighing deeply.

Hu Wenqing listened attentively to the complaints of each patient and comforted them as best he could. Then he turned to Taiming. "There is a verse of Tang poetry that says, 'In the midst of battle let not your mind wander, not to the sight of death shall you pander.' Perhaps the poet was speaking of a situation like this." His expression was utterly devoid of hope.

One night, Taiming received an invitation from a farmer he knew. The farmer wanted to treat Taiming to a meal to welcome him back to the village after his long absence. Taiming felt it would be ungrateful to refuse such a kindness, so he walked all the way to the farmer's house in the dark of the night. When he arrived, he discovered four or five farmers, all familiar faces, seated around the dim, flickering light of a bamboo lantern. When they saw Taiming, they all stood up and offered him a seat. As soon as he was seated, one of them asked him, "Sir, wasn't it rough living in the city where there are no mountain pigs?" "Mountain pig" was slang for black market pigs.

Now another man spoke. "Sir," he called, and then he dropped his voice to a whisper. "Tonight, here at my place . . ." he trailed off, and with his hands, made a motion to indicate killing a pig.

They were preparing a feast for Taiming. After they told him the plan for the secret butchering, everyone sat and waited for the night to advance.

At around eleven o'clock, a brimming pot of water was simmering on the stove and three farmers slipped off to the pig shed. There was a slight sound, and then the stillness of the night was restored. In only ten minutes, they had trapped the pig in a cage. They then dropped the pig, cage and all, into the lake. The pig could not so much as squeal. The only sound was the burble of air bubbles coming up through the water. After a few moments, the bubbling stopped and the lake was still again. The men pulled the cage out and carried it back to the house. Taiming was awed by the simplicity of it all. As a child, he had seen pigs butchered every year for the festival of the dead in mid-July. A sharp knife would be thrust into the pig's throat, and the pig would squeal and squeal at the top of its lungs. When the butchering went badly, it sometimes took a long time for the pig to die. This memory from his childhood made Taiming all the more impressed by the ingenuity of the secret slaughter.

They poured boiling water over the drowned pig, and it grew visibly whiter. When they slit open its belly, neighbors began to show up quietly without having been called, and each was given a portion to take home. Taiming was presented with several pounds. When they were done parceling out the meat, the farmers immediately began to prepare the feast.

"Sir, wait until you taste the flavor of freshly roasted pork," said the one who was cutting the meat. He brandished a piece of meat for Taiming to see, and indeed it looked as if it still might have life in it. Taiming expected the cooking to be amateur and clumsy. When the food was ready, the farmer served up a bowl of it and offered it to Taiming.

Taiming took a mouthful and was surprised at how good it was. He did not know whether it was because his taste buds were starving or because the cooking was good, but in any case, it was the most delicious thing he had ever tasted. Now he devoured the meat voraciously and without hesitation, washing it down with saké. As he ate, he listened to his hosts talk and learned that the workings of the black market had become very sophisticated and that it was so airtight that there was no fear of discovery. The entire village was starving, so nobody would think of informing. If there was one thing that every villager agreed on, it was having the black market. In addition, everyone anticipated even worse times ahead, and they were keenly aware of the need to rally together as a community. This was how the weak protected themselves. Like the starving chicken in the fable that persists in stealing food no matter how much it is beaten, starving people, too, have no fear. It was a lesson for Taiming.

The next day, Taiming went to visit his elder brother, Zhigang, at the office where he worked. The arbitrators were meeting to discuss the ration price of duck meat. Each district, which consisted of ten households, was to be allotted four ducks. The black market price for ducks, however, was actually ten times cheaper than the regular market price, so nobody would be willing to buy the ducks for that amount. The officials were trying to devise a strategy to solve the problem. In the end, they decided to mark down the ducks toward the black market price and let each household absorb some of the losses.

After reaching this decision, one of the older men turned to Taiming and complained, "Sir, we are always having to pay illegal taxes. In the old days, there were outlaws who stole from the rich to feed the poor, but now they rob the poor and feed the rich. I'm seventy years old, and I've never experienced anything like this." The man was referring to the fact that Japanese people and families that spoke Japanese received extra rations of meat and vegetables. In his eyes, this amounted to robbing the poor to feed the rich.

Overhearing the man's comments, Zhigang immediately rebuked him. "What are you saying? Even our children do not belong to us. They belong to the state. Think of the people who have been drafted before you complain about something like rationing."

The senior arbitrator apologized profusely. As always, Taiming felt alienated by his brother's attitude, and he left without even saying a proper good-bye.

Then there was another incident. One day, Taiming was taking a walk near a pond that was owned by Stingy Wang, the village miser. Several unfamiliar young men wearing the national uniform were fishing in the pond. At first Taiming thought that they were policemen, but then he saw that they were civil servants. Each of the men had several large mullets in his basket. As Taiming watched, one of the men caught another one.

Stingy Wang will be furious if he sees this, thought Taiming. But after walking a little ways, Taiming ran into the miser himself. As it turned out, Wang already knew about the young men fishing in his pond. "Those dogs from the municipal office, they're like the devil incarnate!" he sobbed to Taiming. Even Stingy Wang was unable to stand up to this bunch. They oversaw everything from the rationing of rice to general mobilization. If a person got on their bad side, they would repossess more of his assets and deal him other underhanded blows. Since the beginning of the war, the municipal officials had acquired even more power, and now they were as fearsome a bunch as the police. The gang from the municipal office and his brother Zhigang were all the same, taking liberties with their increased authority.

Taiming also had another unpleasant encounter. After a long absence, Zhida came back to the village from Hainan Island. He brought with him a beautiful young woman who, he claimed, was the daughter of a millionaire. He went from house to house, visiting relatives and friends and boasting. According to Zhida, upon his arrival in Hainan, he had used the shrewdness and tact he had cultivated in his many years as a lawyer's interpreter and made a fortune. A millionaire had been impressed and given Zhida his daughter to be his second wife.

One day, Zhida came to visit Taiming. The girl was indeed

quite lovely. But Taiming, who had spent time on the mainland, could see that the girl lacked refinement and could not have come from a rich family. Zhida was wise enough not to try his big fish story on a connoisseur of Chinese culture like Taiming. Taiming was able to infer from what Zhida told him that in fact, he had been only a military detective for the Japanese. Zhida used to be police officer, so it seemed to Taiming like a logical explanation.

As they were talking, Zhida made a point of showing off his fancy foreign gold watch to Taiming. He claimed it was given to him by an important official. Taiming was repulsed by this display.

After Zhida left, Hu Wenqing asked dubiously, "What do you make of that?" His comment was weighty with meaning and could be interpreted in a number of ways. Taiming considered his father's comment and then replied:

"In the end, Zhida is no better than military notes that have no resources to back them up." By this, Taiming was comparing Zhida to the military notes now being issued in the south, in that both were untrustworthy and would no doubt steadily decrease in value until they were worthless.

A look of agreement showed on Hu Wenqing's face, and he grunted his assent. He added, "It doesn't matter where a person of poor quality goes," openly maligning Zhida's character. Taiming felt that Zhida and all those who were opportunistically profiting from the current situation were the worst kind of hedonistic egoists.

Taiming had been home for only a short time, but he had been confronted with many realizations. However, he chose not to let them upset him. Rather, he considered these developments to be inevitable in light of the current transition. Taiming resolved inwardly to concentrate on being true to himself rather than to indulge in futile brooding.

5. The Lair of Tigers and Wolves

When they had unexpectedly met some time ago, Sato had suggested to Taiming that he visit him, and Taiming decided to take him up on the offer. Sato had also asked him at that time to help him with the journal he was editing.

Sato was greatly pleased by Taiming's visit. He was even more pleased to hear that Taiming had left the association. He immediately began to explain that his purpose in publishing the journal was to make a positive difference without falling afoul of the government's extreme censorship rules.

"History has reached a turning point, but for anything to happen, the time must be ripe. Infantile antics aren't going to accomplish anything. We need to settle down and focus our attention on the essentials. It's very easy merely to take a stand against the status quo, but it's also self-defeating, suicidal in fact. Instead, I think it's necessary to pretend to cooperate while gradually making our readers understand the truth."

Taiming agreed with this view. He began to feel tremendous respect for this man Sato, whose sensibilities were so far removed from those of the other Japanese he had met. He decided that the two of them together could truly accomplish something.

He immediately joined Sato's journal. His job was to visit intellectuals in Taipei to commission articles suitable for the journal. It wasn't terribly difficult work, but it did take quite a bit of effort to establish connections with those people. As he got used to it, however, he came to feel that it was far more worthwhile than the time he had wasted at the association. He felt real excitement at the mere thought of sending their journal out into the world.

During lulls in their work, Sato would often share his predictions about the course the war would take. Taiming was left speechless by his penetrating analysis and insight, and indeed, things unfolded just as Sato said they would. The Allies landed at Normandy, and then came the string of reports from the Pacific that Makin, Tarawa, and Saipan all had fallen in "honorable defeat." The political developments were just as chaotic as the military ones: in the face of such harsh reality, complacent official pronouncements about the certainty of victory soon disappeared.

A sense of foreboding began to fill the air. One day in the midst of all of this, Taiming and Sato were walking together down the street. The summer sunlight glistened on the baking hot asphalt. They heard a chorus of voices coming up behind them, singing a Pacific War marching song: an Imperial Training Squad made up of young Taiwanese cadets was passing through. Because the two men were walking slowly, the squad quickly caught up with and passed them. They were marching in four orderly columns, but their uniforms were in tatters and their appearance in general was almost pathetic. As he watched them march past, Sato remarked, "Just look at that. They look like the battered leftovers of a defeated army. And those women!"

He was referring to a group of Japanese women walking along the road in their finest kimono. "What a contrast, eh?" he said to Taiming. No further words were necessary for them to know that they were thinking the same thing.

For a trenchant critic like Sato, everything, but everything, presented an opportunity for a blistering remark. That included the training drills of the Home Fire Prevention Group, which, according to him, were a perfect example of the mind-set of the hopelessly unscientific Japanese, a product of idiotic spiritualism.

Come to think of it, he added, the long, winding lines of finely dressed Japanese housewives and pompous gentlemen in front of the sweet shops and restaurants would soon have those superior expressions wiped off their faces and come to feel the same misery as did the Taiwanese themselves.

The two of them reached the Sakae district and walked into a coffee shop. Although it was a large place, it still was packed with customers. Sato, who appeared to be a regular there, stood at the door as he scanned the room trying to see if he recognized anyone. A man in the corner stood up and beckoned to him.

"Hey there," Sato shouted out. Taiming accompanied Sato toward the man, who appeared to have a companion also. They both were newspaper reporters, and Taiming noticed that they were wearing badges showing that they were members of the Literary Patriots' Association. Taiming was honestly impressed at the thought that here were two bona fide authors.

When they all had settled into their seats, the conversation soon turned to literature. Taiming enjoyed classical Chinese poetry, so he certainly wasn't uninterested in the topic, but he didn't know very much about contemporary and foreign literature or recent literary trends. Everything they said seemed fresh and new to his ears, and he tried to listen with a modest, unassuming air. One of the two writers, noticing his interest, began expounding on Maupassant, Balzac, and Russian literature. The writer's tone was somewhat patronizing, but Taiming couldn't help but feel overwhelmed by his extensive knowledge. He was elated to think that he had caught a glimpse of a new and unknown world.

In due course the four of them got up and left the coffee shop. Sato let his two acquaintances walk in front while he whispered in Taiming's ear:

"Hu-san, you're really impressed, aren't you? Don't be. I'll let you in on a secret: he's just regurgitating what he read in the introduction to some anthology of world literature." There was that pitiless tone of disparagement again. Although Taiming had great respect for Sato's critical eye and keen powers of observation, in this case he found Sato's insistence on bursting his bubble to be distasteful. Even something as valuable as exposure should be kept within certain limits, he thought. After spending some time with the reporters at the offices of their newspaper, how-ever, Taiming felt he was beginning to understand what Sato was trying to say.

It appeared that a deadline was approaching and the reporters at the office were busy at work finishing their manuscripts. They didn't care a whit that visitors had entered the office and pre-tended, with crass self-importance, to be absorbed in their work. The two reporters led Taiming and Sato through the office to a corner where lay a bound book of slogans. Made at the request of the Propaganda Bureau, these were intended to whip up war sentiment. The more "literary" of the reporters flipped through the pages of the book, stopping at each example of his own hand-iwork and asking, "So what do you think of this one? Pretty good, huh?" while he looked back and forth at Taiming and Sato. Taiming realized that no real man of letters would behave in this way. Sensing something unspeakably vulgar about the man, he couldn't stop his expression from growing stiff and cold. At the same time, he began to recognize just how superficial and preten-tious the lecture on literature back at the coffee shop had been. Sato had been right after all. The slogans, too, seemed like noth-ing more than insincere puffery, which of course made the man seem even more disagreeable. He had avoided the sacrifices of practical action while using his pen to give everything a glossy sheen. Braggarts like this man, Taiming felt, were the ones who always took the easy way out. He wondered how many naïve young men this fool had misled with his empty rhetoric. All these thoughts somehow made the air in the newspaper office difficult to breath.

"What a bunch of jackasses," Sato spit out when they finally were able to leave.

He looked at Taiming and continued, "Hu-san, back at the cof-fee shop you were almost in awe of that man. The thought that *he* represents the spirit of literature would be enough to drive a real literary man to tears. Writers today can't have a conscience. If you *do* have a conscience, you can't write. Back during the Russo-Japanese War, authors still had a measure of humanity and could produce superior works like *A Common Soldier.* But people whose eyes are as clouded as those of our writers today simply cannot see the sheer horror of reality, and so they happily dance around as the army's marionettes." He stopped as if he had suddenly thought of something and then continued, "Remember when he said that you have to do such-and-such to succeed in literature? He seems to think of literature as some kind of business. Literature is not about whether or not the individual 'succeeds'; it's about whether or not you make some kind of contribution to humanity.

"Worthless people like him have no business working on a newspaper. People are constantly writing these days about what to do with the Taiwanese. For anybody who knows the true state of affairs, it's a ridiculous question to ask. The current system just imports worthless cowards from Japan. Even the lowliest Japanese reporter makes a base salary of 195 yen a month, I hear. Add to that a 50 percent bonus. An editor in chief makes 1,000 yen plus a bonus of 500 yen. Yet a first-class Taiwanese section chief makes only 140 yen plus change. And they dare to splash big headlines in the newspapers about 'Improving Treatment of the Locals.' It seems that they want everybody in the world to work for them for such a pittance. What do you think, Hu-san?"

He was indulging again in one of his characteristic diatribes. But this time Taiming didn't feel the same resistance as he did before. He felt that those writers of the day who had lost the true literary spirit, who merely turned out "timely" works that answered the demands of the age but had no deeper substance, would probably be flayed by the critics of a future era. And he swore to himself that he wouldn't write for fame and fortune, that in such times it was best to be honest and uncalculating.

After Saipan fell, Taiwan's entire population of 6.7 million was called on to help fortify the island's defenses, and all Taiwanese up to the age of sixty were mobilized to build fortifications.

Taiming also received a mobilization order and, as instructed, attended the meeting of the Homeland Defense Volunteers' Association. The draftees were packed tightly into the main auditorium of the town hall. There were seats on the second floor for those who, for whatever reason, were incapable of participating in a volunteer unit. Thanks to a special arrangement that Sato had made on his behalf, Taiming went directly to wait on the second floor with a certificate of exemption in hand. The meeting began with the usual playing of the imperial anthem and words of greeting from the presiding authorities. The military and bureaucratic representatives then explained the goals of the volunteers' association, followed by rallying speeches made by the heads of the Imperial Service Association. Taiwanese employees of the empire took turns exhorting the group to sacrifice themselves for the great cause of defending the nation. Thunderous applause greeted each of these rallying cries.

Once the main meeting had ended, the thousands of citizens present were divided into their various fortification construction units and assigned to unit leaders. The only people left unassigned were the thousand or so people on the upper floor, all of whom were carrying exemption certificates or were sick or disabled. Almost all those with certificates were local males. Taiming waited along with the others for the officials to come and check his papers.

Eventually, five or six officials from the city government came up to the second floor. They looked like Japanese reservists. One of them stood in the middle of the group and started giving directions. He was wearing a veteran's badge conspicuously on his chest, and from the very beginning he exuded quite a menacing air. He was nearly shouting as he angrily explained to them how to line up to have their papers checked. The group listened in frightened silence. The supervisor then raised his voice higher to say:

"Everybody line up now. Starting from the first row, those on the left side go to the left, those on the right side go to the right and wait in front of the inspector."

Since he didn't make clear whether he meant the first vertical row or the first horizontal row, people in both rows started moving. The people in the left column began standing up from front to back while those in the first row began standing from left to right. The supervisor ran over and started to box seven or eight people on the ears, excoriating them for not following orders. One of the men dared to retort, "But we did what you told us!"

Without waiting for him to finish, the supervisor screamed "Idiot!" and slapped him on the cheek. Nobody said anything, but they all felt burning indignation at the supervisor's brutish behavior. One could sense a silent resistance beginning to crackle within their ranks.

After about two hours, Taiming was finally able to leave the town hall. He was in a daze, perhaps because the stress and commotion of the assembly had worn him out. The others leaving the building with him all looked ashen.

Half a month passed. Taiming received yet another order to attend a meeting of the Homeland Defense Volunteers' Association. This was a full-day Sunday meeting that required all government employees and stipend recipients, Taiwanese and Japanese as well, to attend.

Sunday eventually arrived, and they all assembled at 5 a.m. They were split up into work squads and set out. Taiming was given a gardening hoe and joined the rest of his group.

They looked as lifeless as a herd of sheep being led to slaughter. They had barely gone half a mile when they were so tired that they broke out of formation and were walking so slowly that they were overtaken by a group of farmers.

Even though they were carrying all their heavy tools, the farmers were full of life. As they passed, they turned back to look at Taiming's group, and one of them said, "Even a bunch of pale weaklings like that is being mobilized. Things must really be getting bad."

Finally they arrived at the public grounds where another group was already at work. They were a Patriotic Volunteers' Squad that had been mobilized from the countryside, and they were digging and lifting with great vigor. Taiming's group from the city, however, didn't have all the required tools and so had to dig out lumps of clay with their bare hands and pass them in a relay from one person to another.

Taiming's squad was made up entirely of government stipend recipients. The squad leader divided them into one group whose job was to move clay using wheelbarrows and another group whose job was to dig. Taiming was sent to the wheelbarrow group, where his partner was a young, healthy Taiwanese municipal employee. The young man was incredibly energetic, trying to run from one place to another while Taiming slowed him down with his own, labored pace. Eventually his partner lost patience and went so far as to complain to the squad leader that Taiming was slacking on the job. The leader immediately demanded an explanation.

Taiming quickly replied: "I've been having stomach problems since last night. I can't help it." This was a complete lie, of course.

"I see. I guess if you're ill, there's nothing to be done." The squad leader was unexpectedly understanding. "Take a break then, since you're sick."

Thus released from his labor, Taiming sat beneath a tree and watched the others work. "This is not shrinking from difficulty—this, too, is a form of passive resistance," he thought to himself. Two Japanese passed by without noticing him under the tree. One said loudly to the other, "We should let the chinks do all the work, they seem to be pretty good at it."

"Yeah. They're like oxen."

Taiming felt the blood rush to his face.

The next day, Sato joked, "How's the work coming? Have you been able to build an airfield with that hoe yet?" He continued seriously, asking, "So what do you think about these fortifications? Are they really going to slow down the Americans?"

Taiming replied, "I think the Japanese army wants to fight from Taiwan. In that way they can take advantage of the resources and people here. During the Wushe uprising, for example, they persuaded people from the surrounding Fanshe tribe to attack the Wushe and even got Wang Jingwei involved from the mainland. Basically, their strategy was to 'use the barbarian to defeat the barbarian.' What's more, Taiwan is uniquely suited for these kinds of fortifications. But the problem is that the Americans don't consider Taiwan very important: it's not going to have much effect on the main theater of combat. Although the fortification of Taiwan won't help the Japanese much, it certainly will help the Taiwanese."

Taiming had shared all his thoughts without pause or hesitation. Sato laughed and replied, "So, in other words, Japan's evil intentions will reap good effects." He seemed to approve of Taiming's interpretation. He leaned back in his easy chair and looked up at the ceiling. Another thought seemed to occur to him:

"Let's charge the wolves' den today!" he said, tossing away his cigarette and jumping to his feet.

Taiming assumed that by "wolves' den" Sato meant the headquarters of the Imperial Service Association. He simply followed him without asking many questions and thus was surprised when they arrived at their destination: the university.

"Why is this the wolves' den?" he thought to himself. It was only after Sato finished his business there and they left that Taiming understood what Sato had meant.

Taiming recalled that four or five days earlier, the chancellor of the university and one of the professors had published a piece on Japanese-language education in the newspaper. They argued that in order for the process of colonization to be carried out, the Taiwanese language must be completely eradicated. It was a preposterous notion, unbecoming of any scholar worthy of the name, and spoke volumes about the degree to which these scholars for hire would say anything to toe the party line and curry favor. Considered in that light, this place was indeed the "wolves' den." Many of the recently appointed imperial functionaries were graduates of this university, and many of the advisers to the Imperial Patriotic Association had been drawn from its professors. This university was the headquarters where the rationalizations and the psychological weaponry for colonial exploitation were devised. The professors here were faithful to neither their academic disciplines nor the truth but to policies handed down by the colonial administration—so that when they were told, against all reason, to standardize the rice-planting methods across the entire island, the university's agriculture department didn't utter a word of protest. The spirit of scholarly inquiry was already dead here: the supreme achievement was to be a stooge for colonial policy. While wearing the mask of a sanctuary of learning, it played the role of a bestial predator.

At the beginning of October, there was a massive air raid.

Since the main targets were military facilities, though, the civilians in the city were not in danger. The American invasion of Leyte followed soon thereafter. This in turn started a ferocious counteroffensive by the imperial forces. It was around this time that the Japanese started looking hounded by fate. Even the building of the governor-general, the symbol of Japanese imperialism, appeared to be dressed in doleful mourning clothes.

The situation for the Japanese grew progressively worse by the day. One day Sato suddenly exclaimed, "The Germans at this point are doing nothing more than putting up brute, animal resistance. It's all just senseless sacrifice. Watch closely: we're seeing a major turning point in history."

After sharing his critique of the state of the conflict, he added, "I'm actually thinking of returning to Japan."

He felt that he had to return to Japan now to prepare for the new circumstances that lay ahead. Taiming could guess from Sato's everyday words and actions just what he meant when he spoke of "new circumstances." Taiming was sad that he and Sato would have to part, but he also knew that Sato was firmly set in his decision and that there was nothing he could do to stop him. He had to allow Sato to find the place and the opportunities that would make his work most meaningful. He had to do the noble thing and give Sato the best possible send-off into his new life. Now that Sato's journal had more or less met its stated objective, there was no reason for him to remain here any longer.

When the time finally came for Sato to leave, Taiming invited him to a modest farewell dinner. The two of them drank heavily and talked into the night. Sato took Taiming's hand and said:

"Hu-san, I like honest people like you, I really do. I won't forget you as long as I live. But you're too much of a poet, you're too pure, you're not good at dealing with reality. Please try to work on that from now on. Theory without practice is just empty, you know."

That was his parting advice, given from the heart.

6. The Sorrow of Imperial Sympathizers

Taiming returned to his hometown again. He had remained in Taipei for a while after Sato's return to Japan in order to put the journal's affairs in order, but once that was done, it was time to go back. He was sad to see the journal discontinued, but a shortage of materials and other factors had already made it impossible to go on. In any event, the aims with which Sato had started the journal had already been realized to some extent.

He had no regrets: they had fought with all they had. When the time came to return home to his birthplace, he was satisfied with all they had accomplished, but he had to suppress a bit of sadness as he boarded the train.

Two or three days after he arrived home, Deputy Mayor Azuma and a couple of officials came calling at Zhigang's arbitration office, demanding donations. All the stingy citizens of the precinct were called. Unfortunately, Hu Wenqing was in bed with the flu, so Taiming went in his father's place. Once they were assembled, the deputy mayor began his oratory.

"Our village has been able to make great strides since entering the Great Pacific War. We have progressed from merely devoting ourselves to the cause to accepting the great duty of dying for our country. This voluntary mobilization effort is a true manifestation of the idea of 'A Hundred Million Hearts Beating as One.' You all have done me, your humble deputy mayor, a great honor. In particular, a certain doctor in our village donated more than ten thousand yen. Now, today, I've walked a long way around the village, but if those of you assembled here today could see fit to make a contribution, however small, yours would be the greater honor," he said, and glanced around at all the men.

Then he continued, "Right now, our country is truly facing a crisis. No, it is facing mortal danger. The enemy is peering at us with the eyes of a hungry tiger. 'Fortress Taiwan' could turn into 'Battlefield Taiwan' overnight, and that would just be the beginning. Our 6.7 million people must rouse themselves to action, united as one. We must be willing to endure any sacrifice and suffering that is necessary to meet the demands of the situation. This is our duty as citizens. Since you all are good, loyal citizens, I'm sure you already understand the aims of this general mobilization effort. There's no need for me to give you a tedious lecture. The point is simply this: if you don't want to be censured as being unpatriotic, it would be *best* to understand what the times call for and step forward of your own volition to make a donation."

The word *unpatriotic* resonated especially strongly in people's minds. The officials from the municipal office started going around from person to person asking for contributions. After listening to the deputy mayor's veiled threats, nobody could really be sure what to do. Nonetheless, they all asked to be excused, citing household financial circumstances and other reasons, but to no avail. Two or three of them continued to make relentless appeals, and in the end they were forced to affix their personal seals to promissory notes agreeing to pay later. Since Taiming was there in place of his father, they came to him last. Hu Wenqing was a doctor and was therefore expected to pay more than twice the average household tax, or a thousand yen. Taiming insisted that his family should only make the normal contribution, since his father was a doctor of traditional Chinese medicine and therefore made much less than a doctor practicing Western medicine; furthermore, Hu Wenqing could no longer make house calls because of his age and was losing income because of that.

The deputy mayor turned red. "Mr. Hu is a graduate of the top college of this country and has even studied on the mainland. He is one of the pioneers of this community. Never in my wildest dreams did I imagine he would make such limp excuses."

Taiming started to feel himself boil over at the deputy mayor's disagreeable remarks but was able to suppress his anger and maintain his composure. He replied, "Mr. Deputy Mayor, you are using that doctor you mentioned earlier as the standard, making an unwritten law out of his example, and then attacking us for not living up to it. There is a significant difference between doctors of Western and Chinese medicine.

"Western doctors receive medicine rations from the authorities at prices set by law. Despite that, they've recently started making a profit by selling those same medicines at three or four times the price they paid. As if that weren't bad enough, they go so far as to wrap the medicine in red or blue paper and tell their patients it is 'special medicine for the nobility' and then charge an additional five or ten yen per dose. In other words they squeeze their patients dry. *Of course* it'll be easy for them to come up with ten thousand yen to contribute. A doctor of Chinese medicine, on the other hand, is paid only for examinations and diagnoses: thirty *sen* per visit. Even if you see ten people, you'll barely make just three yen. Ten patients per day is about the best that a doctor can do here in the countryside. The practice of medicine is supposed to be a humanitarian act, not some moneymaking scheme. Thinking of it as such is the first mistake, from which others will inevitably follow. Surely a man as wise as you can understand that much," Taiming calmly explained.

The deputy mayor had no intention of giving up that easily. He brought up Hu Wenqing's property holdings and repeated his demand for a larger-than-normal contribution. Taiming once again had to launch into an explanation, making clear that after taxes, national savings deductions, and other unreasonable levies, barely one hundred yen of income from the land was left. Yet the deputy mayor refused to stop grumbling and complaining. Taiming finally lost his temper and shot back: "Mr. Deputy Mayor, in asking for our contributions you have mentioned that other doctor as an example, which is all well and good. But I would expect that a venerable and patriotic man of character like yourself must have made a truly sizable contribution as well. I know it's terribly rude of me, but might I ask you to enlighten us by making public exactly how much *you* contributed?"

The deputy mayor backed down. Taiming had realized that the man was a hypocrite who would never do as much as he demanded of others. With that, the sum required of Hu Wenqing was reduced to the same amount demanded of everybody else. The rest of the group took keen delight in the way Taiming had put the deputy mayor in his place and mercilessly made fun of him. One of them said, "'Deputy Mayor!' Hah! A native gets a little bit of status and now he couldn't care less whether we all drop dead."

There were quite a few people like the deputy mayor, but there were also those who sincerely wanted to assimilate and very honestly tried to bridge the gap between the Japanese and the natives.

Taiming's friend from public school, Instructor Li, was one such person. One day he came to visit Taiming. They hadn't seen each other in twenty years, and Li had aged so much that he looked like a completely different person. He had even taken the Japanese name Yoshimura. He was still working as a teacher, but recently he had been feeling unfulfilled in various ways.

"I've been teaching for twenty years now, and I've even been fortunate enough to be decorated for my service. This entire time I've worked faithfully for the colonial assimilation movement. It goes without saying that I've also worked for the adoption of the Japanese language; I even changed my name against my parents' objections. It was easy to do when I considered that the sacrifices of our generation would turn into wealth and good fortune for my children and grandchildren. But is that really the case? It seems that the harder we work to move in that direction, the further we are from the goal. The Japanese have a long tradition and history, but we Taiwanese have neither. That's a difference that can't be overcome no matter what we do. It seems like I'm working as hard as possible to do something that no amount of human effort can accomplish."

He smiled sadly. He couldn't bring himself to say, simply, that all his efforts had been foolish and in vain. At the very least, though, here was a man who was nursing a worry in earnest, a worry that was bound up with the tragedy of the Taiwanese people. Taiming could say nothing to comfort him and so remained in a state of gloomy silence.

7. A Certain Decision

Zhigang's son Daxiong suddenly returned home from the university one day. He had decided to enlist in the army. Zhigang, who was intoxicated with the whole idea of assimilation, was quite happy to hear this. His wife, on the other hand, tearfully tried to persuade him otherwise, but Daxiong was firmly resolved on his course of action, and his mother's pleas fell on deaf ears. On the contrary, he merely dismissed her incomprehension with a curt "Don't be so old-fashioned."

She didn't give up. She went to Hu Wenqing, asking him to use his way with words to sway her son, but neither his theoretical reasoning nor sheer persuasiveness was enough to change Daxiong's mind. Finally she turned to Taiming, who replied, "OK, I'll see what I can do."

Taiming met with Daxiong. Daxiong assumed that Taiming, like the others, would try to make him change his mind and came to the meeting with a rather stubborn attitude. Taiming sensed this and so he began:

"Daxiong, let's have a leisurely little chat today. Here is some famous tea I brought back from the mainland. It's quite unusual, so you really should try it. I don't have anything else to bring to send you off on your new life, so I hope it will be enough."

Taiming laughed casually and Daxiong's mood began to soften.

Taiming continued: "Daxiong, enlisting in the army is truly a noble course of action. I'm just curious, though; would you mind telling me what made you decide to do this?"

Daxiong enthusiastically began to explain his convictions. The time had come, he argued, for the Taiwanese to endure great tribulations in order to prove that they could become real Japanese. The litmus test would be how well they fought in the "holy war" (he used those words) that was now being waged. It was his generation's great ambition to sacrifice themselves for the liberation of East Asia's one billion people.

As far as theoretical justifications go, his was really elementary. "Here we have yet another credulous young fool!" Taiming thought to himself, staring painfully at his nephew.

Daxiong was no different from those young men who marched loudly through the streets singing war songs—crude, violent lads who had forgotten even their own humanity. Taiming always felt a chill when he saw their faces, one indistinguishable from the other, all of them like robots. Yet Daxiong was his brother's son, his own flesh and blood. More than that, Taiming felt he had to try to somehow save this sorely misguided young man. An indescribable feeling of urgency began to well up within him when he considered what was at stake.

He began by explaining that the idealized notion of "Reforming the Self, Regulating the Household, and Governing the Nation Leads to Peace under Heaven" had been overtaken by militarism long ago. This happened because the nation's fundamental ideology was nothing more than a mess of contradictions, and things had been corrupted even more in recent times. Capitalism was the foundation of this social formation, which had developed by seeking out colonies and oppressing weaker ethnic groups. Nazi Germany was locked into an even more narrow-minded worldview than Japan was, in which delusions of absolute racial supremacy had given birth to dreams of world conquest. In the midst of all of this, Taiwan was being exploited not only materially but spiritually as well.

"Daxiong. Look at the reality in front of our eyes," Taiming said in an increasingly vehement tone of voice. "They tell us to become Japanese, and at the same time, they run the country like gangsters, making us helpless to do anything at all. Isn't that so? Right now you're planning to go throw your life away fighting this war. For what? For whom? Please think it over very carefully."

Without his noticing, Taiming's tone had become very passionate, but there was nothing he could do about it. He was naturally a ruminative sort, and he rarely could explain his beliefs to others with such flowing eloquence. This time, however, he had a clear objective: to save a young man from the depths of delusion.

The mass murder that had taken place during the war had been rationalized and even made heroic in the name of "the nation." Every possible contradiction had originated in the belly of "the nation." Taking "the nation" as a presupposition had distorted the study of history; textbooks were nothing more than propaganda meant to justify the nation and to protect its power. In short, the curriculum from elementary school to university was nothing more than a continual reiteration of that propaganda. This education had accustomed people to the idea of nationhood until it became a custom and then finally a system unto itself. The purpose of such a system is to cast human beings into one identical mold. Those who refuse to be made over in such fashion are labeled heretics and troublemakers. Taiming used the example of foot binding in China to explain how this kind of thing happened. Feet that had been bound had long been regarded as a standard of beauty, and its morality was never questioned. The entire society never doubted that it was something both good and beautiful. But once society came in contact with the more progressive Western culture, that way of thinking crumbled. A new standard of beauty and morality took its place, and with the abolition of foot binding, a chapter in the history of the liberation of Chinese women was closed. One could see from this example how systems made people blind. Once again Taiming seized upon the problem of nations and the confrontations among nations. He declared that if society progressed to the point that those confrontations disappeared, the need for war would disappear along with them. If that time came, war would become nothing more than a barbaric practice existing only in history books.

Taiming's denunciation of war was nothing more than a conceptual abstraction, but at least it was one informed by the highest ideals. And since Daxiong was himself intoxicated by a conceptual abstraction, albeit one of a different sort, and since this abstraction was the foundation of his actions, Taiming's method of countering it perhaps would have some effect.

When Taiming had completed his long and impassioned speech, Daxiong sighed deeply and looked flushed, as if he had just woken up from a dream. Taiming's explanation seemed to strike him with the freshness of a revelation. Barely able to suppress his admiration, he said, "Uncle, your thinking is really quite unusual. The Reds are no match."

"My thinking is neither red nor black. I simply try to accept what is natural as natural and see reality as reality. It's just a matter of admitting the obvious. To have the courage to acknowledge the facts is the first qualification of an intellectual, isn't it?"

Taiming looked at Daxiong and smiled a smile that penetrated the heart. It seemed that his words made sense to Daxiong.

"Uncle, I'm beginning to understand. I'm going to think it through carefully," Daxiong said, staring intently at the ground. Taiming felt that he had finally achieved something concrete in the real world, a genuine act of persuasion, and he felt like thanking somebody for it.

8. Sacrifice

The next afternoon an army truck stopped in front of the Hu house, and a man was carried out on a stretcher. The members of the household ran out in alarm to see what had happened. It was Ah-Yu's son, Zhinan.

Zhinan had been summoned to serve in an Imperial Service Squad the month before and had been working at a construction site that was on public grounds. He had collapsed from overwork. Sanitary conditions at the site were bad and there were no doctors. His health had steadily deteriorated, and when he reached the point that he could no longer work, he was sent back home under guard. He was now unconscious on the stretcher. His gaunt face was deathly pale; he looked so wretched that one couldn't even tell that it was him unless one looked very closely. The thought that he had been forced to put his seal against his will on the so-called Volunteer Application Form was now painful beyond words.

The household was thrown into chaos. Hu Wenqing did a quick check of Zhinan's condition and realized that he needed immediate attention; he rushed to town in a panic to call the Western-style doctor. Zhinan was too far gone to be helped much by Hu Wenqing's traditional Chinese medicine. The doctor quickly arrived and administered three shots of a cardiac stimulant. He reviewed Zhinan's case and gave his prognosis. One could tell simply from the expression on his face that Zhinan was in grave danger.

From the moment that Zhinan was carried in, Taiming burned with a fierce rage at something he couldn't quite name. Who on earth did this to him? It would have been one thing if Zhinan had freely volunteered to serve, but his application had been squeezed out of him by force and deception, and now the state they'd sent him home in . . . the irresponsibility, the outrageousness of it all, was too much to bear.

In the evening, perhaps from the effects of the stimulant, Zhinan finally regained consciousness. He looked at the people gathered around his bed, going slowly from face to face. His eyes rested on Taiming. "Big brother," he said in a feeble voice.

"Zhinan, what has happened to you? Please, try to be strong."

"There's no hope. Please, carry on without me. How unfortunate that it . . . should end like this . . ."

He turned to Hu Wenqing and to his mother, Ah-Yu.

"Father, mother . . . good-bye . . ."

He gasped violently and suddenly, all too suddenly, breathed his last.

Ah-Yu broke into tears. Hu Wenqing, as could be expected,

restrained himself but whispered, "Heavens!" under his breath, his eyes tightly shut.

Taiming felt his body assailed by an ominous feeling that made him shiver to the bone. It was not merely a feeling of sadness but, rather, something much deeper, a cry of grief that swelled up from the depths of his soul. Zhinan's silent corpse, twisted and contorted by his final agony, seemed to Taiming to be making some sort of an accusation.

His brother's death forced Taiming to confront a problem he had long avoided but could not any longer. This was an unnatural death: Zhinan had become a compliant victim and lost his still-young life. He had accepted this as a given, had believed it to be fate, so to speak. Taiming thought for a moment: this fate had taken not only his brother but now was poised to attack himself and his father as well. There was no way out; the only path open was the one leading to death. Taiming tried to imagine what it would be like when all his family had died and he was the only one left. He felt his soul freeze over as if he were in the middle of a living cemetery.

And what meaning was there, after all, in merely living?

When he thought about it, the life he had lived until now had been sadly incomplete. He had tried to live seriously and earnestly, but had he succeeded? He had tried various professions but hadn't stuck to any of them. His love life had been no different.

He had told himself he was living honestly, but hadn't he just deceived himself? He hadn't had the courage to take life by the horns; he merely had made compromises with it at every turn. He had graduated with a degree in physics and received the highest education possible for a Taiwanese, yet what had he done with it? In the end, wasn't he a useless, impotent being, no better than a worm? The shame of allowing his younger brother to die!

Taiming was by habit an introverted and reflective person. Yet rather than being the source of his will to act in the world, this introspection had restricted his actions, turning him into a brooding, withdrawn man who could barely accomplish even a tenth of what he had set out to do. Studying in Japan, and then in the mainland . . . at first glance such actions seemed proof of a robust strength, but they were empty, without substance.

A storm of guilt raged within him. It was unbearable. He could again hear Ah-Yu's pitiful cries of grief. More than just sadness at Zhinan's death, they were a bitter accusation of all the injustices of heaven and earth.

Her crazed screaming infected Taiming in turn. He suddenly felt as if he heard Zhinan's corpse crying out. The dead don't speak, he thought; it must be a hallucination. But no, it was not. Zhinan was emitting a death shriek.

Then, suddenly, Taiming felt snap the thread connecting all his thoughts. A strange chaos began to fill his head. He dizzily staggered out of the room as if his soul had deserted his body; his gaze drifted through space, without focus.

9. The Far Reaches of Madness

Talk spread quickly that Taiming had gone mad, and there were quite a few facts to corroborate that conclusion. The day after Zhinan died, he sat on the altar in the ceremonial hall of the Hu home, his face painted red like Lord Guan from *The Romance of Three Kingdoms*, and wrote the following on the wall in clear, crisp strokes:

> I aspired to be a scholar
> But bowed to thugs—
> Where is the hammer to beat violence?
> As the hero ever dreams,
> The Chinese spirit lives—
> I will lose this life of mine.
> O but how could this be?
> The slave life drips with resentment,

O but how do we suffer brutes?
Comrades, reclaim old hills and streams,
Rise, ye six million, rise ye together—
Your blood simmering die for duty.

Eccentric words and behavior, to be sure, but not yet enough to decide conclusively that he had lost his mind. Given the circumstances, Hu Wenqing found these zealous verses alarming. He quickly hung up a scroll to cover Taiming's writing, but this didn't stop the curious from filling the hall as they came to see what was happening. When Taiming, face still painted red, trundled loudly into the room, they gasped in surprise. He calmly sat down on the altar and shouted:

"Tell all the living things of the world!"

This was unusual to begin with, but even more peculiar was the way he kept the people at bay. They watched him silently as he began to chant in a sonorous voice:

The head of the family is the big brother
The big brother is the head of the thieves
People are skinned
Trees are skinned
Mountains are skinned

The verses filled all the onlookers' hearts with emotion. Just as his verses proclaimed, the mountains they called mountains were stark naked; the barks of the acacia, the mulberry, and the rest, completely shorn. Even though nobody had been skinned alive yet, many people had certainly been whipped like horses. The empathy faded in the next instant, however, when Taiming's solemn tone changed into something different:

Eee, Yaa, Oii!
Bandits, in broad daylight!
Nah, Aii, Roh!!

As he began to sing a mountain song to a disturbing tune, the people began to stir. One could hear them say things like
"He's crazy!"
"He's gone mad!"
"Poor man!"
Taiming quickly rose to his feet and began screaming, blankly staring into space.

> Leaning on the nation's might,
> He gobbles down glory alone.
> Depraved scoundrel
> Daylight bandit
> Punishment for murder is death
> But he goes on killing so many
> And he's a hero! a hero! What?
> You stupid!
> Tiger
> Wolf
> Beast
> Don't you know?

His torrent of abuse pierced them to the bone. Yet he didn't stop there. On he continued:

> Fool!
> You say you're a compatriot
> But you're just a hound,
> Imperial errand-boy,
> Exemplary youth,
> Exemplary arbitrator,
> Praiseworthy teacher,
> Hah!
> Fool!

After finishing that round, he addressed an imaginary person in front of him, "Yes, you! Fool!" He was in a state of complete derangement.

From then on, Taiming was completely insane.

He wandered around the neighborhood day after day. He scrawled "Daylight bandits" on the bulletin boards of the fish farms and estates. This briefly became a problem, as it was clear to whom those words referred, but once it became known that it was the work of a madman, people gave up trying to stop him. There were days, as well, when he just sat meekly in the hall. In due course, the people of the village, busy with their own comings and goings, no longer took much notice of Taiming. And at some point, he disappeared from the village completely.

A few months passed. Nobody knew where Taiming had gone, but one day a fisherman coming through the village told them that a man resembling Taiming had boarded his fishing boat and crossed to the opposite shore. Before doing so, the fisherman had seen him wandering aimlessly by the sea.

Even before that rumor died out, another one appeared that said that Taiming was working at a radio station in Kunming making anti-Japanese broadcasts. Nobody could confirm or deny either of these rumors. Nonetheless, the words he had left behind on the walls of the Hu house remained, and although people were afraid of mentioning them in public, they spread secretly from one person to another. There were many—many—who came to see those words with their own eyes as the war in the Pacific plunged into its final, merciless phase.